I0727198

Jimmy Jazz **III** Complete Works

HOME DESPOT

A NOVEL BY JIMMY JAZZ

Home Despot a Novel

The bird a nest, the spider a web, man friendship.

William Blake

Nobody can protect a house full of gold and jade.

Lao Tzu

A good parasite never kills its host.

Chase

The Woman Up Front

It was an oblong sagging tit unaccustomed to bra support, so that the stretch marks stood out like cross-hatches in a pen and ink sketch by R. Crumb. The woman refused to wear clothes around her own house and would not consider tailoring her habits simply because a young couple moved into the little house behind hers.

Knocking at the sliding glass door had been a mistake, which DuBois recognized late. If she would move the green Buick Skylark in the driveway, he figured he could pull his beat Toyota wagon in and unload the box of books he hoped to read over the summer and clothes on hangers, mostly Aspen's, that he had piled in the back.

"Be a dear and take my keys."

The woman stood naked behind the curtain, a fat bare arm extended a ring with two keys and jiggled it. A shock of hair, bushy and brown, jutted from the pit like dried poppies out of a vase that he was close enough to smell, gritting his teeth to no avail against the obscene body odor, which a screen of patchouli oil failed to conceal. It was like the time he'd been slapped in a bar by a girl he'd never seen before the slap. The same violent adrenal nausea swirled inside him. He'd never liked fruity new-age hippies, but would rather ignore than fight them. Why did this feel like a fight? She felt an expanding sense of intrigue seeing the group of older people looking in at her. She guessed by the way the two women stood with their mouths agape that they had been living in the suburbs long enough that any break in the sameness of life agitated them. The gray-haired, barrel-gut grandfathers stood side by side like salt and pepper shakers and felt like they'd been caught doing something untoward when they'd been safely minding their own business.

"Wanna see my titties?"

DuBois took the keys as she flashed the group and pivoted so the rubber burned on his black Chuck Taylors. As a basketball-playing, skateboard-for-transportation teenager, he wore a hole through the sole of his high-top Cons at the ball of his right foot at a rate of about one pair per month, which frustrated his mother to no end. His mother had been frustrated with him throughout childhood so often that he mistook it for her natural attitude. The tense consternation on her face now made him a child again. This assault on her sensibilities was his fault, he supposed, for living in a city. With his back to the crazy naked woman, he rested the upper part of his face in his palm. From there his hand ran back over his skull and he decided he better get down to the barber.

Aspen's mother's jowls flushed pink. She was embarrassed and tried to recall an incident from her life where a complete stranger had shown like audacity. She couldn't. A painful smile emerged on her face. Mr. Monera's flesh hung loose around his chin like a turkey neck and vibrated like a light breeze through a poplar when he laughed, which he wasn't doing now, but might have been excused. He supposed that he should feel embarrassed, but he'd been in Korea, seen some of the world.

Her father's cheek flesh—the family jowls—as the joke ran, hadn't yet budded on Aspen's branch of the tree. Her skin held its youthful aspect. Turning thirty was the first time she thought about getting old. She intuited, since that was her way of thinking, that age wouldn't creep up on her like a slow dissolve—but the sag, the wrinkle and the fleshy jowl would jump out from behind the years like witches in a jump scare. She couldn't understand why so many Americans got so fat as they aged. This woman's naked flab flapped in the wind. Aspen tried to eat healthy and exercise. She wished she hadn't spent so much time at the beach. She would burn red, blister in the sun and peel like a molting animal. There wasn't anything she could do about her genes. Inheritance was like rolling crooked dice. But the older woman's nude scene felt like a betrayal. Who the hell did this lady think she was? Aspen felt like her own secret stretch marks and dimpled cellulite had been pickled and put on display at the state fair. DuBois looked more pissed off than embarrassed. He etched another black hash in the ledger he had been keeping against long-haired, wild-eyed hippies. A line from a local band ran through his head.

If the hippies all die, I'm not gonna fucking cry.

His whole family had been stripped naked, exposed as prudes, or rendered lecherous. It was horrible. Tragic. Stupid. DuBois's parents looked on with hard faces. It would be easy to read a dour judgment that might not have been there. Mr. Fuller's yellow eyes may have been fixed on the woman or in the service of a memory he'd been forced to recall. Mrs. Fuller stood with her thick arms folded across a demurely cloaked bosom and looked on under a brightly colored headwrap. One could imagine a phrase like, Put your damn clothes on, woman! stuck in her throat like a dry splinter.

"Look, EC, you're my best friend, but I can't understand why you and Toby would buy this house from this crazy nutball woman instead of the lovely two-story villa with the pool. Yesterday, she was taking out the trash in purple lingerie. Today she was naked in front of our parents. Who knows what's under the floorboards?"

"My, oh my, Aspen. Erosion is eating the hillside behind that lovely villa, undermining that pool, and we'd be swimming at the bottom of the canyon within a year. Besides, we love the house on Circle Circle. The rental property in the back, the whittle cottage, will make us truckloads of money. In the meantime, it's perfect since you, Rufi and DuBois got evicted from your pad in Little Italy. Ignore that woman."

"We weren't evicted, we got thirty days' notice. It's not the same thing."

"Ignore that woman. Don't have anything to do with her. I'm serious."

DuBois lingered in the driveway loading the car.

This is Beth Accomando for KPBS radio. Since the local media declared a housing shortage three months ago, landlords all around the city have been executing long-shelved plans to renovate—

"Paint the interior and double the rent."

Aspen disliked his habit of talking to the radio.

Renters are up against a one percent availability…

"What about rent control? In San Francisco, they organize. Damn the laws in this city. Declaration of dependence. Raze the old buildings, raise the rent, as much as the market will bear. Landlords lording over the land: a feudal story. Who's the serf in this scenario? I should have known when I saw those old biddies painting their house…"

"EC, I gotta go. DuBois needs attention. I'll see you over at the house. DuBois Ellison Fuller… Are you grumbling at the radio again?"

"Naw. I just don't like being treated like rubbish."

"We should have bought that house three years ago when they were cheap."

"Babe, I still don't want to fall into that bourgeois trap."

"We're not getting younger. Where are we going to live when we're old? With our friends?"

"Ha. We need to think outside this box they put us in. Aspen, babe, baby, a home controls you, you don't own it. A house owns its owner."

DuBois preferred to use abstract arguments against buying a house. He would say things like, I don't like landlords, why would I become one? He'd rather pitch a tent under a volcano, though he knew better than to suggest they should live any more dangerously than they had been. He wasn't crazy. The trappings of the middle class were traps—steel-jawed easy chairs. It would get tougher to resist now that EC was buying a house. Aspen's retorts were getting more refined every day.

"You don't like landlords telling you what to do, why not take control of your own life?"

"We can't afford a house, babe. We don't have any money."

"I've got a job now, we could get a loan. You're the laziest anarchist I've ever met. You can't live free in somebody else's space."

She was right. He liked to act as if he had a horror of all trades, but not for fear of the work itself. When he worked, he worked hard and did the best job he was capable of. Halfway or half-ass didn't suit him. In need of a quick line that would slay her desire to own a home, he fell short, couldn't think, and realized how deeply held her dream, and so how much deeper his argument would have to go. He needed more time and changed the subject.

"When those old ladies painted their house, the neighborhood was over..."

Aspen's best friend was the first person they knew who bought property. She would move into the main house, built in the Spanish style with a big window facing the street, plastered walls and a red tile roof. The cottage they were moving into stood behind the main house, a tiny afterthought erected in the 70s with a pitched asphalt shingle roof. The two-story apartment building on the block behind had an upstairs window that looked down into the yard. There was no alley. The main house was last painted when mauve was the rage. Underneath two coats of off-white, the house's original brilliant art deco lime green winked at them where the mauve had begun to flake. Aspen fantasized about restoring the house to its original, rodilating lost highway UFO diner glory. And also suspected that EC would choose a shade more earthy, it being like her to confuse subtle with sophisticated. Aspen hoped it wouldn't be taupe.

"Dub, we should urge EC to restore the house to its original green."

"It's EC's house. She can paint it shit brown if she wants. But no stucco. I won't even stay here if she slaps stucco on it."

EC walked up the driveway, came through the gate and went straight back to the cottage.

"Hi, hi."

"Hi, EC, we're cleaning up before we move our stuff inside."

"Sorry, sorry, I'm so sorry. There wasn't time to get your new home thoroughly cleaned."

"No worries. We're glad to have a place."

Aspen had to twist DuBois's nuts. He kept saying that it was a bad idea. Don't you remember what happened when Lucy bought Ethyl's washing machine? Druthers would have them remain cozy in the rented house in Little Italy where they'd holed up the past eight years, but they weren't given a choice.

And until they save a thousand bucks for first and last month's rent, a friend's cottage would suffice.

DuBois found the change invigorating despite the contradiction of his desire to stay put. He had always liked to live as cheaply as possible. Every time you moved house, you could expect to pay more. That's how poor people stay poor. DuBois, Aspen and Rufi had stayed in Little Italy as long as they could, dealt with insane landlords and watched the rents creep up as the neighborhood got safer and blander year on year.

"This is going to be a great summer. It's a time of celebration and adventure. A summer of endless barbecue, alright."

"The homeless can't be choosers. It smells terrible in here, though."

"Yeah, babe. This dump smells like a cat box."

"Wah wah. Have some cheese with that whine."

DuBois threw open the refrigerator door, causing a jar of pickles to jerk free and plummet through space toward the floor, and in line with his secret talent, he caught the jar easily in one hand and set it right in its place back on the shelf. With a carton of orange juice up to his nose, he asked, This juice fermented?

"I don't like to sniff things, strong smells make me nauseous."

He took a sip.

"Blech. Gimme a dollar and I'll take another sip."

"Give it up, Dub."

DuBois poured the contents into the sink, an orange syrup thick as house paint clung thickly to the porcelain. He spit after it.

"I'll clean the kitchen. See if you can do something about the closet."

The carpet inside the closet reeked of cat piss where the previous tenant must have kept a litter box. DuBois dumped a small box of baking soda on it.

"If this doesn't work, can we cut this carpet out with a knife?"

"Sure, sure. Toby's going to replace the carpet after you guys move out."

Aspen pulled the stove away from the wall and found a pile of spilt red beans, like dried vomit.

"Disgusting. Glad this crap's been here long enough to dry up."

"Hey, hey, look at this! Try it on, Dub."

She lifted a leather biker's cap from a hook on the closet door and flung it like a frisbee, which he caught, spun on one finger, and flung back.

"Naw, I ain't wearing that shit."

"Aspen, coming your way."

The biker hat spiraled over Aspen's head and landed in the sink. She flipped it back to EC with the handle of the broom.

"Smells like sweat and Royal Crown."

"Looks like it would fit Toby. Tell him it's a gift from us."

"Ha ha, Dub."

EC pitched the hat into the garbage while Aspen swept up the red bean mess. She couldn't stop thinking about the woman up front. How she took out the trash in that loose purple negligée. She told EC that the Homeowner's Association at her new townhouse didn't accept cats—she had four—and said her contract allowed her to stay until she found suitable housing. She kept the curtains drawn shut day and night, so it was impossible to see if she'd sold her furniture as she claimed or packed anything at all. Maybe she had no intention of moving. EC had to delay her own moving plans and cram her treasured possessions into a storage unit. Moving back in with your mother always felt like failure.

"What are we going to do about that lady? I think she's nuts?"

DuBois couldn't respond at first, bewitched as he was by the way Aspen's skin smelled of raspberries. Captivated by that smell, he couldn't hold her close enough.

"I hear that. She's a bowl of mixed nuts on the table at Xmas. Nutcracker and all. Did you see the look on our mommas' faces when she answered the door naked? I thought, stroke coming on, call the ER, reservations for four."

"Your daddy laid both of his eyes on her."

"Naw, not sexually at least. My dad? I mean, you see a bloated corpse floating in the river or a house engulfed in flames— everybody looks. That doesn't make a man a murderer or an arsonist."

"So, it's only your father's son who gawks at nude women?"

"Hey, little brown eyes, I didn't want to go to that strip joint. Hayduke dragged me up there. And Pops pretty much hates people—naked or clothed."

"I don't think he likes me. I mean, is that supposed to make me feel secure? Especially with you more like him than you admit."

Aspen's blouse revealed an enticing bit of cleavage. DuBois didn't respond to her as she straddled his lap and kissed the trigger spot behind his ear. She knew his weak spots and how to stoke his desire. Maybe she didn't expect an answer. He couldn't answer. There was no answer of his that she would accept. She dug her small fingers into the muscle of his neck. Stress evaporates. A second kiss was interrupted by an unexpected KNOCK.

"Hell-ooo!"

She was still wearing that loose purple chemise, with her feet bare and heavy tits that hung down on her stomach. She was holding a large plastic cup and Aspen smelled cheap beer.

"Hola, kids. I was wondering if I could have the shower curtain from your bathroom. I bought it for Jacques, who used to live here, and I need it for my new townhouse. Oh, speaking of Jacques, your new landlords didn't give him much time to get out, he left in such a hurry, if you find anything that might be his, I'd be happy to pass it on."

Aspen glanced at DuBois who shrugged. The mildewed tarp had been piled into the garbage earlier in the afternoon.

"Uh… Sorry, we threw out the shower curtain. It was…gross."

"It was practically brand new. Bought two months ago. And the color. That chartreuse is simply gorgeous. I picked it out myself at Bed, Bath & Beyond."

Aspen didn't know what to say, and DuBois wasn't even listening. She looked over at him and got nothing back. The awkward silence was accusatory. She almost volunteered to buy the woman a new shower curtain, but considering their bank account and how DuBois worked two days a week and Rufi, of course, would need new clothes for summer because she'd had a growth spurt, and considering how long it had been since she'd had new shoes herself, well, her mood grew bitter. She thought about her tatty underwear and who did this woman think she was, besides the former owner of this property? She drew strength from EC's admonition to ignore the woman.

"Well, it was gross and we threw it out."

Aspen looked back for DuBois, but he had left the room and was making himself a shot of espresso in the kitchen. She felt nervous, chewed her thumbnail.

"It's in the trash bucket right out there, I can have DuBois fish it out for you."

He might have said, I'm not digging that moldy shit out the garbage, or might have said, I hate to waste, and fished it straight out, but he wasn't listening and continued making coffee.

The woman sipped her cheap beer.

"That's alright, honey, don't worry about it."

She took a sip and a breeze lifted the light material of her chemise and exposed two thick, hairy thighs. Each hair was like a tiny black leather whip curled at the cusp.

"Oh. That reminds me. I demand my privacy. If you need me for anything, call me on the telephone. Don't knock on the door. I have a gentleman friend who also likes to prance about the house naked. That's the way Jacques and I handled things."

Aspen wanted to shut the door in her face.

"We don't have your number."

"I wrote it down."

The woman proffered a lilac-colored slip of stationery on which the number had been neatly written in calligraphy.

"Okay… Uh. Thanks."

"I'd offer you a beer, but I only have five left, need to run to the liquor store, and simply can't manage clothes, not today."

Aspen's need to shut the door had grown compulsive, but the woman showed no sign of retreat. DuBois carried his espresso out the side door. Aspen watched him over the woman's shoulder as he kept walking through the gate and down the driveway toward the car. The parents had gone home after lunch without mentioning the burlesque show, and Aspen had already called EC to tell her all about it.

"You'll never guess what the woman up front did—"

"Oh my gosh, oh my gosh. What a…I hate that B. Her outrageous demands are making us crazy. Stay away from her. She's like one of those fish that feeds on attention, maybe she'll go away. The sooner she goes, the sooner I can move into my beautiful new old home."

"Ask her if we can be rude."

"I heard that. No no. Don't give her any cause. Don't be rude, don't be nice, ignore her so she'll go away."

The woman sealed off the cottage doorway and told Aspen the plot from a video she'd seen, but Aspen was more concerned about where DuBois had gone. How did he always manage to disappear? And where was Rufi? Tasked to unpack a box of Barbie dolls in the other room, she likely sat playing with them on the floor. DuBois was the same way with books. He got fired from a job at the library because he got lost in reading the books he was supposed to shelve. A few of her friends had quit dolls, and Rufi resisted the impulse to wear make-up and pretend boys were cute.

"Arrgg, Serving Wench Barbie, get me a beer out of the fridge."

"Get it yourself, Pirate Barbie, ya lazy cripple."

"Arrgg, her majesty's man took me leg with an iron ball."

"Well, I got drunk and dyed my hair."

"Harr, harr, you think you're punk but you ain't shit…"

Punk Barbie's synthetic blonde hair had been cropped the summer before with the kitchen scissors to spiky, evenly spaced sprouts, which Rufi dyed an exotic shade of blue using the last of the Kool-Aid powder. Rufi currently had thirty-one Barbies, acquired in the aftermath of Xmas and birthdays with competing grandparents buying Ballet Barbie and Peg-leg Sailor Barbie. For whatever reason, it was easier to buy a whole new doll than an outfit. When fortune amputated one of Sailor Barbie's legs in an accident at sea, her daddy, rescuing it from the ashcan, told her that handicapped dolls had as much right to play as any. DuBois made a miniature eye patch and wooden peg leg and Pirate Barbie, by turns, came back a scourge to her own country. A pink and white jolly roger flew above the yard-arm of the Malibu yacht. Not to be outdone, one of Rufi's grandmothers bought an official Wheelchair Barbie™ in a big pink box because, It might be worth something someday. Her games would grow in refinement and finesse until she quit dolls altogether.

The woman from up front was still delivering a monologue as DuBois walked back up the driveway with his long, quick stride, opened the gate and came up behind her. He could see that Aspen was trapped.

"Someone left a note on my car."

"Did you park in front of the house next door? Probably Bern-eece."

"It says, Hi, Can I get you to do me a big favor and park in front of your residence? I have no parking for my guests in front of my house. I sometimes like to park here and find no place to park. Technically, under the law, you are supposed to be provided off-street parking. I keep trying to be a quiet, considerate neighbor. In the spirit of cooperation could you do me this big favor. Thank you."

"She's such a bitch, that Berneece."

The driveway, which had room for one car, was occupied by the Skylark, which DuBois had moved out and moved back earlier. Aspen's black '67 Plymouth Fury with whitewall tires was parked in front of the house, leaving no other space on or off of the street for him to park. The Toyota had to park in front of somebody's house.

Aspen half-suspected that the woman up front wrote the note sowing trouble in her wake.

"In the old neighborhood, we parked two blocks away on a good luck day. Cheese-n-rice. We've been here two days. Some welcome mat. Where does she expect me to put that car?"

"I despise that bitch. She used to send her poodle into my yard to take its piddly shits. I soaked it with the hose and Berneece wanted me to pay to have the little bitch re-coiffured. Ha!"

DuBois laughed, hee hee hee, while he tried to negotiate a way back into the house, but the woman blocked the door with her wide hips and near nudity. Her heavy tits swayed, agitated, with the rest of her demeanor. DuBois wasn't about to risk brushing against one of them. Aspen decided to grab a beer from the refrigerator, which allowed the woman to enter the cottage. DuBois looked at the woman's dirty bare feet and imagined a No Shirt, No Shoes, No Service sign on the front door. The woman situated herself on the futon, which doubled as Aspen and DuBois's bed, tugging the chemise down and crossing her fat legs. DuBois looked away.

"Get me a beer too, babe."

She began the first of several stories about, That vile shrew Berneece. EC's warning to stay clear of the woman remained in the forefront of Aspen's mind, but the horror show that the woman made of Berneece redirected their contempt.

The Call Center

The way the light diffused through the gray curtains in the small cottage behind her best friend's house reminded Aspen of her cubicle. She didn't want to think about work. Couldn't risk dreaming about it. Staring at the popcorn ceiling, she was afraid that the strange light would bring strange dreams.

She focused on the old neighborhood. Reminded herself to sneak into the garden come October to pick the avocado she felt that the tree owed her. The tree hadn't borne fruit, at least while they lived there, until last year when a single gorgeous green bulb-shaped ornament budded. They watched it grow slowly fat like blown glass. Of course, a thief stole into the garden and plucked it before it was ready. Stupid thief. This year they'd watered more often and were dismayed to leave several prospective delicacies behind. DuBois claimed that the landlord had picked her avocado, though it could have been a former resident, one of the kids from the block or the forlorn drifter who raided the trash cans for recyclables. This new neighborhood was quieter and she certainly wouldn't miss the planes roaring in every three minutes. The ample closet space was already missed. Her clothes would stay in boxes here. She wanted to settle into a home of her own more than anything and knew they would need better, more stable jobs. She started this job a few days before they moved but was already feeling ambivalent. DuBois lay half-awake on the futon and she nuzzled into the crook of his arm and set her cheek against his bare shoulder. Rufi breathed heavily as she slept in the other room, while their cat, called Yakuza because of its violent temper, settled in at the foot of her mattress.

"DuBois."

"Yeah, babe."

"What would you say if I wanted to quit my job?"

"Quit."

"I'm not sure I like it—the job, the bosses, my co-workers. I don't like my cubicle or the fluorescent lights."

The brochure for the product was the only spot of color between the gray walls of the cubicle. There was a script, chock full of lies—false promises and purposeful misdirection—that she was supposed to follow until she worked up her own routine. A tray with four ballpoint pens, a bottle of Wite-Out and an assortment of paper clips next to the phone rounded out the emptiness.

"The customers are so rude."

"That's pretty funny, Aspen."

"What?"

"A week before you took this job, you asked that LA Times guy who keeps calling to hold while you got the gold card and you let the phone sit off the hook."

"You cuss them out."

"Telemarketers are metermaids with telephones."

"Promise me you won't cuss them out any more."

"No promises. Your phone's off the hook, but you're not."

She felt warm, safe, skin to skin underneath the thin blanket. Lying next to DuBois at the end of the day made the humiliation of work seem worth it.

"DuBois."

"Yeah."

"EC says we can stay in the back house for six months. Think that'll give us enough time to find an apartment?"

"The contract she wrote, Delineates the rules about what can and what <u>cannot,</u> under any circumstances, be stored in my garage."

"She just wants to dodge misunderstanding."

The two-page agreement was full of legal jargon and fine print. In between lessee and lessor, they were allowed: three bikes, three beach chairs, one Boogie board. And everything else is a no-no and should be kept inside your living space (to wit, none of your funky yard art, DuBois).

"I still can't believe I had to give away the two-hundred-pound white plaster gryphon that Juan Carlos jacked from that office park? He risked his life for that shit."

"Tut-tut, Dubois. No gargoyle statuary. And Aspen, I love you, but none of your pink plastic lawn flamingos."

"EC knows us."

"How long have we known her?"

"Since that day Juan Carlos brought her home after class at City College."

Aspen's eyes felt heavy and the fading gray wasn't yet dark enough for sleep. She tried to think about Rufi, about how fast she was growing, about DuBois and what jobs he could get, about her friend and her new house, but her place of employment kept crawling back in like a spider.

Sanderson Dode made three sales before six. He leaned way back in his swivel chair and let his voice project through the cold air of the office. The middle manager set the air conditioner on "Arctic." To keep you knuckleheads alert and facilitate sales! Aspen was unsure about the middle manager, didn't like being called a knucklehead and hoped he wouldn't repeat it.

"Hey, John, this is Sanderson Dode with Enigmatic Widget. This is a courtesy call to make you aware of a special we're offering to past valued customers on our new model..."

Aspen noticed how Dode used the customers' first names, which reeked of hyper-familiarity, and after his initial lewd proposition, she decided to avoid being caught anywhere alone with him.

"I like your skirt sugar thighs, but it would look better on the floor in my apartment."

Aspen hated confrontation and felt sick inside. What did this dude know about my thighs? She looked down at the carpet, which was gray like the cubicle. She looked around the room and wasn't sure if the others were engaged with customers or cocking their ears for her reaction. She imagined disembodied eyeballs peeking around the edges of the cubes.

"Listen, Dode, I am not the subject of your innuendoes, nor the object of your secret masturbation fantasies. Don't undress me with your eyes, don't peep down my blouse. My boyfriend will rip your head off if you ever say anything like that to me again."

"Sorry. Didn't see a rock."

Insincerity dripped off his apology like sweat from his expansive forehead. The cubicle closed in on her like solitary confinement. She hadn't felt like this since the first day of junior high. Julie and Gloria hashed out plans to get drunk and go dancing with a young guy whose nickname, she might have heard it wrong, was Boring. One of the girls mentioned the disco where Aspen used to get drunk and go dancing before Rufi was born. She thought they might invite her, but they didn't. She suddenly felt old. These kids might have been ten years younger. Was ten years insurmountable? Between thirteen and twenty-three, sure. But the gap between twenty and thirty didn't seem like that much.

Dode went back to his cubicle and had already dialed another customer.

"Hello, Luther? Sanderson Dode at Enigmatic Widget..."

Benny "the Jaguar" Velasquez wore a vintage suit and silk tie but looked too young to be a boss. Aspen was sure she was older than him too. He'd told the training group that he was a professional poet with a corporate sponsor that flew him to readings in other cities on the weekends, and she was sure she heard one of the younger workers in the group blurt out, Dude, I saw you on MTV.

The Jaguar told the group that he took the job at the call center for extra cash and discovered a knack for exploitation. It's all about PMA, he told them once, twice, and again before defining it. The crux of his Positive Mental Attitude denied that one had to move through suffering to reach a goal. He talked to customers as if he'd already made the sale and closed the deal.

A poetry career could only take one so far. It was surprising how, with being a poet and all, clichés ruled his life. The most insidious were: What have you done lately? and Don't quit your day job. Being a famous poet in America wasn't worth much. Resting on your laurels, in this context, would mean teaching. He could vanish into the academy. He could publish with a respectable university press and watch the royalties trickle in. Maybe he should write a hit Xmas song? "Fairytale of New York" or "Christmas Wrapping."

He parlayed the energy he once used to write into selling Enigmatic Widgets—a bold and even insolent move that propelled his corporate escalator up, up, up. On Wednesdays, he shared gleanings from his Tuesday management seminar.

"Today we're going to talk about the manipulation of earnings. The secret to overcoming obstacles—are you listening, knuckleheads? PMA, PMA, PMA..."

When Velasquez was out of the office, the sales floor was ruled by an assistant manager known as The Wrecking Ball—a corporate animal, by serious facial aspect and conservative dress, always in black, she would zip about the office, dancing hither and thither, turning pirouettes in the aisles. Aspen envied her abundant energy and wondered if the Wrecking Ball swam laps or taught aerobics to condition herself. She didn't seem like she was hopped up on coke, but Aspen kept her eyes peeled for any druggie tells—a trace of powder, a rolled-up bill, a razor, a bullet, a sniffle, a jitter or grinding of teeth. She'd known a junkie once who shivered at the word needle. The Jaguar seemed high too, though it might have been an act. The Wrecking Ball said she liked opera and to cook elaborate meals. Aspen thought she overheard a discussion about the vintage of a cabernet sauvignon. Wrecking Ball was an odd nickname for such a cosmopolitan woman. She shouldn't even be working in a telemarketing room. Her family fled Persia when the Shah lost control and settled in Paris before emigrating stateside. Her English was salted with a dash of Farsi and a jigger of *voulez-vous coucher.*

"Sup, Wrecking Ball? Come dancing with us tonight?"

"I went to my share of discotheques in Paris, children. I have to get home, cook a fabulous meal, sleep. You guys will come dragging in here tomorrow wearing your dark sunglasses."

So, it wasn't about age. The Wrecking Ball might be older. New girl hazing? Maybe they were testing her mettle, trying to see what kind of person she was.

"Aloha, Julie…"

Dode addressed the waif with thick glasses, impossibly perky, so likely enhanced, breasts, and three evident pimples under her base makeup.

"You wanna go out to dinner with me tonight?"

"Um, I don't think so. I don't need a boyfriend right now."

"I don't want to be your boyfriend, I just wanna have sex with you."

Dode smiled, running his routine, laughing, and rocking back in his chair. This was about the time he told Julie he could see her beaver dam when she uncrossed her legs.

"Still with me?"

"Yeah, I'm awake."

"Dode reminds me of your dazed high school buddies shouting, Hey, baby, wanna get nasty!"

"I hate the bastard already. When does he stick his tongue between his fingers?"

"In a minute."

Dode had dozens of green papers pinned around his cubicle with the names and numbers of customers he intended to call back. There was also a picture of him holding a surfboard, shirtless, with bushy blonde mutton chops, and flashing a *shaka.*

"I'm celibate right now."

"I've got a thick Johnson."

"Ooooo… gross… Sanderson, it's not a good idea to date people you work with."

Aspen wondered why Julie didn't put Dode in his place. Tell him to stop badgering her. It didn't seem possible that she could be attracted to him. Maybe she needed attention.

"Break time! Back at your stations in fifteen."

The Jaguar sometimes let Wrecking Ball call the breaks. A pack of smokers bolted for the stairs, an older woman tossed her headphones aside and marched toward the restroom while another even older woman kept calling. Most everyone else stayed seated, set their headphones on the desk, and pushed their chairs into the aisle for small talk. When Julie turned her back, Dode held two fingers up to his mouth and wiggled his tongue between.

God, I hate these people, DuBois said, in a sleepy whisper.

"It gets worse."

Aspen felt a knot in her lower back, stood up and tried to stretch.

"Aspen, dear, can I ask how old you are?"

"Thirty-three."

"Thirty-three? You're not thirty-three, thirty-three? When's your birth date? I bet you're a Virgo, Virgos always look so young."

"I don't see what's strange about looking young. Most people don't know what a thirty-plus-year-old woman looks like. Actually, I turn thirty-three on my birthday next month."

The Jaguar thought he saw an opportunity for rapport and made asking one person his or her age every night into a running gag. Julie was twenty-two. Gloria, who looked like a stoner, lived down at the beach and took classes at City College, was twenty-three. Boring, who, lurching with his gangly limbs, resembled a baby Joey Ramone, had decided to try every single kind of liquor at the Keg & Bottle since he turned twenty-one. Last night, he fell asleep clutching a bottle of electric blue Mad Dog on Gloria's couch. The Jaguar did everything he could to entertain the workers. Team-building exercises had become a compulsion with him. One of his tricks was to tag people with a sobriquet, and after it stuck, call them by their given name. So sometimes Aspen would hear him say, Flores, Gloria, Susanna... Ned.

When the break had run a minute longer than fifteen, Jaguar shouted, Okay, knuckleheads, to the phones! Remember that positive mental attitude. First person to get a sale this hour gets ten bucks. Most of the worker bees scrambled to study their green call back sheets. Aspen peered down the aisle and saw Julie passing a note to Boring, which dragged her back again to junior high, though she couldn't picture Rufi, about to enter junior high herself, passing notes in class or thinking about boys or talking about hair like two girls in a nearby cubicle.

"Oh, your hair's so pretty."

"Thanks."

"You should get it layered."

"It is layered, but I need to get my highlights done…"

The call center was rife with managers and manager managers, and the upper-level district manager stopped by twice in a week to, See how things were going. On her second day of work, Aspen signed a card for one of the overseers, she didn't know who, and even when everyone sang Happy Birthday, she didn't know who it was for. After it was over, the Jaguar pulled Aspen aside, said she had a nice voice and suggested she sing louder next time.

At eighty-three, Maggie was the oldest telemarketer in the room. Aspen had seen the Championship Belt hanging from her cubicle on orientation day. She'd sold more Enigmatic Widgets than half the people at the call center combined.

"It's like working on a farm, as long as you know you're pitching bullshit, as long as you accept that, that's half the battle. The other half is persistence. I call them back, even if they said No the first time…"

"If she calls, I'm cussing the old bitch out."

Flores was always trying to play Blue Oyster Cult or Sabbath when it was her turn to pick the music. She liked to wear classic rock t-shirts from concerts she'd attended, and the Jaguar counseled that she would sell more widgets if she dressed appropriately. If you don't take yourself seriously, who will?

"Dub, I know you don't like hippies, but the other day she put on War Pigs and turned it all the way up. It was pretty funny."

Aspen looked up and saw Susanna walking with the Jaguar to write a number next to her name on the tote board and collect the ten bucks. Her hair was pinned back with a white plastic I (heart) Jesus child's barrette.

Gail had charmed four people into buying Enigmatic Widgets with her Trinidadian accent and was still number one on the tote board.

At the end of the week, Zhen Lee and Zhang Wong Smith were the only ones left from Aspen's training group. Ten people had quit and Aspen was starting to think they were smart. Maybe she wasn't being hazed at all, maybe most people didn't last long enough here to invest any energy in. Zhen and Zhang paid more attention to what music would be played on the boombox than selling. Zhen kept putting in Sonic Youth and Zhang brought The Jon Spencer Blues Explosion, which he swore would motivate him to, Sell like a wild man. When Jon Spencer screamed, Baby, baby sure like to fuck, the Wrecking Ball spun over to the stereo, shut off the CD and put Magic 92.5 FM on the radio. An exaggerated male voice announced, The

Big Afro Weekend! And Wild Cherry broke into, Play that funky music, white boy.

"That's way more offensive than Jon Spencer!"

"Shhh, Dub, don't wake up Rufi."

Aspen wondered what DuBois and Rufi were doing at home and wanted to call them but knew the calls were monitored.

"Trust me, babe. Baby, you don't want to know what we do while you're at work, hee hee hee."

She felt guilty after getting paid nine dollars per hour while failing to sell anything. This was more money than she'd ever earned. Her phone rang once before a disembodied virtual voice said, We're sorry the number has been disconnected or is no longer in... She hung up and dialed the next number on the list, even though the Jaguar had told her to slow down because it was too easy to get into a pattern of hanging up so that when a good lead finally answered, her impulse might be to throw the call.

"Try to have a conversation."

Velasquez picked up a phone and dialed a number to demonstrate, Hello, Mr. Bersabé... This is Aspen with the Enigmatic Widget Corporation... Yeah, I suppose Aspen sounds like a funny name, but my friends call me Asp... That's right, like the snake.

Aspen hoped that Snake wouldn't become her nickname. Seven minutes later, Mr. Bersabé had purchased an Enigmatic Widget and Jaguar walked over and rang the bell—DING.

"Success in the cold calling business means overcoming obstacles. I don't care. I – don't – care. If I make a sale, great! If they say, Not interested or hang up, it makes no difference. Because I don't care. Last night my friends and I read poetry on city buses until 2am. Yes, that's right, to practice rejection. It's a skill you can hone. I came home and turned on the tv and imagined what it was like not to have a life. Just kidding. The WWF was on. I don't care about the WWF, but I studied it, I imagined what it was like to be a bad guy wrestler. I saw that love and hate switch on a dime, but overcoming indifference takes real art. How was I able to learn? Because I didn't care. My mind was open to experience. I was in bed, buff-bare if you dare, when the door flung open and my roommates hucked these wet wads of toilet paper…"

His digression came back to the point, eventually, that he lived each moment with intensity and promised success to any of the crew who approached each call with this kind of verve. After another one of his management seminars, he lectured for ten minutes about, Having pride in your work. Aspen tuned out. He couldn't understand the desperation that brought her to this job. Susanna scoffed. Maybe she felt the same way.

"Don't tell me how I should feel about my job. I got carpal tunnel in both my hands. I should be at home with my kids, but I have to be here."

Aspen wondered what would have happened if Susanna had spoken up during the meeting instead of in the break room.

Cecil Trachomatis had a fledgling law practice during the day but moonlighted at the call center in lieu of clients. Julie told everyone that he had asked her out.

"I told him that it was sweet, but that I was busy. Don't you think he looks like Woody from Toy Story?"

Dode laughed above the group. The poor pigeon did resemble Woody, the cowpoke puppet, with his long wooden head, squeezed into a size-too-small suit. Trachomatis overdressed for this job like a singing cowboy from the movies.

"Monday: blue suit, Tuesday: gray pins, Wednesday: blue pins… Friday: casual. That way I get even wear out of my suits."

"Yo, what day is it?"

"Blue pinstripe, must be Wednesday."

"That's cold, Julie."

DuBois's grandfather had been fastidious about clothes. A sartorial genius. DuBois rescued dead men's clothes from the Salvation Army and didn't even bother to separate his laundry. It cycled from hamper to washer to clothesline to drawer as a load. Each day he grabbed whatever shirt, boxers, socks, and trousers came to hand. He put on Chuck Taylors if the day called for walking or Doc Martens if he thought he might have to kick somebody.

"Hello, Mrs. Ho, this is Aspen from the Enigmatic Widget company—"

"Where'd you get my name?"

"Uh…"

The official line was that they were calling previous customers, but Aspen figured out that Enigmatic must have bought the names from a credit card company. She hated lying.

"We call previous customers."

"Junk mail. Junk mail. I've never been a customer. Why are you calling me!"

"To sell you an Enigmatic Widget, so I can pay the rent and feed my kid."

"How dare you? My husband is on his deathbed with brain cancer and you call me to sell me some garbage! How dare you?"

It was amazing how many people suffered from brain cancer. Susanna must have been having a similar night because she told Wrecking Ball to tell the Jaguar that she had a migraine and went home.

Safe California Home

DuBois's foot came down with all its weight on top of a garden snail, crushing the shell with a sickening crackle and cold smear that oozed between his toes as he searched for the phone jack behind the woman's house. The search was impeded by hip-high weeds, nothing a machete couldn't hack, if he'd had a machete, which he didn't. His next footfall, placed with more care after noticing a pair of flies circling, avoided a cat turd half-heartedly buried in a patch of loose dirt. The phone company inspector wanted twenty bucks to look into the matter and suggested that DuBois plug his house phone directly into the box first, and as he did, a female voice could be heard rattling off a series of numbers—arrrr – five – two – nine… He unplugged it and tried the next jack. Heard dead silence. What could those numbers mean? He discovered a loose wire, easily reattached it, and a dial tone signaled success.

His reflection in the window reminded him to get down to the barber. He was glad for the thick curtain the woman up front had hung to block out the sun. In the next yard, a sleepy old orange cat basked in the grass. Shitting beast. A cat could lie about in the sun, licking itself, all day.

Squawk.

An apricot tree with thick foliage and a lemon tree in which bees caressed the flowers had been planted on either side of a low, wooden fence. The mockingbird was up above on the telephone wire, brown with a distinct white tail feather. Its agitated Squawk had been aimed at the thin orange cat like a dart. The bird dropped onto a lemon branch above the cat and SQUAWKED again, sticking another dart before diving into the supine feline to tear away a patch of orange fur.

"Oh, shit."

The cat didn't do more than roll over, as if, to show DuBois the bald patches of scab across its back. The lazy beast had made no attempt to deter the attack—it sat there, paralyzed, plucked, indolent. The cat stayed put, in thrall of the awful siren song or in dotage to masochism, while the bird reset for another dive. DuBois hoped that the poor old cat was biding its time, dreaming violence, plotting revenge.

"Dub, honey, the phone's working and Toby wants to talk to you."

DuBois would have preferred to see what the bird would do next but returned to the cottage. Taking a seat on the threshold, he ran the hose over his feet. The water was too hot at first and then cool. Aspen handed him the phone. He noted the platform heels that accented the muscles in her calves and touched her leg.

"Sup, man?"

"Bro, Studboy. The woman up front called to bitch me out about you tapping into her phone lines."

"Oh wow, our line was dead and…"

"You should have told her you were going to work on the phone."

"She asked us not to knock on the door."

"You should have called, here's her numb…"

"The phone was broken. How would we call?"

"I don't know, walk to the corner store."

"Fuck."

"I know, bro. Stay out of her way. She'll be gone soon enough. Later, Studboy."

"She—"

"Don't worry about him. He's pissed off because their realtor made a mistake that cost them three thousand dollars."

"EC's friend?"

"Yeah, Pia. They went to elementary school together. She offered her commission as a wedding present and you know EC likes a bargain."

"I heard him in the driveway yelling, Damn it, Pia, that's stupid! Stupid!"

"I can't believe he talks to her like that. Wait, hold on. Hi, EC."

"Hello, Aspen, I'm on my lunch break looking at new furniture. I found a nice new puffy couch and a table wiff a glass top made from wrought iron. Do you remember what the living room space looks like? That woman distracted me while I was trying to measure."

"Pia probably knows."

"She's my oldest friend, but I wonder what she knows."

"Sorry, I didn't get a good look at it since that first walkthrough."

"I can't wait to paint the bathroom. I can't stand that pink tile…"

Aspen cleaned off the stove and unpacked a box marked Pots & Pans so she could cook Kraft Dinner for Rufi. DuBois said they should boycott Kraft, on account of tobacco holdings, but Rufi didn't like generic mac & cheese.

"Ah, I love that original vintage tile. What color are you going to paint?"

"White, white… all white. Toby says he can do it, but I know some professional Mexicans who used to work for my dad…"

Aspen's gaze wandered out the window. It looked like DuBois and Rufi were up to their old tricks in the yard. DuBois set Yakuza in the grass under the lemon tree and they ran for cover behind the patio lattice.

"I gotta go Elizabeth."

"Shhh, babe."

SQUAWK!

"Come here, Momma. We're playing a joke on Yakuza."

Yakuza had been part of the family since he nuzzled four-year-old Rufi's hand at the pet store. A last desperate act of affection, not in character, it turned out, as the big black cat had settled into downright ornery, attacking anything of his size or bigger that strayed into the yard, coming home late with abscesses on his belly or a nick out of the left ear like a drunk in a back-alley bar fight. Every time he even saw another cat, Yakuza puffed up like he was getting the electric chair. He'd already made a run at one of the woman's cats and rammed BUMP into a sliding glass door. When they had friends over, Yakuza would move in close courting attention and draw blood on the sucker who reached to stroke soft black fur, Reooww!

Aspen wanted to take the brute back to the pet store that first week but wasn't ready to call the ten dollars they spent on de-wormer, cat food and litter a total loss.

"Check that bird on the wire."

Squawk!

It displayed the same preliminary agitation. Yakuza was in position on the grass. The bird studied this new cat. Maybe Yakuza wasn't beaten down enough, like the old orange cat, to be mesmerized. DuBois wasn't sure. The bird floated down to the lemon branch, tossed another squawk. Hesitated. Before it could swoop, the fat black cat sauntered away, driven by curiosity, toward the cottage to investigate what the humans were doing behind the lattice. He rubbed against DuBois's bare leg. Stepping off the branch, the mocking bird's wings carried it up and over the neighbor's house.

"Ha ha, wait, look, a gopher."

A small rodent, with big front teeth and twitching whiskers peeked his head out of a mound of recalcitrant soil.

"He's so cute."

"I know a murder of crows and a flock of seagulls, but what's a group of gophers called?"

"A solitude. Gophers are solitary creatures, they can't abide other gophers. Like Yakuza."

"That little guy made all these holes?"

"He has his own underground world."

"Hey, babe, I got another load in the car. What should we keep here, what should we store?"

"You know that you aren't grown as long as you have shit stored in your momma's garage? What's left?"

"Toby helped me with Rufi's bed, so a few books and toys."

"I say we keep the toys."

"Well, I say we keep the books."

"I'll vote with Rufi—she's gonna outgrow the toys before you outgrow your books."

"Two against one."

They all missed their old house. They had paid the rent on time for eight years, Aspen figured $52,000, and the bastard gave them thirty days so he could paint and double the rent. They suffered through the noise pollution of landing jets (every three minutes) and worried that the air was lead-heavy from jet fuel rain and the freeway exhaust stained the patio furniture gray, so what did it do to the lungs? DuBois read about a factory at the bottom of the hill fined for spewing toxins. Maybe they were lucky to be forced out. But for the money, the house in Little Italy had been a palace—two bedrooms, enclosed yard, spacious balcony. The view of the downtown skyline at night, tall ships docked in the blue harbor, and, they hated to admit—the grim undercarriage of monster aircraft screaming down to the airport made their home unique. They would be hard-pressed to find anything comparable.

"I don't want anything out in the yard. I don't want this place looking white trash."

EC took down the clothesline on day one so Aspen wouldn't be tempted to air her clean laundry. It didn't matter so much since there was a washer and dryer in the garage. DuBois said they should hang the laundry anyway because it was better for the environment and easier on the clothes, but Aspen was so excited about not having to go to the laundromat that she didn't think to take EC's jibe personally.

"What's up with that white trash shit, EC? You know Aspen's uncle-cousin and grandma-aunt never left Arkansas—"

"Ha ha. I don't want any of your funky trash either, D-String."

She'd tried to get everyone in the punk scene to call him D-String, which hadn't caught on. They'd known each other for twelve years, and even though she split up with his friend Juan Carlos, he felt like they were friends in their own right. She was a punk at heart, went to shows, liked the music, even if she dressed like a preppy. Hadn't he pushed her to do her first stage dive at a Fishbone gig? She could have been a poseur, a lot of kids who went to punk shows in those days were just trying on the clothes. Her better-than-thou self-love was a different kind of pose. Aspen felt like making an excuse for her friend and said, I think she has high expectations. This is the house she's always dreamed of. Still, that her friend worried about what the neighbors might think was a shock.

Aspen fancied many of the houses on the street. She fancied houses, period, but prices were going through the stratosphere. She kicked herself for not trying to buy a house even one year before when the prices were a hundred thousand dollars cheaper. Toby had already given a lecture on property values, but DuBois figured if you can't do whatever the heck you feel with your place, like paint it shocking blue, well, is it really yours?

The only thing that excited him about the neighborhood was the pirate flag that had been raised on a pole three doors down. The house had a motorhome parked out front. He had never seen who lived there, had never seen anyone on the street. There were no kids playing ball, no elders on the porch hunched over a checkerboard, no dealers on the corner waiting to sell a fix, no gangbangers skulking in midnight doorways, no Mexican ladies carting laundry home from the mat. No smells of fish or garlic or anything delicious wafting out of kitchens. A picture of anonymity. There were thirty-six houses, in four models, basically all the same, though many of the places had achieved subtle distinctions of character over time with room additions and a variety of landscaped yards. Even on Sunday morning when they expected to be woken up early by lawnmowers and leaf blowers, there was nothing but birds singing. Once in a fortnight, landscaping crews slipped in unobtrusively to care for the yards, while the automated sprinklers kept the blades of grass sharp and green. An assiduous eye might glimpse a resident stepping from his or her car after work, though with on-street parking discouraged, even this would be difficult.

"It's so quiet here."

"I like the quiet. It feels safe."

"I don't know, Boo-daw. It feels like a ghost town. All the people disappeared."

"Yeah, I like to see kids running around, riding bikes and laughing."

"Will we disappear, Daddy?"

"I don't know."

"Do you think Toby and EC will disappear when they move in?"

"Naw Boo-daw, we'll always be friends… Hey, I know how to make my girl laugh. What's black and white and red all over?"

"A newspaper."

"Naw. A penguin in a blender."

Rufi laughed, but her facial expression held the same concerned grimace. Her momma pulled her in close and gave her a hug.

Toby came over that evening with a red wheelbarrow, a tall ladder, a short ladder, and a device to wind up the backyard hose, which previously coiled like a gopher snake under the spigot. EC came up the driveway behind him.

"What are you doing?"

"It's going to rain, so I thought I'd put these boxes in the garage. My Pops will drive the van down Thursday night and take the books to his place."

The first ample droplet from the sky marked the cardboard like a bullet through a road sign.

"No no. Don't put them in the garage. The woman up front hired junk dealers to take all her stuff away and Toby has already filled up the tool shed with new toys from the hardware store."

"All right."

"Don't look at me like that, you signed a contract that says: three bikes, three beach chairs and one Boogie board in the garage. We made the contract to avoid situations like this. To protect our friendship."

Plenty of people had warned them not to move in with friends. DuBois turned about-face and set the box down inside the cottage.

"I told you to get rid of those things a month ago."

"I can sell these. That would have been like throwing money away and you know it. Don't start with me. You turned out my favorite green chair like a bitch on the sidewalk, I fit that chair, and some lucky bastard scored and they got my—"

"Your napping couch, I know, I know, poor baby. I have to go to work, but please, please put those books where they won't topple over on us while we sleep."

"Not such a bad way to go out."

DuBois loved books more than his own music. Dag. Did she know how difficult it was to find a napping couch that fit your body? It was like finding the perfect sex partner—like luck, like chance distilled, shy of a miracle.

Toby surveyed the property, thinking about what tools he might need before the big housewarming party. He tugged at his goatee. A garland of beaded sweat stretched around his forehead underneath a Padres baseball cap. He got out a tiny slip of paper and scratched out a list: hedge clippers, sledgehammer, crowbar… The woman up front offered to sell him her lawnmower, but the blades needed sharpening. Sorry, I'll get my own, he said.

The First Barbecue

The first match bounced and went out. The unexpected rain had soaked the charcoal, washed everything, and left the evening air scrubbed for the first bbq. Aspen pulled an extra pack of veggie dogs from the freezer in case any other vegetarians showed up. Toby and EC bought pollo asado at the Price Club for themselves.

"Studboy, you have to leave airflow under the coals."

"Dude, shut the fuck up. I know how to arrange charcoal. Like Pops always said, Build it like a house and it'll burn. These coals were left out in the rain, dig?"

"Try more lighter fluid."

DuBois shrugged and saturated the coals with another squirt of fluid. He struck a match and held it to the corner of a brick until the flame snuffed between his fingers. The hibachi grill was crusted with rust and carbonized chicken fat. DuBois banged it on the patio, knocking off a shower of black flakes, and decided it was clean enough to cook on.

"I think I saw a gas can in the garage."

"Gasoline? Man, don't poison us."

"I know what I'm doing."

Toby's buddies in college called him The Owl. It couldn't have been for wisdom. He had put in extra time at the gym, since he met EC which showed in his chest and arms. He must have been in his late twenties, wore stonewashed jeans and white topsider shoes. He had his hair cut short and wore a goatee. The goatee was probably a fad. Toby seemed vulnerable to fad. Du-Bois bet that he carried a Pet Rock around at school when he was a kid. And a Rubik's Cube he never solved. He had small feet, small hands, and thick fingers. And kept a class ring on his left pinkie.

Rufi invited Brenda, a friend from school, over to play and Brenda's mother asked if her son could hang out with them while she went shopping. Aspen said it was okay, and since the morning clouds had burned off and the sun was on high, Rufi led the kids outside to run through the garden hose sprinkler, but DuBois told them not to waste water, so Rufi and Brenda got squirt guns and chased the kid brother around the yard.

"Brenda, run along the barracks and cover the left flank."

Spencer, aka the enemy, ran a circle around the portable fire pit, which Toby had picked up on sale at Megatool Outlet. The kid sought cover behind Toby as Rufi and his sister snuck up along the perimeter with their squirt guns poised for action. He stuck out his tongue. The girls caught him in a crossfire while he held up a stubby middle finger. Rufi shot for the crotch so it would look like he peed his pants.

"Knock it off."

"Sorry, Toby—collateral damage."

DuBois laughed and picked Spencer up by the arms, using him as a shield while the girls soaked him. Spencer squealed, kicked, wriggled free and hit the ground running.

"I'll get you back, DuBois."

He leapt the fence into the neighbor's yard and sent the sleepy orange cat darting for cover.

"Yo, kid! Stay out of that yard."

Spencer had picked an apricot off the ground and was getting ready to huck it at his sister, who was refilling her squirt gun with the hose. Spencer dropped the fruit, jumped back over the fence, and dashed for the cottage.

That kid is hyper, Toby said to DuBois as he poured gasoline on the coals.

"He's not hyper, he's a normal, active kid."

"No, I've seen kids like that before. He needs medication. He's out of control."

"That's ridiculous, man. Fuck a Prozac nation. Putting kids on medication…"

DuBois remembered his mother telling off his fourth-grade teacher, That boy doesn't need drugs, send him out to run laps around the school. While the other kids did math, DuBois did laps—he felt best when his heart beat as fast as his brain. His teacher was ecstatic when he came in from a run and scored a perfect 100 on the math test. She couldn't imagine that he practiced calculating as he ran—doing long division in stride.

Toby struck a match and tossed it on the fire, sending flames up four feet—the coarse black smoke made everyone cough—EGG-HHH, EGGHHH—before the fire snuffled out.

"These coals are beat. I'm going up to the store to get another scuttle-full. Cheese-n-rice!"

Toby looked defeated and went into the cottage where Aspen and EC prepared a salad, grabbed a Lowenbrau, and sat at the kitchen table. Thinking about fire safety, he blew out the green candle, under which Aspen kept a stack of lottery tickets.

"Aspen, babe, we need anything from the store?"

"I invited some friends from work, maybe more beer?"

"Slice the cucumbers thinner."

EC, holding a large knife, looked up at Toby like he was insane.

"You should find a task other than telling us how to make salad. I cut the cucumbers in this family."

EC wasn't used to taking suggestions from boyfriends. She couldn't remember her own dad ever going into a kitchen. Juan Carlos would have played DJ, with a beer in one hand, taking off one record before it finished and playing another and leaving them scattered about for EC to put away in the morning. Aspen noticed that EC sliced the next cucumber thinner and the next one thinner until they were like tracing paper.

Toby got a broom and went out to sweep up the carbon flakes that DuBois had knocked off the grill onto the patio. Pushing them into the dustpan, he squinted at the concrete to see if it had been discolored. Nothing a little muriatic acid couldn't obliterate. Always good to have a gallon on hand. And one of those coal chimneys for the bbq.

DuBois walked two blocks looking at the thirty-six houses, wondering what the people were doing inside, wondering why they never came out.

Once he got to The Dirty Boulevard, as they called it, the atmosphere changed: city bus #42 pulled up and an old lady hobbled out, leaning on her handcart, bound for the grocery store. Traffic was frenetic—a car that smelled like it needed oil honked in the intersection. A boom car, lowered almost to the asphalt, blasted bass heading east and six teenagers practiced grinding skateboards on the concrete planter at the street side of the store. The slap of flipping skateboards was the official sound of the era, echoing in the background of every scene. Two snot-nosed rugrats rode a grocery cart across the parking lot toward the dumpster where a street bum was digging for a gourmet cheese or slab of meat just past its expiry date. Six kids were piled on the coin-operated mechanical elephant in front of the store, their combined weight forced it to move slowly like an old drunk.

The store was too bright inside. DuBois left his sunglasses on as he picked out a bag of EZ Lite charcoal, hot dog buns, two limes and a six-pack of Bohemia, his favorite Mexican beer, which was on sale.

The clerk had long fingernails, bedazzled with rhinestones, so that she could barely key in the tender. Her smile reminded

DuBois of his sister, but the way she looked him up and down made him feel like bacon on a doughnut.

"Thanks."

"No problem, sugar."

She turned her head and watched him leave the store. He felt hungry and wondered about Aspen's new friends from work. She'd talked so much crap about them, he was mystified when she suggested they host a barbecue.

A police cruiser rolled through the intersection as he waited to cross the street. On the north side of the boulevard, apartments had names like Par*dise Arms and Tropical Mano* with many signs missing at least one letter. On one corner, a junk car, absent its engine and windshield, sat up on blocks in the parking lot of a smog test station. An adult bookstore occupied the opposite corner. That the grass grew greener on EC's side of the boulevard was not a toothless old saw. There were more trees and fewer tv antennas poking out of the roofs. About halfway down the block, he felt like he was being watched. He didn't see any signs of life peering out at him from the houses. The street felt deserted until he spotted the police cruiser out of the corner of his eye, pacing him down the block. A second later the car pulled onto the sidewalk in front of him. An officer stepped out and adjusted his belt.

"Is there a problem, officer?"

"You tell me. Set the package down slowly and put your hands on the car."

DuBois was careful not to make any sudden moves.

"Are you a gang member?"

"Naw."

The cop patted him down. Took a comb from his back pocket and put it on the roof of the car like he'd confiscated a switchblade.

"Let me see your ID."

"I don't have to show you my ID. Are you arresting me?"

The peace officer folded DuBois's right hand behind his back and clapped a handcuff to it. A car drove past blaring old-school Chaka Khan and DuBois felt their eyes on him.

"There was a robbery call on Euclid and University and you fit the description. The suspect fled on foot."

The cop peered into the brown paper sack. He put DuBois's left hand in the cuffs and left him leaning against the car while he put in a radio call. The black body of the police cruiser wasn't hot enough to raise a blister. He lifted DuBois's wallet from his back pocket and took out the ID.

"What do those tattoos mean?"

DuBois had a portrait of Malcolm X on his right arm, a skeleton with a smoke in one hand and a sloshing martini in the other tattooed on his forearm, and two kinds of barbed wire inked onto his wrists. It had been a long time since he'd been pinched in the cuffs, but it wasn't the first time. He didn't respond and the cop made a TTTTSSK noise before unlocking the iron bracelets.

"I guess you can go? But keep your nose clean."

DuBois picked up his sack, jammed the comb back in place and didn't look round to see if the peace officer was watching him.

Aspen's friends from work had arrived. Susanna brought a huge bowl of her secret potato salad. One of her kids, missing a front tooth, played Barbies with Rufi and Brenda in the dirt around the side of the house, which they had declared their clubhouse fort: no adults allowed. The kid brother was up in the lemon tree, looking down on the scene.

Zhen and Zhang had already put the CDs they brought into the boombox. Brenda's mother was back from the store and playing dominoes with the woman from up front who managed to pull a pink and orange flower-print muumuu over her nudity. She slapped her dominoes in place, laughed and drank her cheap beer from a plastic cup. The young guy called Boring was sitting in the corner drinking from a bottle of Chivas that he kept tucked in his belt.

"What's she doing here?"

"I don't know. Maybe DuBois invited her, he thinks she's funny. Looks like she's having a good time."

"I don't want you hanging around with her, we need her to move out, remember."

"You know why she's selling this place, don't you?"

"No, and I don't want to know. I want her out."

Zhen and Zhang were dancing to Chumbawamba on the patio.

"She's dying of cervical cancer. She has maybe a year to live."

"She told you that?"

"Uh huh."

"And you believed her?"

"Why would she lie?"

"You said yourself she's crazy."

Toby walked into the kitchen to grab another beer.

"What's she doing here?"

"Ask DuBois."

"What's taking him so long with the charcoal? I should have drove up there myself."

"Relax, Toby. The party doesn't start until everyone arrives."

"Hi… uh, Aspen. I made two plates of brownies, one for the kids and one for the adults. Do you have cats? I never even knew this neighborhood was here. It's like a little yuppie enclave in the middle of the city."

"The last tenant left that awful smell."

Toby didn't know what to say, so he walked down the driveway to look for DuBois. EC set the pan of adult brownies on top of the refrigerator. Flores smiled, revealing a gaping hole where she was missing a tooth.

The woman from up front had been drinking her cheap beer all day while she conducted whatever business she did over the phone with the curtains drawn tight. She had an oblong crystal hanging from her neck and hadn't bothered to put on shoes. She slapped down one of her dominoes and laughed for no reason.

"I can't believe they bought this shithole for $300,000."

"It's a good neighborhood. I wish we could afford to live here."

Susanna wanted to slip her sandals off but didn't feel comfortable yet. Maybe later, she thought.

Toby gathered wood from the side of the house and piled it into the new fire pit. Stacking the logs with precision, he sprinkled a handful of Kindling Lite (splinters of pitch-pine) which he picked up at Megatool Outlet. The sun was setting and everyone was hungry.

DuBois walked up the driveway carrying the charcoal.

Jaguar and Wrecking Ball came together. She brought a venerable wine and a brie to bake and he had made them stop at the store for a bag of baby carrots and a bottle of Evian Spritz since he didn't drink alcohol.

DuBois set to work on the hibachi and Aspen stood over him and rubbed his shoulders massaging a knot of tension.

"What's the matter, babe?"

"Nothing."

"Is it my coworkers? I didn't think they'd all come."

"Naw."

He leaned over and planted a long kiss on her forehead. Toby was talking about the virtues of middle management with the Jaguar, who wore a vintage short-sleeve checkered shirt, crisp black jeans, and Doctor Marten shoes. His hair remained slicked back in precision style as it always was at work. Aspen thought she heard Toby say, Those people don't want to work.

EC fell, tipsily, into a slow, solitary dance with Zhen and Zhang on the porch. Zhang said he was in the mood to smoke a bowl and sway to some grunge, but his brother, who had really been into darkwave lately, slipped Dead Can Dance into the CD player. Everyone was drinking and the music floated through the yard and a good time was underway.

DuBois laid three veggie dogs on, and Toby plied on his pollo asado, which sizzled on the grill as the fat dripped into the fire. Aspen put the Mexican rice in a bowl with the rest of the food on the patio table. EC debated with herself whether to organize the buffet by color or food group. She ended up putting the meats that everyone brought on the far end from dark meat to light, the grains in the middle (which included the hotdog buns and the rice) and the salad on the extreme side. She lined various condiments along the back behind their respective counterparts.

The woman from up front finished another beer but didn't do the alligator onto the dance floor until Flores put on a Jefferson Airplane tape.

"Remember, what the dormouse said..."

They held hands and spun in a dizzy circle. Boring must have gotten drunk because he was crawling up under the Jaguar's chair and slyly tying his boss's shoelaces together. Brenda's kid brother, recruited into the machination, told the Jaguar that Aspen wanted to talk to him in the kitchen. He fell for it, onto one knee in the soft dirt spilling his Evian Spritz.

"That wasn't funny, Ned."

Susanna stopped laughing long enough to say, I thought it was.

Aspen made a quick circle of the yard, stuffing limp paper plates into a Hefty bag. The woman from up front had the Jaguar cornered.

"I'd invite you in, but I'm getting ready to move."

"Boring."

"Excuse me."

"Yeah, boss."

The Jaguar slipped out of one conversation he didn't want to be in and into another. He thought he might treat the party to a poem, but after a full day of reading, study, and silence, he wasn't feeling his usual loquacious self. If they asked him to, he acquiesced that he would oblige. The Wrecking Ball was arguing about the best California wine with Toby. Jaguar saw the red wheelbarrow in the garage and smiled. The woman from up front asked for a sip of the Chivas, which Boring pulled out and handed over, reluctantly.

"I've got the cancer, you know. Yes. But I met a mystic healer who swears he has the cure."

Boring looked around for some old goat to foist the woman onto. He could smell her thick breath and false perfume.

"You wanna know a secret?"

She wet her middle finger between her lips and traced it, like a solipsistic guitar solo, in a meandering S over the rotunda of her chest, over the hill of her belly toward the swampy vaginal delta below.

"This crystal has healing powers when I slip it into my cunny."

Boring blushed. DuBois and Aspen held hands in front of the fire pit.

"Your coworkers ate all of Toby's pollo asado."

"Yeah, there's still a bunch of veggie dogs left, though."

Susanna sat down in one of the lawn chairs. Her butt and hips squeezed out the sides.

"Susanna, that was the best potato salad."

"Thank you, honey, it was my momma's recipe."

"You'll have to write it down for me."

The Jaguar found DuBois's punk records in the cottage and put Stiff Little Fingers on the turntable.

Everybody's dying in the centre of town. We're doing nothing wrong, we're only hanging around... They treated him like shit, kicked him in the head and then laughed when he bled...

"Thanks, Aspen. Nice meeting you, nice meeting you, nice meeting you."

"Bye, Zhen, bye, Zhang."

Susanna decided it was time to get her kid home to bed. Brenda's mom caught Spencer by his t-shirt and wiped ketchup off his face. They slipped out without saying goodbye.

Rufi brushed her teeth, ran a comb through her explosion of hair and climbed into her bunk without being told.

"My girl's growing up."

"Goodnight, Daddy."

Out on the patio, the mood had shifted, relaxed.

"Pot brownie anyone?"

"Yeah, let me try one of those."

"No thanks. None for EC either."

"Dope makes you dull."

"Don't be a fuddy-duddy, boss man."

"I'll totally mack one of those bad boys."

"No, thank you. I haven't even smoked since Paris."

The woman from up front took two brownies and staggered into the main house.

"Toby, we are going home."

"Just a minute."

He pulled the garden hose from the hose winder and doused the fire in his new fire pit. A hiss of steam rose.

Aspen put her healing hand on DuBois's shoulder and he slumped back into his chair with his legs splayed and took the last swig from his Bohemia with lime.

"I'm going to sleep, babe."

She slid The Selecter record into its proper sleeve and slipped another rocksteady side onto the turntable. About a half hour after everyone else had gone home, Sanderson Dode showed up with a 12-pack of Keystone Lite. A couple of guys DuBois once played in a band with were sitting around the cold fire pit, softly tapping on bongos. They drank Dode's beer and smoked hand-rolled cigarettes until three in the morning.

The Yard

A dozen cigarette butts littered his new mobile fire pit. Toby had come over early with his new lawnmower, intending to cut the grass. He hadn't planned to dump the ashes until after the second fire, since that would be more efficient, so he resolved to pick each butt out of the dust by hand. After one or two, with gray fingertips, he decided it was easier to dump the ashes into a plastic garbage bag.

Rufi was watching *Apocalypse Now* and DuBois had gone back to sleep in her bunk—helicopters reverberated inside his head as a napalm hangover defoliated his gray matter.

"Morning everyone. Can I borrow a socket to plug in the mower? I don't want to disturb the woman up front. I bought a new thirty-yard extension cord from Megatool Outlet so I can mow the back and front yard grass without unplugging. I can't use the garage plug because the wires are frayed. I'm going to have to replace the whole circuit box in there. Going to have to do a lot of rewiring around here."

Rufi didn't look up from the tv.

"Hi, Toby. The plug's over near the door."

"Morning, Aspen."

"Wasn't she supposed to move this weekend?"

"That's what I thought. Pia fucked up the contract. Legally, she can pay rent for 90 days. We've got her paying sixty-nine dollars a night, so you'd think that would motivate her ass, but all that junk is still piled in the garage. I don't know. Who parked their Cadillac in the driveway?"

Aspen walked out in her thin robe with the frilly pink collar and stuffed animal head slippers with most of her hair piled up in a disheveled beehive. She didn't like the way the windows in the two-story apartment behind them looked down into the yard like a guard tower. She didn't care that Toby saw her before she was dressed for the day. He planned to marry her best friend, and that made him like family. Peering over the gate on tiptoe, she could see the white convertible Cadillac parked in the driveway.

"Nice car."

A minute later the lawnmower motor whirred to life, causing squiggly lines to roll down the tv screen. The fog of war. Toby set to work on the front lawn as the sun began to rise in the sky. It was going to be a hot day.

DuBois sat up in Rufi's bed and stretched his arms. The fanfare of the lawnmower seemed too loud.

"I thought the helicopters busted out the tv."

He scratched himself, wondering what was on the agenda. I'm supposed to do something today, he thought, but I can't remember. The tv held Rufi's attention like frozen sea ice. DuBois slipped down onto the carpet and crept up on his daughter like a tiger, slowly, slowly. On the screen, Kilgore said, Charlie don't surf… DuBois pounced with the stealth of a wild beast, rolled, wrestled, and tickled the piano of her ribcage with the index fingers of his large hands.

"You shake my nerves and you rattle my brain..."

She was caught off guard by overwhelming force and debilitating laughter. Her hair was in his face like a smoke screen. Tumbling over, he got a leg lock around her waist. She tried punching his arm, pinching his skin between her nails, but his hide was like armor. He applied pressure until she said, I... sur... render.

"How's daddy's little Boo-daw this morning?

"Fine, Daddy, I'm watching *Apocalypse Now.*"

"Again? Not like the Saturday morning cartoons when I was a kid. *Quick Draw McDraw, Underdog, Johnny Quest...*"

"You're still a kid. I'm making coffee."

"Yes, please."

"How late were you up last night?"

"Shoot. I don't know. The boys came over and we rapped with some goofy friend of yours from work. Dude said his name was Dode. He asked Rodrigo how big his Gomez was. Hee hee hee."

"He showed up? I'm glad I went to bed. Rufi, pause that movie and bring your breakfast tray into the kitchen. And comb out your hair."

"Yes, sir, Colonel Momma."

The cottage smelled like fried eggs and Nag Champa. Aspen used a cookie cutter to make a heart shape in the bread. When she dropped the yolk in, it took the form of the heart. The left-over heart shapes, fried in butter, were Rufi's favorite part.

DuBois reached for the crust she hadn't eaten on the tray.

"Goofy muthafucker. He brought a 12-pack, though, so we invited him in."

"What's so funny?"

"Oh shit. That fool must have been drunk, 'cause the woman from up front stumbled out to tell us to knock it off—they talked and—"

"Does he drive a Cadillac?"

"Hee hee hee."

DuBois got up from the beige carpet and followed Aspen toward the bathroom.

"It's still out there in the driveway. They're perfect for each other."

"People crack me up."

"Excuse me."

"Let me grab my book."

He reached past her before she could shut the door and picked up the paperback. Aspen smelled good, so he kissed her. Out in the yard, Toby was starting to work up a sweat and had taken off his polo shirt. His chest and back looked like a thick brown carpet, which glistened above his pale skin. He pushed the lawnmower along the length of the Cadillac, taking care not to scratch it, and was about to mow the back lawn when Dode and the woman came through the sliding glass door. Toby took off his cap and wiped his brow with his polo shirt.

"Hi, Bro, I'm Sanderson Dode."

They shook hands.

"I'm Toby Saint-Malo. She told you I bought the house."

"Yeah, she was telling me."

The woman was wearing her purple chemise and holding Dode's hand. The smile on her face showed that the planets had cosmically aligned.

"Sandy's going to help me move, aren't you, Ducky?"

"Sure thing, Jello-puddin.'"

Toby turned a shoulder to their kiss but couldn't escape the sloshing bucket of lips and tongues. The kiss might be less disgusting, he thought, if she had waxed her mustache hair. The woman had proffered the word he most wanted to hear—Move—and he didn't want to jinx it.

"Uh, I have to get a few things done around here before I have to get to my second job."

He pushed the start button on the lawnmower, which swirled into action. Stooping to pick up a dish of dry cat food that had been set out for the old orange cat, he dumped it in the rubbish bin.

"Nice meeting you."

The couple didn't see Toby or hear the lawnmower as their embrace grew more intense. Aspen and DuBois watched the scene through parted mini-blinds.

"I wanna look. Yikes! Toby needs a shirt or I need sunglasses."

"It's like Def Jam Comedy around here."

When Toby finished the back grass, he cut the engine. The yard was dotted with more than a dozen gopher holes. DuBois finished his coffee and set the mug in the sink. Dode stepped out of the main house wearing a leather biker cap and licked the woman's dried saliva on his lips. He piled an art deco lampshade into his Cadillac next to the chartreuse shower curtain. He was whistling like a tree full of house finches.

Aspen and Rufi passed through the gate, skirted the eight-foot brick wall, and made their way down the trash cans, fast, continuing down the long driveway and leaping into the Fury while Dode was still in the house. Thus, avoiding him altogether. She had no idea what to say to him, but was sure, as word passed around the office like a collection plate, that it would dominate the docket at the call center on Monday.

Toby knocked again.

"Studboy, I'm going to grab the cord. Gonna have to re-sod the whole yard."

Toby wiped more sweat from his hairy body with the polo shirt.

"Who's the dude with the sweet Caddy?"

"Some creep from Aspen's work who came to the party after you split. She came out and they hooked up."

"Okay. Oh, don't leave cat food out for strays, you'll never get rid of that mangy riffraff."

"Shitting beasts."

He looked at Toby and knew Juan Carlos wouldn't like him. He would size him up and write him off, as they'd done to his predecessor—the Frat Boy. Juan Carlos used to hold a special antipathy for fraternity brothers—Frat boys don't think about anything besides chugging, hazing, and date-raping. Every business major I ever met only took Shakespeare because it was required. Cliff and Biff Notes. This moniker even though Robert had never been in a fraternity. Robert had a liberal arts degree and worked as a line cook in a sandwich shop. He was conventionally good-looking, friendly without being a gregarious creep. There was nothing wrong with Robert, which was the problem. He was all foreground and no shadow. Anyone who didn't come out of punk rock, Juan Carlos would say, was basically a frat boy with capitalist consumer values. DuBois laughed along but wondered if Juan Carlos had wanted to get back with EC. Especially when he said things like, She's changing, man. Not the girl I lived with. She's becoming her mom. Juan Carlos thought that you either became your parents or you didn't. And there was no way in hell he would.

EC, for her part, tried to be a socially conscious adult—she recycled cans, bottles, and newspapers. She even rinsed out the cat food tins. If it polluted the air or was unkind to animals, she was against it, which didn't stop her from driving a Suburban Utility Vehicle or eating hamburgers.

Toby wound the extension cord carefully. He looked back at the main house. Surveyed the yard.

"Dode reminded me of this guy in my fraternity from college."

"You were in a fraternity?"

"Omega^2."

"Huh."

"I wanted to be a film major but switched to business admin when I couldn't get in."

"Yeah, I thought about film school once. Had a plan to make the next *Raging Bull.*"

"That's funny. I wanted to work in film colorization. I had a plan to colorize *Raging Bull.*"

"Huh. That movie was so intense I saw red. Even though they used chocolate syrup, I saw red blood spraying off De Niro's face. The mind, man. They should make more films in black and white... Have you seen *Nosferatu?* The silent *Faust? Häxan?* Shadows like deep, dark knives, man. You can't film that shit in color. Life should be in black and white."

A sledgehammer moves with a fixed rate of downward torque. A crack—both sound and splinter—boasts success, and so the unwanted curb of cement in the backyard was destroyed. Toby handed the ten-pound hammer to DuBois, who rubbed his hands together, gripped it, and swung high with the leverage of his long arms punishing the unwanted concrete.

"Nice shot, Studboy."

A piece broke off and he lifted it easily into the wheelbarrow. He used the teal polo shirt, which had been tucked into his belt, to wipe the sweat out of his eyes. The two men worked for over an hour hammering until the cement was gone and a flattened dirt furrow remained between parcels of grass. Their conversation wildly roved from film appreciation to air pollution to the work at hand.

"It's cool. I do it just to get aggression out. You know all this pent-up—"

DuBois wiped sweat from his hairline.

"My body's gonna send hate mail, though."

"I know what you mean, Studboy."

Toby wiped his own sweat and lifted the hammer for another knock. Toby was thinking that DuBois's body was built for swinging a hammer. He conducted a short internal debate on how the comment might be construed, didn't want to sound homoerotic, so kept it to himself.

"They say buying a house causes more stress than anything next to getting married and you're doing that too… I don't envy you, man."

DuBois felt a cool sense of satisfaction helping EC and Toby prepare their nest. He also felt a blister bubble up on his palm. He understood the need to change a space and make it your own. Toby felt like he was putting his acquired muscles to use, though the sledgehammer found some he had neglected in the gym.

The woman from up front got the last of her things loaded into Dode's Cadillac. EC took one look at the inside of her new home and called the cleaning lady her mother used. Her future husband experienced the satisfying feeling for the first time that the ground he toiled on was his own.

Communal Living

The broken chunks of unwanted curb were stacked beside the house in a well-thought-out pile. Toby gave himself fifteen minutes to drive to his part-time job at Chinese Furniture Showroom. On Sundays, there wasn't much traffic. His job inside the warehouse was to keep the furniture displays throughout his area neat and organized, looking like a model home rather than a home people lived in. As soon as he got the pillows arranged, a family would roll through with kids like gale-force winds. In the first hour, a Caucasian male, average height, with unremarkable features, wearing an LA Lakers jersey, tried to open a pullout couch the wrong way and broke it. Toby's supervisor wasn't happy.

"It's your job to make sure this kind of thing doesn't happen."

The rest of his shift was spent in preventative, N-n-n-n-n, Don't touch that! Let me show you how this works…

On Circle Circle, DuBois relaxed in a patio chair and read a novel while Yakuza turned about on his lap like an animated puzzle piece searching for its place. DuBois knew the exact extent of the danger the situation presented. The cat's claws padded about his legs, poking him just shy of breaking the skin. The story was intense so he read with the courage of the oblivious. The last time they spent a lazy Sunday like this, Yakuza tore into his flesh when another cat came into the yard. The lazy beast didn't snare birds, bat grasshoppers, or chase down mice, preferring to let them do their own thing, but another cat, any cat, foreign or domestic, sent him into an inexplicable rage.

DuBois sipped herbal iced tea from a tall glass. He squeezed the last drops from the lemon he picked earlier off of the tree and stirred with the appropriate long spoon. EC had given them her old utensils, which was good since the aluminum coating on Aspen's flatware was flaking. EC gave them a set of chipped dinner plates and two wine glasses that didn't match.

"I won't have that tired stuff in my new house."

After DuBois broke the last wine glass in the sink, Aspen couldn't be bothered by the glassware's pedigree. She was happy not to drink out of a plastic cup.

"What's the point of washing the dishes if you're just going to break them? Might as well put them directly into the trash."

"I don't set out to break the dishes."

He smiled, trying to accept his clumsy side. EC gave them a cabinet from Toby's college dorm, which DuBois envisioned as a bookshelf. Since it wouldn't fit in the cottage, they decided to keep it with the ragtag fugitive fleet of their furniture at his parents' house. Most of their things were handed down by parents, strangers, or friends. Their possessions were like a star map of the city's finest rummage, of which they were long-time denizens. DuBois had even played in a band called Garage Sale Score! which lasted about two weeks and broke up after their first gig.

"Girl, you always make your boyfriend get rid of his furniture when he moves in. Five years on, he takes nothing but a duffle bag with his clothes. Ha ha huh."

They'd seen it happen to Juan Carlos and Robert and wondered if Toby would fall into the pattern. He had four and a half years to go.

"This ugh-wee cabinet doesn't match my decor."

"Maybe we can paint it."

Aspen ran her hand over the fake wood texture.

There was no way DuBois would let her get rid of his things. Wasn't it bad enough that his momma threw away his Star Wars figures? Aspen wanted to get rid of his old holey red jeans that he'd worn to most of the gigs he played with Welded-Steel Chain Fastener. She wanted to burn the photos of his ex-girl-friends that he kept in a shoebox at his mom's house and recycle the letters Virginia Fontanelle wrote to him in the ninth grade.

Hey DuB,

I'm in Mr. Fuckingham's class. It's kinda boring but Mr. F just threw chalk at Doug Fulbright because he was talking in class and hit Stacie Raddison who never talks in class. So funny. Do you wanna go to a movie Saturday night? My dad will drive us. He'll probably make us bring my little sister, but we can ditch her in the arcade.

Luv Gini

As far as DuBois was concerned, those letters were innocent ar-tifacts of an age gone by. Vague documents with the power to invoke elaborated memory that would die with his body or his faculties. He wondered what happened to Gini—to Roy, Mikey, Marla, Dee, Tawnja. To all his friends from those days. He couldn't remember what movie they saw, but the heavy block of black darkness in the back of the car was still vivid. Her father's huge head watching the road, how he never spoke or played the radio. The quiet and her hand squeezing through the darkness between his legs and his own hand slipping between hers. A dangerous stiffening. The soft cotton of her sweatpants. His relationship with Aspen was a living artifact separate from the past, like a neoplastic sculpture garden distinct from old things dug out of the sere sands of Egypt or wrenched from the clay of ancient Greece. Each unimpeachable by the other.

DuBois looked up from his book when EC came through the gate.

"Don't mind me, Dub. I'm here to pull weeds."

DuBois read until he reached the end of a chapter—didn't want to put the book down, but found it taxing to stay focused while his friend worked. He lived here too and didn't like looking at the weeds. Shoving a yellow envelope into the book to mark his place, he went into the cottage and came right back out cradling two stereo speakers in his arms. The radio, set to an old-school station, played Roy Ayers "Everybody loves the sunshine…"

"Weed-pulling music. Hee hee hee. You want a glass of iced tea?"

"Please, please."

DuBois handed her a glass, which she threw down her throat in one gulp. EC had strong, broad shoulders and shoulder-length curly black hair.

"You got an extra pair of work gloves?"

"Sure, sure. You can use Toby's."

The weeds didn't come up easily, moored to the earth as they were with thick and tangled roots. The sun clicked upward by the hour until it bore down overhead. EC had a new gardening hat, which was UV resistant, that Toby picked up for her at Megatool Outlet. Despite the heat, she smiled as she worked.

"You guys are already doing too much work and you haven't even moved in."

"We have to. We're having the housewarming party in two weeks."

"Two weeks?"

"Yeah, yeah. I'm registered at all the department stores so everyone can get me wots of nice presents for my new home. And Toby signed up on the registry at Megatool Outlet in case you and Aspen want to get him something we need."

After about an hour, the patch of ground looked a little less like a jungle and a little more like a Zen garden. The woman up front must have lost interest in the yard several years before. DuBois figured that she quit the yard with most things in life after her diagnosis, but for all he knew, she had always lived like this. Eventually, the last bush had been pruned, the last weed extracted. EC raked the topsoil with the titanium alloy rake she bought at Megatool Outlet while she chose assorted plants.

"Let's put these plants in the ground. Do you think they go with the other plants?"

"What do you mean, go with?"

DuBois picked up a shovel and was glad EC offered him the gloves because the blister on his hand felt raw and open.

"I meant aesthetically. Do the colors go? Also, does this genus fit with that genus taxonomically? How about the first one right here?"

"Juan Carlos would be a better judge of the colors."

"I don't want to hear about Juan Carlos."

She pointed to an open patch of dirt and he jabbed the spade in. Before the hole was a foot deep, they examined a severed earthworm writhing around. Don't worry, he'll get over it. EC shook a plant loose from its plastic pot and set it into place. DuBois pushed dirt in around the edges and tamped the soil.

"Wow, that looks beautiful."

"Hi, hi, Aspen's here. We've been working hard."

DuBois removed the gloves, black with dirt and sweat and flakes of skin. He leaned the shovel against the wall. The three friends surveyed the day's labor. He leaned in and she pulled back because his body odor smelled rich but gave him a quick kiss anyway.

"You smell like aged cheese, babe."

"I haven't been wearing deodorant since that last office job."

"Toby has a can of Right Guard you can spray, Dub."

Before he could speak out against the chemicals they put in that antiperspirant shit, Rufi scampered up the driveway. He pushed away a skein of her explosive brown locks, which had slipped into her eyes.

"Daddy, a metermaid's putting a ticket on your car."

"Shit, that was what I was supposed to do today."

California had labeled him a "gross polluter" since his battered Toyota wagon couldn't pass the smog check and now whenever he drove it, he felt like he was doing something evil. The mechanic said $450 might help it pass the test even though the car was worth about that much. It didn't matter since they didn't have the money.

"Excuse me, sir? You gave me a ticket two days ago. I'm aware that my car needs to be registered—I'm saving money for repairs."

The metermaid didn't answer because he was too focused on entering the license plate number into an electronic ticket book.

"Hello? Hello?"

"You have to park this car off the street."

"I don't have a driveway, man."

"You must put this vehicle in storage. I can issue a ticket every two hours."

"What the hell is wrong with you? Are you human?"

"This is my job."

"Screw your job, ass clown."

The metermaid pushed another yellow envelope with a ticket under the windshield wiper and climbed into his vehicle, which looked like a golf cart.

"I do not enjoy being called names, sir."

He'd been called a jackbooted brown shirt fascist thug by a lady in a Volkswagen parked at a red curb and a commie pinko agent of the state by an elderly man waving a cane who had parked his Ford Taurus in front of a driveway. Every day people harassed him—children threw rocks at his cart, ladies flipped him off with obscene gestures. He missed the old country. He missed the quiet life he had as a country doctor. Though sometimes he pretended he was ten years younger and that this job was an internship for the police academy or the FBI. On payday his pretenses fell apart, as he looked in at the kitchen and caught a sad smile on his wife's face. The golf cart whirled off like a popsicle stick in a gutter torrent. DuBois let the ticket stay on the windshield, wondering if the guy was dead enough inside to come back in two hours and lay another one on top of it.

EC and Aspen walked down the driveway. He knew what Aspen was thinking. She didn't have to say it and to her credit, she didn't. He thought EC might say things happen for a reason and was glad her mind was on something else.

"Hi, hi. We're going for an exercise walk around the neighborhood."

"EC wants to see how people have remodeled over the years."

"It's funny that the parking meter guy would come down this street on a Sunday."

"Especially since there aren't any meters on this block."

"There, there, D-String."

DuBois still didn't know what to do about the car. He walked back up the driveway, into the yard and found Rufi reading one of her Oz books. He picked up his own book and tried to read but couldn't concentrate. He kept thinking about the car, about the repairs it needed, about the 200,000 miles they'd driven together. He weighed the pros and cons of public transit, the bovine, lethargic ages between bus stops in a city designed for cars. Eventually, the plot of the book shunted the plot of his life aside and he melted into the story and out of reality.

EC and Aspen walked at a brisk pace, moving their arms to tone the haunting flab. They passed an immaculate lawn like a putting green, turned on a perpendicular street and pushed up an incline.

"The same thing happened when I introduced Toby to my mother. He charmed her. That's one of his strong points, he can win anybody over."

"I don't think he cares about winning us over. I don't think he likes DuBois. Remember when you brought him to Undersea Planet to watch DuBois's band? He was playing bass and singing, Daylight comes tally my bananas, for the tourists."

'Toby liked the music. He bought a cassette."

"I know, that's what I mean. DuBois hates the trendy covers he has to play at Undersea Planet, it's for tourists, a gig he only did for money. It's not his art."

"Yeah, yeah, but you like it too."

"True, we both like Harry Belafonte, he's fantastic, but, you know, the starfish and seahorse costumes are embarrassing."

"I think they're called sea stars. I mean, they're not fish."

"Whatever, a seahorse isn't a horse, either. Ha ha."›

"Look, here's a house for sale."

"What's the asking price?"

The girls walked up onto the lawn to pick up a flyer from a box nailed to the Sunny Day Realty sign.

"Let's look in the window."

"Wow, it has a fireplace!"

"Those hardwood floors are like yours."

"Wouldn't it be cute if they made this into a picture window?"

"We could have gotten this place a year ago for half the asking price."

They walked for about forty-five minutes up and down the surrounding streets. Every fourth house had a For Sale sign in the yard. They looked in all of the windows. When they got back, Rufi and DuBois were still reading.

"I could have bought one of these houses for a hundred thousand less…"

He heard Aspen's voice. Caught himself not listening. She'd tried to pull him out of the book, off the page. He didn't like to hear the summary of her conscious dreams any more than her unconscious ones. Like this morning, she dreamed that six circus clowns were trying to rob the house—they hit him over the head with a bat and took the VCR. The effort to listen was like doing a pull-up at the park. Like lifting all of his own weight. He got his chin over the bar in time to hear her say, I think we should save up and buy an old house in Golden Hills before they go up too.

"It's Golden Hill, no s."

Toby got off work from Chinese Furniture Showroom as the sun was setting and came to the house to make sure that the woman up front had gotten all of her stuff out. He planned for the painters to come in Monday so that they could move EC's furniture the next weekend.

"What did you do? These plants are no good with the tropical ones and why did you cut the bush back so far?"

"We worked hard today."

"We? SIGH. No wonder my gloves and tools were left out."

He picked up the shovel and put it into the tool shed.

"This is stupid. Stupid…"

DuBois heard the dispute from inside the cottage where he was making peanut butter and fried plantain sandwiches. The sizzle was pleasant on the ear as the sugars boiled inside the fruit. He flipped the sandwiches with the black spatula and pressed down. SZZZZ. SZZZZ. Eating them out on the patio while the sky turned pink would have been lovely, but Aspen took up her sandwich and moved closer to him on the futon couch to listen to the argument like it was a Friday night fight on the radio.

Cold Calling

The inside of her mouth was as dry as the empty water cooler in the break room, which one of the guys had already tipped to one side. A lesson in futility. Even a horse won't drink from a stagnant pool. There were sodas in a machine, but she didn't drink soda. Hadn't since she was a teenager. The Wrecking Ball had brewed some kind of brown liquid earlier that afternoon, which remained in the pot on the warmer, but the idea of drinking from a Styrofoam cup made it impossible. She couldn't bring herself to drink anything out of Styrofoam.

"Hello, Mrs. McCaffery, this is Aspen with the Enigmatic Widget Corporation…"

"I'm sorry we're not interested."

"Hello, Mrs. McDaniel, this is Aspen with the Enigmatic Widget Corporation…"

"I'm busy watching tv—please, please don't call again."

Aspen set the phone in its cradle and leaned back in her chair. Pushing into the aisle, everyone in her row had focused their attention on the Jaguar who stood in front of Julie's cubicle.

"What happened to Zhen and Zhang?"

"Those clowns aren't coming back."

It was the second day they hadn't shown up for work. Aspen found the Jaguar's smug air distasteful. He seemed to take pride in speaking forthrightly, but whenever bosses talked about employees behind their back, she had to wonder what they said about her. In this young boss, it could have been inexperience or an inability to care what anyone else thought.

A stuffed toy flew out of Dode's booth and hit Boring in the back of the head. Boring had grown to loathe Dode, hated the sound of his voice, his stupid blonde hair, his clothes, everything. He chucked the toy over the top of the cubicles to the next row. It flew all around the room, like boys tossing around a tennis shoe in the locker room.

"I went to Vegas once, and this stripper asked me if I wanted a lap dance, and I said, No thanks, I'm running out of money. She got all offended and said, You could have told me that I was beautiful but wanted to stay by the stage. Women want to be lied to…"

Julie rose from her seat to get a sheet of fresh leads. She wore a tightly fitted top and flared pants with faux fur on the cuffs.

"Yeah? Well, Sanderson, maybe fat skanks want to be lied to."

Aspen hoped that Susanna was out of hearing range. Julie liked to whisper about the food Susanna consumed in the break room—Ooo, McDonald's soft serve? It's so gross. Julie called her Big Susanna and Aspen assumed there must have been another Susanna or Little Susanna in the office. Julie looked so thin, she might suffer from anorexia. If you could look past the boobs, you'd see ribs and hipbones and frail arms. At home, Aspen avoided talk about body image in front of her daughter. She worried about it, though, and hoped puberty wouldn't hit Rufi like a bomb.

Flores took off her headset and leaned toward Aspen. She smelled like nicotine and break room coffee.

"I had fun at your barbecue, but when I went out to my van, I found this note."

She passed the note as the Jaguar sauntered up the row. He intercepted it like a seventh-grade math teacher, with sarcastic bravado.

"No passing notes in class, children. Do I have to separate you two?"

After he said this, Aspen realized that Julie was no longer sitting next to Boring. They had talked for a whole hour the Friday before without making any calls. No calls, no sales.

"I've been calling, Boss. Nobody's home."

Aspen studied the marks on her sheet.

"I talked to lots of people. MacGowan, not interested. McCallister, not home. McAvoy, not interested, McDougall, McHenry, McMordie, McTeague, McTell not interested, not interested, not interested, not interested. I made a new rule: five not-interesteds in a row, take a break."

She smiled. It was the first time she had asserted herself in front of a boss. She felt liberated, like removing shackles or slipping off your life vest to accept drowning.

"You have to take a breather after that kind of rejection."

"That's good. That's right. I don't want you to be like Hot Fingers Susanna."

When Susanna heard her name, she peered out of her cubicle and saw the Jaguar getting ready to make a speech. He jumped up on the filing cabinet so everyone in the call center could hear him.

"Listen up, everyone. That's right, headsets off and ears up. You don't want to dial too many numbers an hour. I keep telling you guys to slow down. Try to start a conversation with the customer, but not with each other in the aisles. That cuts into productivity. Establish rapport. That's what I used to do when I was cold calling. If you get into a pattern of hanging up, your impulse will be to hang up, it's the safe way out. Don't take the safe way out. You have to treat it more like a game, a challenge. There are strategies. It's like poetry. There are ways to win. Try something like, Can I ask why you're not interested, ma'am?"

"These leads are bogus."

"Try asking them if they earn over one hundred thousand a year. If they do, they'll start boasting. If not, the leads are bogus. Move on."

Aspen was always surprised by the personal things people told her over the phone. I'm giving my son a bath. You sounded like my ex, she left me, but I still care about her. I'm sitting on the toilet, hold on a second... Oh snap, I thought you were my drug dealer...

The Jaguar opened the note, seeing an opportunity to boost morale.

"Okay, okay. I caught Flores and Aspen passing notes, and we all know what that means…"

"Read it!"

"Okay, listen to this. Dear whoever, I don't know who you are or why you parked in front of my house. Please park in front of the house of the person you are visiting. I have worked hard to keep my yard green and orderly. I hate to look out my window and see cars… Ha ha ha. She lives in a city and doesn't like to see cars. What a maroon. One of Aspen's neighbors left this on your van? Next to the peace sign? Ha ha ha. Whoever wrote this has a stick up their ass. They should move to Wyoming. I should write a villanelle…"

"Big Take Over!"

A cold caller from another row yelled. It meant that they were close to a deal and needed help closing it. The Jaguar jumped off the filing cabinet and sprinted to take the call before the Wrecking Ball.

"I hate this job. Children? TTTSK, I'm forty-seven years old."

"Flores, sorry about my neighbor, I've never even seen the woman."

"No worries."

"Can I ask you a question?"

"Sure, honey, go ahead."

"Have you ever seen an Enigmatic Widget?"

"They keep promising to take us on a tour of the factory, none of the bosses here can be trusted. Including the poet. Never trust a poet or a manager. They act the same way toward their employees that they do toward the customers, tell 'em what they wanna hear. Fucking panderers."

"Wow. You don't talk like you enjoy this, so, uh... why work here?"

"Aspen honey, I'm trying to buy a food truck and need cash."

"Wow."

"Susanna wants to buy a house and works two jobs, Cecil wants to start his own law practice—everyone has a goal... Gloria plays flute in the symphony."

"Stoner Gloria? I had no idea!"

"Ho oh, no. I'm the company stoner. Jaguar said he smelled dope smoke in Gloria's hair, so pinned the handle on her, but I'd given her a ride to work, it was my joint. Do you smoke? I'm high right now. No, you don't look it. Julie's going to school to be a model, she's got the snooty-bitchy part down. You have to have something else here or you'd go crazy. And Dode's in luv, l-u-v, aren't you, Dode?"

"Oh, I met the perfect woman. She's beautiful. Even if she's a bit older. And she doesn't mind my extra emotional energy. In fact, she nurtures it. We spent every minute together this weekend until I had to come to work. This job's not so bad. But I'm looking at this as an entry-level position. I have a degree in middle management from State…"

Dode kept talking until he discovered that everyone had gone back to work.

Julie was on the phone and listened intently to a guitar riff play on an answering machine: Hello, this is pop sensation Brittany Spears…

She copied the number and walked across the room, hoping the Jaguar was still on that call.

"Yo, Boring, check out this answering machine. It's Brittany Spears."

Boring took the number on a tiny yellow Post-it and punched in the numbers. He heard the same cheap and sleazy guitar riff followed by the same message: Hello, this is pop sensation Brittany Spears… which was interrupted by a man's voice, Hello?

"Oh hi, uh, this is Sanderson. Is Brittany there?"

"No, she's at drama practice."

"Thank you, sir. Could you tell her I called? She should have the number. Bye."

Boring sat back in his chair.

"I talked to Brittany's dad. I'm going to call her back tomorrow. I bet she's hot."

He wrote the number down on his desk calendar. It was common practice to save numbers, especially if a customer was rude. Boring took them with him and signed people up for dildo catalogs from the back of Hustler and wrote the numbers on the walls of public lavatories. Most people didn't realize that he had their address, their credit history, shoe size, favorite color—everything.

Over in his cubicle, Dode called a number of a person who had been rude to him three months before, Mr. Rittle. You order Chinese food. You pick up now!

"What are you talking about! This is the Little residence. Little. Barbara, did you order Chinese?"

"You order Chinese food, Kung Pao chicken, pepper beef, flied lice, assho–"

Click. Mr. Little hung up.

The Wrecking Ball had put one of her opera CDs in the player and was humming an aria as she circulated through the call center looking for a Big Take Over. The championship crown for top seller of the week was hanging on Gail's cubicle. She had moved to the corner because she didn't like to make small talk with the trainees saying, I prefer to stay focused. Every week ten new people came to work and most fled by week's end. The Jaguar said that every once in a while a young poet came in with the new hires. This was difficult for him, he claimed. I can't show favoritism, even if they make goo-goo eyes at me for an entire shift.

Gail counted herself lucky to beat Susanna by one sale the week before and spent the hundred-dollar cash bonus at the new Body 18 store at the mall. She also worked two jobs. Gail was saving money to bring her family to the States but wasn't about to tell the call center that. An hour later, Aspen had called a whole page with the surname Chan, thirty-two Chans in a row. Aspen drew on the calendar while she dialed. She sketched a quick pentagram, hoping magick might help her sell an Enigmatic Widget. She doodled a pirate flag, a vase with flowers and a fairy that looked like Tinkerbell. Finally, she drew a human form and scrawled the phrase Voodoo Dolly next to it. She didn't want to accrue bad karma but decided to jam a pushpin into the eyes when the next customer was rude. A lot of the people in the call center skipped over the Asian names because they didn't speak English or pretended not to. Aspen lost her place a few times and called the same Chan twice.

"Hello, Mrs. Chan, this is Aspen from the Enigmatic Widget Corporation…"

"No English."

"That's okay, bye."

She was making a conscious effort to say thank you or goodbye to each caller so that it seemed like she had a full conversation.

"Hello, Mrs. Chang, this is Aspen from the Enigmatic Widget Corporation…"

"Sorry, I am not interesting."

She took a deep breath and dialed the next number.

"Hello, Mr. Chank…"

"Um, um, um, uh, can you hold on?"

The voice was male, probably the son of Mr. Chank. Whoever it was set the phone down. Aspen waited patiently, spacing out. She forgot who she had called and ran her finger over the list. She heard a noise in the background, so turned up the volume on her headset to see if he was coming to the phone.

"Hello? Hello, this is Aspen from the—"

BAMMM!

A terrific shock knocked Aspen backward out of her chair with a crash and her head bounced on the floor like a bowling ball. She clutched her right ear with both hands. A sound like an exploded firecracker had rocked the phone line. Everyone looked around. Dode saw Aspen writhing on the carpet. He craned his neck, trying to figure out if he should call 911 or laugh his ass off.

"Oh my gosh, what has happened?"

The Wrecking Ball knelt over Aspen's fallen body. She looked so small, fallen into a fetal ball, crippled. A face twisted with pain. A concussed grotesque. She pried Aspen's hand away from the side of her head and the cold callers who had gathered around saw the blood trickle from her shattered eardrum. A tear followed gravely, at its own pace, from her eye. The blood dripping off of her cheek onto the carpet would leave a stain.

Litigation Nation

Aspen thought she remembered Toby talking at her damaged ear. Had EC been holding her hand? She couldn't be sure. Toby's lips formed words, she supposed, but without sound. Waves of air sloshed through the torn drumhead and rattled the auditory cortex, but meaning eluded her. DuBois breathed consciously, glad to be alone in the elevator as it rose from the lobby. The elevator was slow, labored. At least that Muzak wasn't playing. He imagined all his favorite punk songs arranged as instrumentals with a string orchestra. *I'm about to have a nervous breakdown—Hm HmHM h Hm h HmHm. HmHm.* The elevator itself smelled like a bucket of sterilizing chemicals, which made him think of sick people. The doors opened on the fourth floor where a series of hushed conspiratorial tones emanating from the various rooms turned out to be television blare mixed with the moans of the sick, the dying and the mad. He followed the numbers, searching for her room. A doctor in a white coat conferred with a pair of nurses wearing matching scrubs in the hall. As he passed many of the rooms, he could see the blue tv light as well. It was like walking through an opium den with addicts, stretched out on fetid canvas cots, kicking the gong around. It all felt very 19th-century sanitarium. He expected to witness a bloodletting, dodge escaped leeches, and smell ether wafting out of the surgery. He was glad that the tv in her room was off. Then again, it made him think that she must be seriously fucked up, since she was missing *Felicity* on the WB. Aspen slept with the bed elevated. The stillness was impressive, the room dark except for a faint glow of amber neon from outside. It was hot and Aspen's painted toenails protruded from under a thin sheet. DuBois thought that invalidity suited her, that the white gauze wrapped once around her head added a perverse quality to her beauty. DuBois sat on the edge of the mattress and touched her hand, careful not to wake her. He sat with his baleful eyes closed until a nurse came in.

"Go on 'ome. Aspen can leave hospital in the morning."

He didn't want to leave, but did. At home, he found anxiety, the worry in every tick of the amplified clock. The awful wonder whether she would hear in stereo. The ugly do-nothing hopelessness of hope. He hadn't run in a long time, his ligaments suffered atrophy, but in his mind he ran, all the way back to seventh grade. He ran through puberty, he ran from cops, he never understood what the cops had against him. Supposed it was some kind of anarchy in his posture, a lawless countenance. He ran down a steep embankment in his dream through a garden that needed watering and climbed the spiral staircase of an underground tower until he came to a treasure chest. He stood there stupid, afraid to open it. He ran. He ran away. Passing mundane realities, he ran toward ridiculous, vivid adventures and kept running in his sleep until he woke exhausted.

DuBois and Rufi came back the next morning. Rufi climbed up into the hospital bed with her mother, who was awake and asking for coffee. They had given her a sleeping pill the night before, so she was still groggy. Rufi grabbed Aspen by the torso and squeezed.

"I have a surprise for you."

Aspen wished that Dubois would step around to the other side of the bed and repeat what he said to her unbandaged ear. His face looked so forlorn it must have been sweet. He smelled of talcum powder, a pleasant change or maybe it called-up a memory from a happier time. She came to life with her smile, taking on an air of leisure. The hospital pajamas might have been a terry cloth robe and the pillows propped behind her back of pure satin. She might have been stretched out on a chaise poolside under a friendly sun in a modernist Palm Springs case study house. She'd never been to Palm Springs and hadn't worked on her tan since she was a teenager, but that same youthful glow came into her face with the smile. Her coworkers sent a vase of assorted flowers, which brightened the dull, functionary room. The nurse came in with a roll of bandage.

"You might learn this, luv."

His large hands moved carefully as he wrapped the bandage once around her head and looked to the nurse for approval. She smiled and he continued to wrap five or six yards of fine white muslin around her head to protect it. Round and round like a turban. DuBois stepped back to admire her swaddled brain. He lifted her hand and kissed it.

Rufi snuggled deeper into her momma's bosom. Her massive kinky hair was pulled back in a ponytail. Aspen almost laughed.

"Child, your hair would twist into dreadlocks and your teeth would rot in your head if I wasn't there to nag—brusha, brush."

Rufi didn't mind being scolded. She'd had a rough night too, brooding over a life without her momma.

"I'm sorry, Mummy."

"It's okay, Boo-daw. We'll brush it when we get home."

DuBois extended a green velvet jewelry box in one palm. Aspen looked like she might choke on sentiment. He lifted the lid.

"Your grandmother's brooch?"

"Yeah, I'd forgotten about it."

"She gave it to us when we were going to get married."

"Mmm."

He pulled back the lid on the box, revealing a shamrock green stone set into a silver berthing. His hands shook as he fumbled with the pinback.

"Okay, don't move."

He managed to pin it to the turban. The nurse brought a hand mirror.

"Lovely, can you try standing, dear?"

Rufi pulled the sheet to the side and Aspen scooted to the edge of the bed. DuBois gripped her hand to steady her. She was wearing purple hospital pajamas with gold paisley teardrops, which tied in the back. One foot touched the floor.

"It's cold."

Rufi jumped over to her momma's valise and brought out the animal-head slippers. She situated one on each foot.

"Thank you, Boo-daw."

Aspen stepped with one slipper. DuBois swung an arm around her waist and gripped her hand. As she began to list to one side, he eased her upright.

"Let's blow this medicine stand."

"What did you say, Boo-daw?"

"She said this tongue depressor gets her down."

Aspen looked at them like they'd been speaking a foreign language. She wasn't sure herself if she had heard them wrong or hadn't been able to comprehend. It was no time for puns. DuBois held her hand as she walked all the way down the hall, into the stale gray elevator, through the lobby and out the automatic doors to the car.

Aspen was only laid up in the hospital overnight but had to stop working at the call center since the hearing hadn't come back in her right ear and the telephone headsets weren't reversible. The Enigmatic Widget company dropped her.

"There's nothing we can do. She never sold anything for us, didn't make it through the probationary period, she wasn't an official employee. It clearly stipulates… We'd like to help, but…"

The only lawyer that Aspen knew was Cecil Trachomatis, who had worked at the call center with her. DuBois thought that it might be a conflict of interest, since he considered Enigmatic Widget as culpable as the bastard who'd been playing games with the phone. He had no way of knowing where Trachomatis's loyalty resided. He didn't know where to begin, so he agreed to hear the attorney's pitch. Cecil arrived wearing his blue pinstripe suit, which told Aspen that it must be Wednesday.

"Can you take the case?"

DuBois looked over the scrawny man, wondering if he could handle it. He remembered Aspen describing the characters at the call center—it was true that the lawyer resembled Cowboy Woody from *Toy Story*.

"Sure, Aspen. Don't you worry."

The lawyer patted her hand like her whole body was on the verge of collapse.

"Stop treating me like a delicate flower."

"I'll see it through to the end."

He felt sorry for her and wanted to offer comfort. He also felt embarrassed because her button-down dress showed cleavage.

"What? Whadja say?"

"He claims he's got our back. We appreciate that, Mr. Trachomatis. Trachomatis, what is that Greek?"

"It's funny that you ask that…"

The lawyer relaxed into the chair as he told them a meandering tale about his family's diaspora. After the long story, DuBois and Rufi walked him out to the curb and watched him climb into a Mercedes that was parked in front of the note lady's house. DuBois looked at his little girl and said, Did you catch that?

"What, Daddy?"

"He parked in front of that crazy lady's house, but she didn't put a note on the Benz."

"Why not, Daddy?"

"Good question, Boo-daw, good question."

Back inside the house, DuBois hit a button on the answering machine: Sent Saturday, April 17 at 12:54 p.m. Hi, darling, I'm leaving a message to you and yours, this is your Grammar. It's Saturday about one-ay, about one o'clock. I wondered what you guys are all doing and how you're doing. It's a beautiful day here and everything is fine and I hope it finds all of you the same. Keep in touch, love ya, bye bye.

"Rufi, you should draw a picture for Grammar."

The little girl hesitated, so he sat down with her. Pushing her hair out of her face, she wondered what to draw.

"We should draw a picture of Momma so she knows what's going on in our life."

They sketched a picture of Aspen in a yellow bandage turban with the broken crayons that Rufi brought from the other house. He colored the sky green and the grass red. She added her great-grandmother astride a horse and at the last minute threw in a B-52 flying over dropping a bomb. When they finished, DuBois wrote, We love you, Grammar at the bottom, folded it and stuck it in an envelope. The hard part for him would be finding the address, sticking a stamp on it and putting it in the mailbox. Aspen asked for a glass of water, so he set the envelope on a pile of boxes and forgot about it.

Trachomatis came by the next afternoon in his Mercedes, which he again parked in front of the note lady's house.

"Sit here on the couch, Momma. We rented movies for you at Video Rush. *Johnny Got His Gun, Spartacus, Full Metal Jacket…Stripes?*"

"I almost got *Chicken Soup for the Soul: the movie* but it looked stupid."

Rufi fluffed a pillow behind her mother while the lawyer sat in a patio chair that DuBois dragged inside and crossed his legs. Aspen said, Thanks for coming. My hearing isn't great yet, but the mystery is killing me. I have to know what happened.

"I started by tracking the name and address from the call sheet. I wanted to find out if the Bomber had any assets we could attach."

He paused to chuckle.

"I also talked to a district attorney who wasn't sure if there was enough evidence for a criminal case. He suggested that we

pursue it in civil court where the burden of proof isn't as strin-
gent."

Cecil tapped the yellow notepad he had taken out of his brief-
case.

"I wasn't able to find much of a paper trail leading to anyone
named Chank in that part of the state. Certainly, no assets. The
phone number was linked to a dive bar, rural delivery. There's
not much out in that part of the world, a gas station, sand,
miles of road, cactus and, of course, the sun. It's really hot out
there. I called the number again, but no one answered. Suing
the monster who crippled you, Aspen, could be a waste of energy."

"He shouldn't be on the call center list unless he makes over
$100,000 a year, right?"

"Enigmatic Widget buys those lists from credit card compa-
nies."

"Can we sue them?"

"I don't think so."

Cecil looked down at his wingtips and noticed a speck of mud,
which he flicked off with his thumb.

"Those were bum leads. The credit card company copied the
darn phone book in a rural area. I don't think this Mr. Chank
has anything."

"So, what's going to happen?"

"Well, I'm not sure. I mean, um, well. Maybe someone should go out there and try to track him—Darn-it, Aspen! I don't know anything about this kind of law, you'll have to find a private investigator to undertake the case. Or call the sheriff out there and see if he can help."

"I thought you were going to see this to the end."

DuBois folded his arms. He never wanted to get the system involved. He clocked Trachomatis's weak will from minute one. People living up to their physiognomy really bugged him.

"Well, I can't. I, I–"

"Cheese-n-rice! You're not being straight with us, Jack."

DuBois stood up with his fists clenched.

"DuBois, stop."

"Cecil. My name is Cecil. Not Jack. This is bad timing. One of my buddies from law school called, his firm wants to hire me. I have to go to Los Angeles for a final interview, maybe live there. My father was named Jack. Uh. This is a once-in-a-life-time offer. I'll be making literally one hundred times what I was making at the call center. He preferred to be called Jim, though. His friends called him Jim. I called him Father, or Sir, I mostly called him Sir, until he died. I don't know how to explain it. Aspen, you know how we had that Finder's Fee program? If you could get a buddy to come on at Enigmatic Widget, you get fifty bucks. Well, my lodge brother will take five grand for my head. That's what we're talking about here. I'm sorry. I hope we can still be friends."

Aspen was still wearing her turban.

DuBois was pacing the cottage. The beige carpet looked worn by heavy traffic. His incessant pacing aggravated it. If he paced long enough and pivoted sharply enough, he might be able to wear through the carpet, through the floorboards. Once he hit dirt, it wouldn't take long to form a ditch and for the ditch to grow into a chasm. He remembered EC saying that Toby was going to rip out the carpet anyway, so he didn't worry about it. DuBois didn't care if the chasm went all the way to the center of the earth and hot magma spewed forth. At least the lawyers would burn up. He stopped mid-pace and looked at the lawyer with contempt.

"You mean you're dropping us for money?"

"I'm afraid so. I— I don't know what to tell you."

Grammar

DuBois used both hands to set a wicker basket into the cavernous trunk of the Fury. It was loaded with snacks: hummus, bread, nuts and seeds, olive tapenade, fresh fruit… The road always made them hungry. He'd already packed Aspen's clothes, Rufi's clothes and dolls and his sleep roll. They had a full tank of gas and were headed out on the highway northbound out of the city, away from the beaches, which were sure to be crowded with spring break tourists living for the sun. DuBois told the band he was through. The boys would be pissed, he knew that. He might never see them again, and was only slightly ashamed that he didn't care. Before the on-ramp, Aspen said, Oh look, a house for sale.

He acted like he didn't hear. The thing DuBois liked most about the freeway was that there were no houses for sale, so there would be no arguments. Even if there was a house on the side of the freeway, they would surely be moving too fast to notice, and even if she noticed a blurry For Sale sign as they sped past, he could always say, You don't want to live next to no smoggy, noisy freeway. This, however, was what he called "Danger Logic," and when it came to Aspen and houses, it was safer to take an abstract line. She could easily say, I'll live next to a freeway. I lived under the flight path of an airport for eight years, a freeway is nothing. A freeway sounds like waves breaking on a beach compared to an airport. As long as he stuck with, I don't want to be tied to a mortgage, she couldn't refute his feelings.

They left early enough so that all the traffic was coming south out of the sprawling suburbs. He turned on the radio and flipped away from commercials until he landed on a local talk station:

"The — BLEEPING — homeless are ticks under the skin of hard-working people."

"A lot of homeless people work these days. Whole families live in their cars."

"There's a lot of land between Lone Pine and Independence. Refugee camps are the answer. Concentration camps. Manzanar is empty. Ship the vermin out to rot."

"What the hell is wrong with you?"

"Don't talk to the radio, babe."

DuBois slipped a cassette into the player and turned up the volume on Lightnin' Hopkins "Big Car Blues."

"This tape's older than Rufi."

"You made it for our last road trip—The Blues, The Buzzcocks, and The Blasters."

"Good tape. We did thirteen states in thirteen days."

"Fourteen states, we drove through fourteen states."

"Yeah, but thirteen emotional states."

"Seeing Tom Waits at a bar somewhere in California."

"Sly delight."

"A flat tire in Utah."

"Boredom."

"Making love in Zion."

"In a tent? Awful."

"Funny. Pulled over by the cops in Oklahoma."

"Craven terror."

"Craven, good word. Getting lost in Missouri."

"Misery."

The wind was blowing Rufi's explosive hair and her stuffed teddy bear was in the trunk with a bag full of Barbie dolls. She ran down a scheme to get Grandpops to take her shopping for camouflage parachute pants. She wanted a paintball gun, but didn't think Grandmoms would allow it. All of Grandmom's thoughts revolved around the church, lately. They would be praying for somebody's soul and reading mind-dulling scriptures. She didn't like to take sides but Rufi saw a chance in Pop's old blues albums. She would start asking questions about Big Bill Broonzy, Memphis Minnie, and Victoria Spivey until he pulled out all of the old records. With incredible luck her Grandmoms would consent to make cookies.

"Daddy, do I have to go to The More Than Conquerors Church of the Holy Sepulcher with Grandmoms. It scares me?"

"Oh Boo-daw, the soul of sweet delight can never be defiled, hee hee hee. Better you than me. I love music but could never suffer hymns."

His parents had moved to the farthest suburb out, past the wine country even. The last housing tract where each dwelling looked like the one next door. Houses are cheap here, son, his father counseled. Cheap with lots of space. Your mother likes the quiet. She's got to have the quiet.

She traded the sounds of the city, the bus rumble, the neighbors shouting domestic violence, garbage trucks in the alley and sirens for hot, dry inland weather with coyotes coming into the yard to eat the cat.

"Is this it? Is this the right house?"

"I don't know, they all look the same. Like I told Pops, hee hee hee, this plastic gated community may seem safer than the old neighborhood until you come home late from the Elks drunk one night and enter your neighbor's house by mistake. Not a big deal (unless you get shot) until you wake up next to his wife."

"It's that one over there."

"Thanks, kiddo."

DuBois's mother was in the kitchen when they came in. DuBois got Aspen a cup of water. They sat at the kitchen table.

"Where are you kids going?"

"North. We need to get away."

"We love Rufi to stay over. She can go to church with me."

"Yeah, we might stop and see Grammar."

"Oh, you children don't have to do that? We all know how that lady can be."

"Moms, don't start."

"Lord, save her soul."

DuBois's father came in, opened the fridge. Stared. Shut it.

"Well, have a safe trip, son."

He shook DuBois's hand and pressed a twenty into his palm.

"Thanks, Pops. Keep on truckin', Rufi."

"Bye, Daddy. Bye, Momma."

Aspen turned around in the passenger seat to wave to DuBois's parents and her baby girl, as always lined up tallest to shortest waving and blowing kisses.

"Your parents are a riot."

"Mmm."

"They didn't seem happy to see us."

"I didn't notice."

"Maybe they just looked concerned."

"They always look concerned."

When they hit the freeway, he pushed in the tape and Chuck Berry came on with "No Particular Place to Go," which wasn't right because DuBois had told his grandmother they would pull into her place before dark. Aspen chewed gum and looked out at the distance through dark glasses as they cut through the foothills. Traffic on the interstate was sparse—aircraft, a sign said, would enforce the speed limit. A tagger had used a black marker to add a bomb falling from the plane.

"They don't even bother to give you a ticket out here, just drop a bomb on your ass."

They passed a convoy of army trucks transporting a dozen soldiers in desert fatigues. The middle truck was toting a howitzer that could level a city block.

"Think Rufi will join the army?"

"Nah, it's gotta be a phase."

"I hope so."

They passed a station wagon loaded with kids, camp gear strapped to a luggage rack and Aspen wondered if they should go back and pick up Rufi. She liked camping, would like to chase the squirrels and frolic in a cold melting snow stream. A hawk circled overhead. Brown hills turned into desolate rocky canyons. A song about leaving played quietly on the radio. After about an hour, DuBois pulled over at a Shades Gas to let the Fury's radiator cool. The station looked rundown and forgotten, there wasn't any shade for one thing—the sign, the building, the lettering on the pumps all looked faded like the high desert sun was straining to erase them. They could see the attendant through the window, a teenage girl working alone, under a shadowless fluorescent light.

"The Fury sure sucks gas."

"Style has a cost."

Aspen got the restroom key from the girl. When she hit the light, a roach darted from the corner. The mirror was cracked and she saw herself divided. Straddling the toilet, she tried to pee. Unwinding the turban, she was careful not to let it touch the floor. She peeled the bandage and tossed the bloody piece of cotton in the trash. She ran fingers through her hair, which was matted with sweat, and studied her image in the cracked mirror. She readjusted her black bra straps. Applied lipstick. Her tits were sweating and she imagined running through a sprinkler or dropping into a lake from a rope swing. She couldn't bear the turban and dropped it into the trash. All she could do to cool off was unbutton her blouse, which might allow onlookers from above to see the tiny mermaid tattooed on one of her breasts.

She washed her hands twice.

The sunlight felt extra-brilliant on her face and almost knocked her over like she'd stood up too fast. DuBois was waiting outside the door and caught her up in his arms. She smelled so good. He kissed her like he was reaching deep inside her chest cavity, which spun her head around even more.

"The soda machine only has Crafty Cola and I'm boycotting those corporate fuckers."

"I'm not thirsty. You were right. It's nice to be out here away from everything."

A desert breeze blew fallow dust over the asphalt.

An empty school bus was parked behind the station, which prompted thoughts about the school Rufi attended—ranked last out of a hundred on a proficiency test. Most of her classmates spoke Spanish first and didn't hear English more than six hours unless you counted television, which in itself didn't help them take tests in English. Rufi and her friends were knit like a sweater, but they joked about huffing paint and even the littlest, sweetest ones tossed up West Side when Rufi brought her Instamatic camera to school to snap their pictures. She was a foot taller than one of the boys and tried to crouch in the photo but still towered over him. The kids were laughing and having a great time in every photograph. Her best friend daNeesha had a Band-Aid taped around her middle finger and innocently showed the world. But there was always some kid whose older brother had run away or that boy who called Rufi a "lesbian" lurking in the background.

"Do you think the schools out here are any good?"

"I dunno."

"Yeah."

"See that exit? That's where those cops shot that girl who was asleep in the car."

"That was so sad. Her cousin called the police to help them get her out of the car because she was having an epileptic attack."

"Yup. They saw that she had a gun on her lap and those fool pigs broke the window."

"What did they expect? She had the gun because she was scared."

"They shot her like twenty times. Four cops. One girl. Al Sharpton came down and tore 'em a new one. Did you know Al Sharpton used to manage James Brown and the Flames… It's hard to understand."

"Dub, I have a bad feeling. I think we should go home."

DuBois swerved off the two-lane blacktop into the dirt and slammed the brakes. The tires locked and a cloud of dust rose around the big car. Aspen jerked forward, glad for the seat belt even though it cut into her breasts. They didn't see the dead cow in the muddy ditch whose yellow skull was on a lazy journey to bleached white.

"You want to go back?"

He must have forgotten that she had an ear injury or didn't realize that he was yelling. Aspen cringed and cupped her hand over the gauze protecting herself like a punch was coming in. Like once when they were drunk and arguing about money and she had thrown one of the dishes he had picked up at a garage sale. This was before EC gave them some nicer plates. He rushed to stop her from breaking another plate or maybe just to save his own skull. One of her spike heels drove into his thigh and his hand shot up to strike back. He wanted to smack her across the mouth. Frozen that way, the next plate shattered like hard candy. He didn't bleed much, a cut on his forehead that he probably deserved. He went directly to the closet, picked up a broom and swept the pieces into a dustpan. DuBois had a long-standing habit of cleaning the house when he was upset. Aspen broke him of it one morning after a minor brawl by pointing it out. He saw the danger in that logic because all she would have to do to get the house clean was piss him off. The inside of the microwave hadn't been cleaned since.

He was madder now than he had ever been. The anger wasn't aimed at her. You couldn't solve problems by hitting people— they weren't soda machines. He did pound the steering wheel. And when that didn't absolve anything, he punched the horn, which sounded off like a trumpet. He was about to swear to his mother's god when a passing truck driver answered his call with a low bellow on the air horn. DuBois looked up, the truck driver grinned through broken teeth and waved.

"We can't go back. I told Grammar we were coming."

"I know."

"What?"

"She's scary."

They were twenty minutes from his grandmother's cabin. She leaned over and kissed him on the neck. He was determined to store that anger for when he would need it. He wiped the spittle from his lip.

"Let me redo your turban. It looks beautiful on you."

"No, it's too hot. Should I pin the brooch here? Maybe I shouldn't wear it."

"Don't worry about what she thinks."

"You say that all the time. But when you're not there, she gives me shit. Like why aren't you married? Why doesn't DuBois get a real job?"

"Just say, Ask him."

DuBois turned the Fury up a dirt road and passed through a clump of trees with dry, yellowed leaves suffering a spell of drought. A tarred rope that must have held a tire swing hung down from a high bare branch. The tire had rolled downhill and come to rest in a gully. The sun was low in the sky and a blur of pink hung over the distant hills. The cabin needed painting, like the fence around the yard needed mending, and the weeds in the garden needed pulling.

"Grammar says this broken-down ranch reminds her of back home…"

A big fat gray cat lounged in the front window behind the porch. One of the chickens began to scream and they saw others pecking around the yard. A chill came into Aspen's spine all at once, which might, she thought, be a message from her injured ear—so reaching into the glove compartment, she popped the cap off of an orange prescription bottle and choked down a pain pill dry.

There wasn't another house within shouting distance, but Aspen remembered that Grammar had a good neighbor up the road. They hadn't made a trip out to these parts since Rufi was newly born. Had it been that long? Why did their families live so far away? She thought about her dad and wanted to fly up to Canada right away. She also remembered how strict Grammar had been—they might have had a baby together, but wouldn't be carrying on under her roof. When Grammar said, I'm sure you don't want to get saddled with another mistake, Aspen asked DuBois to splurge for a hotel room. He leapt at the chance with a concupiscent eye on a sexual adventure. The motel that he found wasn't the Waldorf, but it would do.

Grammar must have heard the sound of the Fury crunching up the gravel road. She stepped onto the porch, a big woman with fat bare feet holding a shotgun. Aspen saw a horseshoe hanging above the door, and looking about the yard, saw wagon wheels and rusty tools and painted plaster casts of animals that senior citizens in trailer parks fancied up their lives with. A Norman Rockwell look-at-the-birdie nostalgia for a world that never was.

"It's me, Grammar—DuBois! Don't shoot."

DuBois had an idea to make t-shirts with a big target on the front superimposed by bold print lettering—DON'T SHOOT. He wanted to give them out to homeless people around the city after the third one was shot by the police in as many months. Aspen hadn't made the mistake of getting out of the car. She waited until Grammar set the shotgun down and gave her grandson a hug.

"You can't come into the house right now, my darling. I'm glad to see you. Is that you, Aspen?"

"It's me, Grammar."

"Mmmm. I feel an illness or injury afflicting you, girl. And I see you're wearing my brooch…"

"Moms told you what happened."

"Yes, she told me. I don't know why you can't call your Grammar."

DuBois handed her the envelope containing the picture Rufi drew for her. She opened it and looked at the artwork. If she thought the girl had talent, she didn't say it out loud.

"I'm here Grammar, here in the flesh. What are you complaining about?"

"Thank you, DuBois. Where is that granddaughter of mine?"

"Well, if you talked to Moms, you know where. She's spending a week with them so we could take a vacation."

"A vacation? Doesn't that imply you found a job? Hee hee hee. Oh, my goodness, darlings. Give me a minute to tidy up."

The silver-haired woman went back into the house. DuBois and Aspen sat on a bench on the porch, which creaked. The sun dropped behind the hills and the twilight shifted into darkness with more stars than they'd seen in a decade winking on and blinking off. A yellow moon rose in the east.

"I forgot how many stars there were."

"Me too. I can't remember the last time I saw a star or took notice of the moon. There's Venus."

"It's beautiful."

They waited. Neither spoke or thought about speaking while they looked at the stars.

"What do you think she's doing in there?

"I'm afraid to ask."

Aspen stood up and peeked through a crack in the curtain.

"She's got a broom. Looks like she spilled cornmeal and coffee grounds on the floor. Was she always messy?"

"One of her rituals."

"Or dementia. People stop cleaning when they have dementia."

"Waaaah."

Grammar startled them, waving a severed chicken neck. Hee hee hee.

"You laugh like DuBois."

"My darlings."

She grabbed Aspen, planted a big kiss on her cheek and pulled her into her big body, which was comfortable and easy to get lost in. The chicken neck flapped near her bandaged ear. A flash of fear—in a word, salmonella—dissipated in the hug along with every care, every worry, and every hurt.

DuBois smelled chicken roasting in the oven—a rush of flavor jumped out of childhood. No one could cook like Grammar. He was glad to see that she hadn't lost the skill living out here alone.

He had told her before that he didn't eat chicken, that he was a vegetarian. She must have forgotten. Dinner would be, Chew your food one hundred times, darling. Sit up straight. Get a job. Marry this girl. Act right. No wonder he didn't drive out here more often. She'd set a bowl of her homemade applesauce on the table, which he always asked for as a kid. Her homemade applesauce was almost worth the long drive. When she pulled out a rhubarb pie and set it on the table, he didn't worry about getting fed.

Aspen told the story of her injury. She told how DuBois had been so good in the hospital, talking to the doctors, running to the pharmacy, and bandaging her up at home. She told how smart Rufi was in school, described Rufi's friends and told her all about the swim team. She promised to bring her granddaughter out to see her the next time they came.

After dinner they moved over to the davenport and Grammar brought the rhubarb pie and a sharp-tasting liquor in tin cups. My neighbor up around the way says he distilled this corn whiskey himself. The crotchety old firebrand likes to brag and boast. DuBois suspected that it was Old Crow, which Grandad used to drink, and that if he looked around, he just might find a familiar bottle tucked away. Of whatever provenance, its warmth expanded beneath his ribcage like a torchlit beacon. The hour grew late and Aspen wanted sleep.

"Now let me see if I have a remedy for that ear."

"Oh no, Grammar, the doctor said Aspen will be fine in a couple of weeks."

"Are you going to tell me, darling, that you came all the way out here to this godforsaken desert to visit an old lady? Oh, no. I will not believe it until the day I die and see you crying at my funeral."

The deep shadows thrown up by candlelight looked as if they'd been painted on the walls. The old woman walked over to a shrine, a little altar, set up on quilted cloth: Virgin of Guadalupe statue, seven lit candles, three acorns, a sprig of heather, drying bundles of potentilla, sage, hemlock, violet, and holly. Hessian crucibles and retorts. Tarot cards showing pantacle, cup and wand. A tin of mustard seed and another of snakeroot. Dusty green books containing recipes, diagrams, histories. Odd trinkets of wood, leather and base metals, eerie things in jars and Druidic sigils written in beetroot on onionskin. Phials of oil, the quill of a crow and a penknife. Muscaria, poppy and wormwood. She unscrewed a small glass jar and sniffed the contents.

"Hmmm."

"Don't let her put anything in your ear."

Fear crawled over Aspen's skin like a spider. The air was as thick as water. Apprehension rose in a dark tide. A cord tightening. She gasped, trying to suck air. She hadn't felt like this since she'd tumbled in deep water rough surf at the seaside and mistook down for up. She fought the urge to open her mouth, fearing the gallons of salt water that would surely rush in.

"Really, Grammar, Aspen doesn't need that gunk for her ear. I only wish we could find the man who did it. The guy had the same area code as you. He might be one of your neighbors."

Aspen looked surprised. What was DuBois saying? Grammar looked up from the jar and over at her grandson.

"You're hot-tempered like your grandfather. Revenge makes use of dangerous logic. It's seldom final. Marcus held a grudge against his brother for thirty years. Stir his soul. I miss him. I miss him every day."

DuBois walked to the corner of the room where he found a drum. One hard knock sent dust into the air. A second tap and a third began a lilting rhythm.

"Aspen, darling, you write the name of the man who hurt you on a slip of paper and put it in the circle."

A circle had been drawn in brick dust on the wood floor.

"Close your eyes, my child. We make the music together because together the music is made. Feel the rise and fall of your breath and shift your gaze up to your inner eye—try to manifest what you want."

Grammar listened to the drum. Animated by new excitement, the old woman pinched a colored powder from a jar and drew a symbol on the floor next to the circle with what looked like remnants of ash and spent coffee grounds while a faint song issued, unintelligibly, Aspen thought, from the dry husk of her lips. The seven candles flickered in a draft through the door. The old woman's hips rocked side to side. It might have been a few seconds or a few minutes. Aspen lost all sense of time until Grammar spoke.

"You children need protection. Lo who opens the world for justice, be sure of what you want. Africa in Haiti prayed for light and life. Go back to go forward. Prometheus was cut down in the great basin. One in all in all things. Written out are the twelve names. Lo, these human-formed spirits take as they give. The true leader remains unknown. The true man demonstrates power. Lo the auk, lo the hartebeest, lo the salt sea cow. Walk as the four-footed animals. The tuna swims like the shark. Has the eagle ever soared too high? The worm has no use for the left eye or the right. Turning this way and that. Go down to rise up. Observe the four humors. See, hear, taste, touch, and smell. Sorrow is but as shadows-beauty is of the art. Be so careful what you ask them for, my darlings, for the shades up from the shadows, sisters in harmony, beat and rhythm, may wish to help you."

DuBois concentrated on the drum, on the rhythm, on the beat, with his critical faculties closed against the words. He smiled in a way he hadn't since baby Rufi passed into his arms that first day, and when Aspen looked over at him, she didn't know what to think.

Dan Petro's Bar

Aspen lay awake listening to a lone cricket chirping outside her window. Restless—the pain pills, like acid on a copper sheet, etched on her bones. She must have slept, a little, at least, since she now recalled a vivid dream about her ancestors coming up out of the graveyard like zombies—her perpetually infirm Aunt Alva scratching, moaning, and staggering with the horde. The old woman didn't look much different ten years into death than she had in life. Why hadn't she gone out to sleep in the empty stable with DuBois? Why hadn't he come in? Aspen was startled but not surprised to see a hen flap onto the army surplus cot, which Grammar had pulled out of the closet for her to sleep on. The old woman told her grandson to go sleep in the old horse barn out back and he made a swift retreat—book and flashlight in hand.

Grammar was up early, frying eggs with jerk spice and sizzling bacon in an iron skillet. DuBois came into the cabin looking irritable, scratched his jock and stretched.

"I made my darlings a nice breakfast."

DuBois inhaled and didn't want to stop breathing in because it smelled so good.

"Smells good, Grammar. But you know I don't eat pig."

"Well, Aspen and I will eat the bacon. I think we got enough fresh eggs to fill your stomach."

"Go easy on the eggs, Grammar. I don't eat like a teenager anymore. Have you got coffee?"

She poured boiling water from the kettle into a Chemex filled with grounds. Left it to seep and steep.

"The smell of your coffee invigorates my soul."

"I hope you like it strong and black."

"I'm down with black and strong, but Aspen likes hers with milk and sugar."

"There are cubes in the sugar bowl, darling."

After a minute she poured him a measure in one of the strange tin cups.

"Hold it by the top, so you don't burn your skinny bones."

Aspen washed her face and changed the ear cotton, which, clear of her blood, felt like a little cloud between her fingers. She picked a pair of zebra-striped capris and squeezed into them. She decided to go without a bra and climbed into an accordion-like tube top as well.

"I see that spooked look in your eye."

"I didn't sleep so good."

Grammar came out of the kitchen holding a tall, thin wooden cup.

"I made you a special drink that will heal your ear so good that you'll hear words before they're spoken."

"Oh Grammar, that's enough. Cheese-n-rice. How long can you keep this act up?"

Grammar stopped smiling and put on a mask that would frighten Medusa to stone, clear your sinuses, strip the chrome off a fender, get you higher than you've ever been and leave you with a hangover chiseled out of brimstone.

"Aspen, my grandmother is not a voodoo mambo. She hasn't visited Haiti or even been to New Orleans. She's a white lady from Santa Rosa. Born in 1921 with six toes in a craftsman-style house. She used to say that shamans were born with six toes and called it a portent that led her to a magical connection with the hidden world, but I say it was like a hobble on a horse that left her in a mire of magical thinking. She never finished college and doesn't know how to tell good information from bad."

"You snitch."

"All this, the smoke and mirrors, snakes and ladders, a stolen mishmash of spiritual hoodoo gleaned from movies. And this old book."

DuBois went to a cedar chest and pulled out a dusty, dog-eared Time-Life book—Vodou Rituals.

"She's been playing at Sunday bruja so long she believes it. This book scared me as a kid… Look at this shrunken head. Sorry, Grammar, but—"

"He's as grouchy as a mole in the morning, Grammar. Useless unless he sleeps till noon, you know musicians, it's okay, really,

I have mornings to myself. He doesn't know what he's talking about. He's a dogmatic materialist. This is a practice, an ancient art. I felt something, Grammar. I couldn't sleep thinking about it."

Grammar turned around and walked into the kitchen without saying anything.

"I said sorry! You think Grandfather held grudges! Now I'm going to get the silent treatment. She pulled the vow of silence on him for a whole summer once. My grandfather was a gamblin' man. He would bet on how fast paint would dry, but he always said, Only a fool would bet against a stubborn woman."

Something shattered in the kitchen, glass or possibly ceramic.

Aspen was afraid to look in, knowing DuBois was not about to, she tiptoed to the door. Grammar petted her old gray cat. Pieces of a vase were scattered on the linoleum in a mess of dried flowers. She wondered if Grammar broke it intentionally or knocked it over in haste. It didn't matter.

"Are you happy?"

Aspen took up the wooden cup—its contents smelled like regurgitated grass and the underside of a heavy rock. She took a baby sip, winced. The texture felt like mashed green peas. Aspen picked up her coffee and took a gulp to rinse the sour taste.

"How much longer can she live out here by herself?"

He shrugged. Ran one of his large hands through his hair, which still needed a trim.

"Moms has been trying to get her to stay with them. She won't go."

DuBois packed his sleep roll and Aspen's dirty clothes bag in the car and waited. The morning begged for adventure—the air was fresh and country quiet. They waited for fifteen or so minutes, but Grammar never came out of the kitchen. Even when Aspen went to the doorway and said goodbye, she remained silent. Upset or embarrassed, Aspen couldn't say.

"Let's get out of here."

Aspen punched his biceps hard enough to bruise. She wanted to make him talk to his grandmother, so they could leave with a Goodbye, darlings, and her blessing but "just plain stubborn" was a family value.

"You can be a real ass."

Aspen pinched her nose and choked down the contents of the wooden cup in a single shot. Her stomach wanted to heave it right back out, the thick green liquid climbed her esophagus hand over hand like it was a rope ladder to her mouth. She pursed her lips tight and forced it back down. She could feel it swimming around her stomach until it succumbed—drowned, to the acids therein. The episode ended with a rumbling growl.

"You didn't have to do that. You know there's not a hospital around here for miles in case you need your stomach pumped."

Aspen felt like Thee Midnighters were grooving inside her stomach, rather than pumping out of the car stereo, as DuBois pulled the Fury back onto the highway. He thought about the book he'd been reading the night before and leaned back in the driver's seat. DuBois had taken on an air of grim determination and drove fast without speaking. Thirty minutes later Aspen farted—the pain in her stomach became a memory.

"Man, that stinks. Eye of newt and swamp water."

He drove with his head stuck out the window, like he did when he came home late from a gig with his body demanding sleep. The air felt hot and dry. A sign said—Death Valley. After another thirty minutes of straight driving, Aspen decided that her ear hurt and she reached into the glove compartment for the pills.

"What's this?"

"I found it in the chest at Grammar's next to her voodoo primer. I thought we could shoot bottles out in the desert."

"We don't need this."

"You asked Grammar to protect us with her mojo, but you've seen how she protects herself. If you buy into that magic bullshit, you have to roll with fate. This is fate."

He picked up the gun. Felt its heft.

"Put that thing away. I hate guns, I hate guns. You don't know anything about guns. You're going to shoot somebody, maybe yourself or me."

He looked at it again to check the safety.

"Be careful what you wish for."

He snickered and smiled, without humor. The Bad Brains came on the stereo and he turned up the volume. He remembered one of their gigs across the border in Mexico. EC and Juan Carlos were there. The singer, HR, started the set with a 360° front flip, dreadlocks flying in time with Dr. Know's ripping guitar. "Pay to Cum" was the fastest song in the world. A group of skinheads was trying to control the slam dance pit and Juan Carlos got kicked in the balls. He staggered to the edge of the pit trying to hold his puke. Who kicked you man? I'll bust the mutha-fucker in his grill… DuBois went after a skinhead, an ugly bastard with acne pox down his back. He managed to throw four punches. The other skins jumped in, fists wrapped in flannel shirts, boots hit from every direction. If he went down onto the floor, he'd have to be carried out. They would kick him until the band stopped playing. Luckily, the Bad Brains shifted to a slower reggae number and a greater love overtook the venue. Jah Rastafari Haile Selassie I against I. That same blend of love and rage mixed with thoughts about Aspen and Mr. Chank and hoping they would pick up a clue at the saloon.

"Let's get a beer."

"It's too early."

"We're on vacation."

Dan Petro's Bar wasn't more than a clapboard hut with three barstools and a tiny refrigerator stocked with bottles of Miller High Life. It reminded DuBois of where he'd slept the night before. It didn't have a jukebox, but a staticky radio played

Mexican banda music. A Perry Mason rerun, muted, played on the tv in the corner. A cow skull hung on one wall next to a poster showing a girl in a red bikini selling Miller High Life. A man sat on the porch smoking a cigar. He wore faded blue jeans and a dirty button-up work shirt. His Roughout boots looked like they'd been with him for quite a while. Not past 9am, a wrathful star cranked up the morning heat. A dusty desert wind blew sand across the porch through the open front door.

"Hi."

He didn't respond. DuBois nudged past. Aspen adjusted herself on one of the empty stools, lighting on a precarious balance. DuBois took the twenty that his dad had given him out of the pocket of his black jeans. He wondered why the bartender was ignoring them. He'd painted Fuck the Police on his t-shirt, but that couldn't be it—this joint couldn't afford a dress code.

"Can we get a beer?"

The bartender groaned like his knees and back hurt to stand up. An enormous gut poured over the waistline of the jeans like beer overflowing a pint glass. The guy had been a hippie. The scraggily remnants of his long hair peeked out from underneath a fishing cap. DuBois bet he'd gone bald at middle age. The cigar stayed smoldering out on the porch and two bottles of Miller High Life from the refrigerator were set down in front of them on the bar.

"I hoped for Guinness."

"I hoped for a glass."

The bartender looked at her, reached under the counter and set a pint glass on the bar. She poured the beer herself and sipped the head before it overflowed.

"Thanks."

"So…What's to do around these parts?"

The bartender picked at his teeth with his tongue.

"Not much unless you like fishing."

"Fishing?"

"Where do you fish?"

"The lake went dry, so."

A toilet flushed and the door at the back swung open, letting loose a smell like a pit toilet. A stocky young man fumbled with the buckle, trying to hitch his pants.

"I-I I'm sorry."

Each syllable twisted and twitched into existence.

"I-I I'm not a dirty bird. I had to go potty."

The tone of his voice scratched on DuBois's nerves like an amateur DJ on a cheap record. His short pants were pulled up too far into his butt crack. He'd tucked in the shirt, mostly, and buttoned it all the way up to his thick neck. He wore sneakers without socks. His thick dark hair hadn't been washed or combed, so that dandruff speckled his broad shoulders. He needed a shave, but his facial hair was sparse and sporadic.

"It's okay…We didn't see anything."

"Excuse me, Mister P. Do you think I could have another soda?"

He stood there scratching himself on the neck. The bartender walked out to the porch and put fifty cents into a soda machine, a can of Dr. Pepper rumbled out, which he set on the counter.

"That'll be seventy-five cents."

The stocky, slump-shouldered young man took out a Velcro wallet connected to his belt by a string and held it close to his face to look for the right bill.

"You–you keep the change."

DuBois sipped his beer from the bottle and Aspen downed her swill in a gulp. The bartender went back out on the porch to finish his cigar.

"Do you think he's Chank?"

Aspen looked over at him, his back faced the door and a puff of smoke rose around him. She tried to place herself in the moment of the phone call. She strained to match his voice to the one that asked her to hold on a minute, but it had all happened so quickly.

"I don't know if he's Chank, should we ask him?"

"Did you, um, did-did you, um, say Chank?"

"Yes. Do you know someone who lives around here called Chank?"

"I-I don't want to go in the closet."

"The closet?"

"Mr. Chank said if I was a dirty bird he would put me in the closet."

"Is that bastard on the porch Chank?"

"I-I I'm not a dirty bird. Mr. Chank lives down on the farm. Mr. Petro doesn't like small talk."

DuBois sat back on the barstool. Aspen reached over and touched the funny, round-bellied young man on the hand, who shied away as if he had an allergy.

"Don't worry. I'm Aspen and this is DuBois."

"My name is Dooby and I'm not a dirty bird."

"Anyone can see that, Dooby."

Mr. Petro came back in and asked if they wanted another beer for the road and he charged Dooby seventy-five more cents for another soda.

"A boy ran away from home. Mr. Chank gave him a job on the farm. He said there wasn't much work to do since all the other kids left and they stopped planting."

Every time DuBois asked about Chank, Dooby repeated his bit about not being a dirty bird and not wanting to go in the closet.

DuBois took out his wallet, shoved Jackson in and pulled Lincoln out. He set the five-dollar bill on the bar under his empty bottle. When they got up to leave, Aspen pushed the door to the shitter, which smelled so bad that she decided to hold her pee until the next stop.

"You want a ride back to the farm, Dooby?"

"Sure, sure. But I-I I don't really want to go to the farm—yeah, okay."

Aspen got in the passenger side and Dooby clambered into the back seat. He set his bundle of possessions on his lap and tried to figure out the seat belt. Mr. Petro stepped out on the porch to watch them drive away and said, I wouldn't go messing around at Chank's place if I were you.

The Stucco Shack

When they got to the big tree Aspen said it was a poplar and DuBois said it was a cedar and Dooby didn't know, but said it was the best place to park. They sat listening to Curtis Mayfield and Parliament-Funkadelic and DuBois wanted to let the motor run so he could hear Disposable Heroes of Hiphoprisy, but killed the engine and the cassette player spit out the tape.

"Are you sure there's no road that goes to the farm, Dooby?"

"Um, yes, I mean, I'm sure because Mr. Chank said we don't have a car, so why do we need a road?"

It had turned into a lovely day—scattered clouds absorbed the cruelest part of the heat and the hot wind had dissipated. The shade of the big tree invited them to stop and have a picnic. Dooby stuttered, I-I I'm hungry, and DuBois figured a picnic would give them time to think. He popped the trunk and spread a blanket under the tree. Aspen reached one of her delicate hands to open the snack basket and couldn't help but laugh out loud.

"Dooby, you look like Yogi's pal Boo Boo bear."

"I'm not Boo Boo, I'm Dooby."

They each had a brown banana and bread with peanut butter. Aspen packed more than enough food. She wished they had brought a bottle of wine, but since Trader Joe's stopped carrying their favorite three-dollar bottle of Bull's Blood, they hadn't found a brand to replace it.

DuBois stretched out on the blanket and decided to finish a chapter from Oscar Zeta Acosta he'd been reading the night before. Zeta and his pals were gearing up to firebomb the Safeway. The wrong book to read before confrontation. Aspen stretched out in a sun patch and thought she might try to get a tan. She hadn't been out in the sun since the summer before and felt her pasty whiteness like wearing someone else's skin. Vulnerable to sunburn, a fear of skin cancer, like a wraith, assaulted her peace of mind. After her moment in the sun, she scooted under the shade of an overhanging limb. Dooby sat on the blanket like a trained circus bear waiting to go on stage. After they were done eating, the wind carried in a rancorous stench that reminded DuBois of the Tijuana River after a heavy rain. DuBois and Aspen tried to pinch their nostrils shut—Aspen recalled Grammar's potion and felt nauseous.

"Fucking hell? Cheese-n-rice."

"Um, I don't want to go swimming today. I-I I don't like swimming."

DuBois tucked the gun under his belt and Aspen put the basket in the trunk and made sure all of the doors were locked. She pulled a pair of white socks over her painted toenails and picked up her black canvas Converse sneakers.

"You might want to check your shoes for scorpions out here."

She tapped sand out of one shoe. And then, sure enough, a scorpion fell onto the ground from the other. Oooo! She shrieked and sprung straight back. Closer inspection revealed that it wasn't moving.

"You bastard."

"Hee hee hee."

Dooby led them around over to a bush on the brink of a twisting canyon and pointed at the trailhead. DuBois thought he smelled sage... and what? A stink bug? A dozen golden briars hooked onto his pants around the cuffs. Nature showed its most brutal aspect: snakes, scorpions, tarantulas, thorns, briars, brambles, barbs, needles, and too much sun. Way too much indignant sun. Why would anyone try to farm Death Valley? He turned over a rock and watched a centipede scurry for cover.

"The farm is down this way, but I-I I don't want to go to the farm today, okay, I'll go."

"Watch out for snakes. They come out of their holes when it gets hot."

At the bottom of the descent, they came across the shell of a burned-out automobile. The glass was broken out and the frame was charred inside and out.

"Whose car is that, Dooby?"

"I-I don't know."

He led the way with Aspen in the middle and DuBois as rear guard. As he stumbled over loose rocks, Aspen wondered why DuBois let him serve as their guide. Looking back DuBois's gaze jumped around like he was expecting an ambush. They walked a crooked quarter mile and the sulfurous smell grew more intense with every step. The untrodden trail led them through a heavy patch of scrub, which Aspen hoped didn't con-tain poison oak—they'd rubbed against it on their last camping trip and once was enough. Coming to a fork, Dooby scratched his neck and decided to take the left prong. DuBois guessed that both paths realized the same destination.

"Hold up there a second."

He wished they had brought a canteen. An unknown creature hissed at them from the bush and Aspen wondered if it was a snake, and it might have been, but a lizard, six inches includ-ing the tail, scampered into view.

"I do as I'm told, I'm a good boy. I don't catch lizards anymore. Their tails fall off."

"I know you are, Dooby."

Aspen smiled, patting him on the shoulder. From this point they could see what looked like a house hidden from the trail by a canopy of trees. About thirty yards south they saw a pool filled with dark liquid. The place looked deserted. An observa-tion that didn't relieve Aspen of an uncomfortable feeling.

"I bet the smell comes from that pool."

"I-I I don't want to go swimming."

"Can't blame you there, dude."

A compacted dirt path ran from the sludge pool to the shack, which turned out to be no more than a square stucco box with a shake shingle roof. Somebody with a baroque sense of humor had hung a sign over the door that most likely once spelled out

Thou Shalt Not Enter. It hung by one corner and looked like a strong wind could finish it. Dooby led them right up to the front door. Aspen looked through the window, but the moth-eaten curtains were drawn, and glowed with a familiar blue light. DuBois scanned the nearby foothills. Inside the house, a phone was ringing. They all waited for someone to answer it.

"This house wouldn't be so bad if you painted it and planted flowers."

DuBois looked at Aspen like she stepped out of her mind and stood before them in her psychic skivvies. It was like staring at the sun to discover how vision works. Her want for a house had grown into a blind compulsion.

"Yup, maybe set up a white picket fence and cart away all the bubbling fecal matter."

The phone rang four times, but no one answered it.

"Dooby, where's Chank?"

"I-I I don't know where Mr. Chank is. Maybe he went swimming."

DuBois and Aspen looked over at the pool. Filled with detritus, bigger than a swimming hole and smaller than a pond, the rotten smell emanated from its still water. It might have been filled with sewage. One couldn't imagine swimming in it.

"I-I—"

"I know, Dooby, you don't want to go swimming."

The phone rang in the house again. Dooby opened the front door. DuBois pulled out the gun, which still felt heavier than it looked. He and Aspen followed him up a short ramp made from a piece of warped plywood and a brick. A tv was left on in the corner and Montel Williams said he would be right back after the ketchup commercial.

A colorful poster hung on one wall—thousands of dots titled "Rainbow."

"I don't see a rainbow, do you?"

"Hmm."

When the phone rang again, they froze like statues. Dooby copied them. They stayed that way while it rang three more times.

"This Chank's a popular guy."

The dirty couch looked like it had been picked up at the curb, one of the cushions didn't match and the others were torn and soiled. There was debris strewn all over the cement floor—paper plates and cups but also rusty car parts dragged in from a junkyard. Aspen pictured a hundred roaches scurrying for no lack of cover if the lights flashed on bright. The phone rang again. Aspen picked it up and held the handset at a distance from her good ear.

"Hello."

"Hello, this is Daniel from the Four Seasons…"

"I'm sorry we're not interesting. CLICK. I don't think the phone works. I could hear the telemarketer, but I don't think he heard me. The bottom half of the handset looks black. Smells burnt."

There wasn't much. No back door. A single window at the front. Somebody had scrawled willy nilly with red crayon on the wall opposite the poster. DuBois suspected Dooby. A hot plate and an icebox accounted for the kitchen.

"Where's Chank?"

DuBois held the gun close to his chest like he was posing with it and Dooby pressed his hands over his ears, looked scared and bared his teeth.

"Put that away before Dooby gets scared. You look stupid any-way."

"I'm not allowed to play with guns. I don't want to go in the closet."

A knot of tension had built up in DuBois's neck and he wished Aspen would put her healing hand on it. This Dooby character was too far out—he couldn't be sure it all wasn't a surreal dream.

"Maybe Chank's outside."

He peered out the door and moved with stealth between blades of sunlight. The smell from the muck pond fouled the air.

"Hey, man, what is that slime in the pool?"

"I-I I don't want to go in the pool."

DuBois peeked around the side of the house and saw a man sleeping in a wheelchair in a shady spot. He had one leg and one arm. His bald skull was scabbed and blistered. He looked soiled, like the couch. A calloused and pink hand hung limp. And the pores were inky black. His arm stump was dirty. It looked like he had urinated, leaving a puddle under the chair, which saturated the dragging empty flap of his corduroy jeans.

"Mr. Chank is asleep."

"That's Chank?"

Aspen couldn't go near him. He could stay asleep, forever, she thought. She couldn't imagine how he could answer the phone, much less set off any kind of bomb. Or a gun? Maybe someone fired a gun. She tried to remember how it all went down. She unwound her memory from DuBois standing over her with a bandage in the hospital. Rufi was there. EC and Toby had come to visit. She remembered sprawling on the gray carpet at the call center. Dode got to her first. Did he crane his neck like that to look at her panties? She couldn't be sure. Her coworkers— Wrecking Ball, Jaguar, Julie, Flores, Susanna, Cecil, Maggie— stared down at her like she'd been found dead at the river's edge.

The phone rang again and Dooby went into the house to answer it. DuBois kept one eye on Chank and one hand on the gun.

"Hola, soy María de Mondo Telemundo. ¡Eres la ganadora del sorteo! ¿Hola? ¿Hola?"

"I-I-I, don't understand."

"That's it. Oh, no. It was—"

She lost her balance. Desert heat, dirty pool, Mr. Chank—spun in and spiraling around the mind. Desert, pool, Chank. A wound in a wheelchair. Stumps. A phone. A gun. A sequence of open sores. The blistered pink flesh. She remembered when her mother decided that children ought to do chores and ordered her to clean the toilet for the first time. She thought about period blood, about virginity lost and found again. Flashes of birth and afterbirth. The infernal bridegroom and the eternal husband. Cracked, growled, roared, howling all in a merry din. She slumped against the house to keep from falling over. Her elbow scraped on the coarse stucco—shredding skin and raising capillary blood.

"Ow. I think maybe…Dooby did it."

"Dooby? I don't know if he's an idiot, an imbecile, or a cretin, but he wouldn't do anything malicious. You can see that in his dumb, fat face."

Dooby ran through a series of lugubrious facial expressions and scratched the back of his neck like he was confused.

"What did he say about playing with guns?"

"Huh."

DuBois shook his head like it all made sense, like all the pieces in the puzzle fit together. He picked up the phone and put it back on the hook and Dooby remained in the corner.

"Hi, Dooby, can you come out here? I want you to tell me if you've ever shot a gun in the house."

"I-I I don't want to go in the closet."

"You won't have to go in the closet if you tell the truth."

Aspen felt ridiculous trying to bluff Dooby, since the closet he kept talking about was nowhere to be seen. The room didn't contain a wardrobe or even a cedar chest. As a mother, she never made a threat she couldn't follow through to execution. Stop crying, or we're leaving the park, saw them exit posthaste. Clean up your room or no tv, assured no one would be watching all their favorite shows.

Dooby stared at his Pro-Keds.

"Where's the gun now?"

"I-I I threw it in the swimming pool."

Aspen and DuBois both exhaled a breath of relief. DuBois hadn't taken his eye off of Mr. Chank. He walked up to the wheelchair, reached out and poked Chank on the shoulder.

"He's dead."

The phone rang again.

"Chank must be on all the lists. He probably bought an Enigmatic widget. Every telemarketer in the world calls here, including you, Aspen. Let's get out of here."

Dooby rocked back and forth in the corner. Aspen had many questions, all pointless curiosity.

"Shouldn't we call the sheriff or an ambulance?"

"The phone's broke."

About halfway up the trail, on the way out, a rattlesnake slithered onto the path. DuBois pulled the gun from his belt, leveled it, aimed it, lowered it, and tucked it right back into his belt.

"You can't even shoot a snake."

"I wanted to shoot it."

"I know. I'm proud of you."

"I know."

They walked off the trail, keeping the snake at a distance. By the time they got to the Fury, the sun arced overhead. Its heat blanched the blue out of the sky. DuBois burned his fingertips on the steering wheel; Aspen seared hers on the seat belt buckle. Dooby climbed into the backseat which was unbearably hot against bare patches of leg. Overhead, the lone poplar or cedar looked sinister silhouetted against a copper sheet.

"What should we do with him? We can't leave him here."

"Wow, uh, I guess he's coming with us?"

DuBois opened the driver's side door and slipped into position. While adjusting himself in the driver's seat, a vision of Chank's arm stump left a bad taste in his mouth. He turned the key, pushed in the tape and The Disposable Heroes broke into their cover of one of his favorite bands, which improved his outlook fourfold.

Come and join the surf and sun… And keep California number one!

To Aspen's delight, DuBois drove straight to Motel 69 and got them a room. He asked Dooby to stay in the car, so he could sneak him in later and save six dollars.

Motel 69

DuBois and Aspen took off their shoes and bounced from one double bed to the other in the motel room. Dooby wanted to jump on the beds, too, but was afraid he might get in trouble, so found a corner and watched.

This whole experience reminded Aspen of the first time they drove into Mexico and got lost in the hills. She'd been afraid then too. DuBois didn't want to stop and ask for directions, but the dirt roads got more confusing and the potholes got bigger, so big that one of them jarred the right front hubcap loose from the tire. Eventually, they stopped and tried to ask, Which way to the United States? The woman looked at them like they were insane. Aspen tried, ¿Donde esta los Estados Unidos? But the woman didn't know or didn't care and simply shrugged.

"Dooby, do you have any extra clean clothes?"

"I'm not a dirty bird."

"Try these."

She held up a pair of DuBois's jeans and a band t-shirt with "Adolescents" scrawled across the front. The faded shirt, which DuBois bought after a gig at Wabash Hall thirteen years before, had a small rip near the shoulder.

"Go on and take a shower now, Dooby."

Aspen looked over at him and wondered if he'd be able to squeeze into DuBois's clothes. DuBois was tall and wiry whereas Dooby was squat and soft.

"DuBois's baggy pants actually fit you."

Dooby smiled and closed the door. He pondered the controls on the shower, leaned in to turn one of the knobs and a stream of water soaked his head. Reflexively, he turned it off. This action repeated several times, wetting his hair each time before he figured out how to lean back before the water hit.

"What's he doing in there?"

"Search me."

"Not a bad idea."

"Stop. You know I don't like being tickled th-"

"Fine."

"Oh shit."

"What?"

"I dropped my gum in your hair. Sorry, honey."

She picked at the gum in his hair, but it only got worse.

"Remember that time we were at Magic Mountain and my gum fell out on the Revolution loop and landed on the dude in the front car?"

"A blue wad stuck to a bald head."

"When he protested, you called him, Gumskull!"

"Gumskull...Hee hee hee."

She gave up on the gum and cuddled in on top of him. But when she pressed her lips against his, he tilted his head to watch tv over her shoulder. Her mouth tasted sweet. She closed her eyes and he ran a finger across her eyebrow. They continued kissing while the news anchor described a horrific scene. Two kids in Colorado shot up their school. An analyst described the ending of an epoch and claimed that human character had changed for the worse. Sure, murder, disaster and confusion were nightly fare, but this terrible crime, he insisted, marked a low evil place in the history of a depraved nation. They interspersed video of the school under siege with a song by pop singer Marilyn Manson. One of the commentators said guns don't kill, people do. Another one said Lucifer had returned to earth and tempted those boys toward murder and mayhem, which sounded like a marketing gimmick. Maybe they were trying to sell records with a revival of 1980s-style Satanic Panic.

She heard the shower cut off, sat up and straightened her tube top. They were both feeling solemn when Dooby came out of the bathroom and Dooby worried that he had done something wrong—his hair was washed and face scrubbed, he looked clean. The jeans Aspen gave him dragged on the floor, but could be rolled up at the cuff.

"I-I I'm a clean boy now."

"You're a handsome boy too."

"Give him a goatee, and he'd look a little like Toby."

"I'm not Toby, I'm Dooby."

Dooby sat down in front of the tv and DuBois went into the motel bathroom. He took his shaving kit and decided a shower would do him good. Aspen flipped through the channels and found a Bugs Bunny cartoon. They settled in to watch. After about ten minutes, the shower came on in the bathroom. Three minutes after that, DuBois opened the door and a rush of steam followed him out.

"Oh my gosh! D-string."

Dub emerged from the bathroom with a mohawk, which harkened back to his days in the punk scene.

"Dooby, is that the funniest haircut you've ever seen?"

"I-I I think that's a funny way to cut your hair."

"I couldn't get the gum out…"

"It's more punk rock than last time."

Last summer, he shaved most of his hair and cut graphic lines into the fade so that the back of his head looked like a lie detector test. People expected him to whip out a piece of cardboard and breakdance. Who's your favorite turntablist, bro? Will Crazy Legs make a come-back? *Jockin' Mike D to my dismay.*

"When we get home, I'm going to listen to all the old records—Bags, Plugz, Zeros. EC still has Juan Carlos's albums. They were in storage, after that fucking cat of theirs used them as a scratching post. Waste of great music. Those bands started in the garage and ended up there. I don't even think she has a record player."

Aspen gathered up the clothes she wanted to sleep in and went into the bathroom.

"Oh wow! If we can make it back by Saturday, they should be having their housewarming party."

"You think they got everything moved in?"

"Sure, sure, ha ha, unless Megatool Outlet went out of business."

"No way Megatool Outlet goes under with customers like Toby. Out of stock, sure, sure, but out of business? Fuck no."

Aspen went into the bathroom to take her shower.

"What are your plans, dude?"

"I-I don't have any plans."

Dooby opened his weathered canvas sack and laid its contents on one of the beds. He had a videotape, a filthy stuffed animal, a box of Barnum's animal crackers, a ball on an elastic band that had broken off the paddle, a paddle, a National Geographic with a giant rodent on the cover. DuBois asked if he could look at the magazine—Dooby looked unsure but said okay. A nurse extracted a Guinea worm from a man's leg by winding it around a stick. As soon as he turned the page, a photograph fell out onto the bed. A much younger Dooby stood amidst a group of hippie teenagers, gathered around an older man with a beard in a white linen tunic and another old man wearing a huge smile.

"Hey, that's Timothy Leary? They shot his ashes into orbit…"

"Um, well, those were my friends and Mr. Chank was my friend. Do you want an animal cracker, DuBois?"

"No, thanks. Is Mr. Chank this guy with the beard?"

"That was before."

"Before?"

"Um-uh, before something went wrong. Can I um-uh, can I have an animal cracker?"

"They're your crackers. You don't have to ask anyone. Leary once said, Water is addictive. And too much will kill you. So, don't eat the whole box."

Aspen always said she wanted another child, but DuBois wasn't sure if Dooby could fill that need. He set the magazine back in its place.

"I like capybaras."

"Yeah?"

"I think my ear's all better. I can hear out of it."

"Must have been Grammar's magic potion."

"I'm going to be sure and tell her that so she can rub it in your face. What are you boys up to?"

"Dooby showed me his things."

"What's this? A movie we can watch?"

"I guess you can watch my movie."

Aspen put it into the hotel VCR.

"Says here, we can get porn from the night clerk."

Dooby's tape started with gray static. After a few seconds, a film flickered into life. It might have been shot by student filmmakers on Super 8 or on video by a low-budget documentary crew, but it wasn't homemade. A group of young people, maybe the same ones in the photo, came on the screen, arms aloft like wings and flying down thigh-high golden grass along the gentle slope of a hillock. Wooden troughs, abundant with flowers, overflowing green with tomatoes, potatoes, peppers, eggplant, and huckleberry, stood in front of the stucco shack—whitewashed in the video and glimmering in the morning sun. There was a dormitory or bunkhouse and a shot of a guy waving the camera away as he went into the outhouse. The presenter, also a hippie, held a mic up to a man with a beard. A title flashed: Dr. Roland Chank, LSD.

Hee hee hee.

"Shhh."

"Well, yes. My children and I live communally. This is a loosely organized commune where each lives for all. We aren't religious nuts or nationalist separatists. Our study group has taken deep dives into Saint-Simon, Stirner, Landauer, we've looked at Bellamy Clubs, read *News from Nowhere*, stolen bits of Fourier's phalanx and Proudhon, Brook Farm, New Harmony, Fruitlands—I'm personally attracted to Bronson Alcott—Llano del Rio, Home, Kellog, Graham… If someone has a utopian thought, we'll study it. Ivan and Jane are great. Even Bucky

Fuller has interesting things to say. But in the end socialism, communism, capitalism don't hold water. There's too much work to be done. So, if we have one rule it precludes ists and isms."

The filmmakers cut in more shots of young people frolicking around the hills. Sitar music like water dribbling over river stones played over the top, and long slow shots dissolved between talking heads and youths at work in the green fields.

"We explored LSD early on, but it hasn't led to the kind of mind expansion we hoped for."

"Is that Dooby? Is that you, dude?"

A boy on the screen, who looked to be about fourteen or fifteen, showed the camera crew around the compound. They stopped by the pool and took a hit off a joint.

"I know how homeboy got his nickname."

"Shhh."

Dooby sat on the bed and stared at himself like he didn't recognize the stranger on screen. His younger self explained how the mushrooms, fish and exotic plants in the pool cleansed sewage. Of course, you can drink it. It's filtered. The commune's long-range plan promises clean water for the whole region. He knelt down and used his hands as a cup to drink from the pool.

"These people are seriously stoned. Like Mormons or Moonies."

Chank's voice appeared over a montage.

"We are trying to cultivate a mycelium that will ameliorate depression. One day it will filter the mind just as it filters the water. People are well within their rights to be depressed. Existence, as we know it, is full of sorrow. The world is depressing. From the bomb to Vietnam, what a drag the world can be. A total bummer. Permanent bliss could be how we avoid mutually assured destruction. If we don't crack the mind, the cracked mind will crack the world."

"I left home when I was sixteen, knocked about the country, tried my hand at odd jobs, rode the rails across the Midwest, and ended up here with Mr. Chank. He's a brilliant man."

Two girls, like vixens out of a Russ Meyer film, streaked naked across the screen and leapt into the pool. One of them dove under the murky water and came up from the depths holding a gnarly black mushroom.

"Those must be some sick mutha-fucking mushrooms."

Another girl twisting at the long brown braid on her shoulder came on the screen.

"Our commune isn't a cult. Mr. Chank doesn't call himself a guru. We come and go as we please. The idea here is to get free, silly. To free our minds and our bodies. Mr. Chank has a plan."

The video took a dark turn, a shot that must have been inside the stucco house showed Chank with a hand drill boring a hole into his own skull. A little blood rose around the sharp flutes of the bit.

"Trepanation is an ancient ritual of body modification practiced by the Incas and the Egyptians and in the late 1960s by friends of mine…"

The video cut to a close-up of skin, healed over, which rose and fell with a pulse.

"I'm talking about reversing the pathways. Undoing our misery. An idyll, an ideal. A permanent state of innocent ecstasy, like a baby before the sutures in its skull fuse together. Blood volume increases, hence more oxygen is delivered to the brain. Heightened perception. Plato in Delphi, the truth beyond the veil of experience. The utopia inside. Ritual use of LSD, trepanation and our mushrooms will save Earth from its people."

"I-I I got a hole drilled in my head."

Aspen and DuBois looked at each other and didn't know what to say.

Housewarming

The faded yellow ticket on the windshield of his Toyota had been joined by a pink tow-away notice. DuBois crumpled it and squeezed it in his big fist. Everything should be great: Aspen's ear felt better, Chank, being dead, hadn't caused any trouble and a party to celebrate EC's new home was under way up the driveway, behind the gate in the backyard. This should be a time for jubilation. Yet, while they were out in the desert, everything changed. When they picked up Rufi, DuBois's father wasn't there. Moms said he went to live in a hotel. On top of that, Aspen's mother called and said that her father had had a heart attack. His doctor released him from the nursing home, but he didn't feel up to visitors. Aspen shouldn't worry, her mother said, about coming to visit. At least not right now. Winds were blowing offshore. Big things piled upon little—an overwhelming wave of doom—their fathers, his broken Toyota, the look his mother gave when she saw his haircut, the grief she made blatant about the thirty-year-old boy they had in tow. Plus, the rent, gas, and phone bills, plus his lack of suitable employment coupled with Aspen's existential desire for a house of her own. Daughters grew up faster than fathers could process—and he felt disconnected from his little girl—discontent and alienation darted about like barracuda inside the wave. On the news, another postal worker killed his colleagues. DuBois slammed the balled-up notice into the street and headed up the driveway. The wave came crashing down and he needed to swim. Swim to the cottage before he killed somebody. Water,

water everywhere. His own voice and bass line echoed out of the stereo speakers.

Daylight come and tally me bananas…

The tape Toby bought at Undersea Planet played for the party guests. DuBois hated it, hated that they recorded it, hated that Toby bought it—an empty promissory note on a bankrupt scheme. There's a point in every mailman's career when zip codes dance a polka. DuBois came unglued. His lips turned white, his jaw tightened. Pearls of sweat formed at his hairline. Aspen said that when he got anxious, he made the same facial expression his father made. Mothers everywhere were correct when they scolded, Keep making that face and it will freeze that way. They didn't tell you how it set crushed into the dry wrinkles of age, but what youth could understand that anyway? Years of worry about money and getting ahead bought Pops high blood pressure and high blood sugar. DuBois had done everything he could not to trundle down the same wheel-rutted trail. What the heck was the old man doing? Leaving his mother? After all this time? It made no sense. But first he had to traverse the path from the street to the cottage.

Aspen, Rufi and Dooby followed him single file up the driveway. The girls carried their overnight bags, Dooby toted his canvas sack. Aspen wasn't ready to explain Dooby. Still figuring it out in her own mind, she hoped EC and Toby would be distracted with their other friends. The tourist music and party conversation roiled over the fence. DuBois opened the gate. It felt like everyone looked at them. Three teenage boys looked up from a vintage *Silverball Mania* pinball machine in the driveway. Toby manned the grill, searing his beloved pollo asado. EC worked diligently plating several side dishes galore in the kitchen of the main house with her aunts. A dozen other people in scattered cliques drank bottled beer. One freckled lady sat in a patio chair wearing dark sunglasses and showed off her pregnant belly.

Flames danced on tiki torches placed strategically around the yard. Another group gathered around the blender to indulge in strawberry margaritas.

A time of celebration.

DuBois nodded at people as he slipped through the crowd, like navigating a carnival funhouse. The lines of good-natured men and women, whispering to themselves about his mohawk, recalled a venturesome stroll on the boardwalk in Mission Beach in the summer of '81. He was with Juan Carlos. You expected verbal abuse when you cut your hair short, since just about everybody wore theirs long. The heavy shoes, the black trench coat, the dark glasses expressed how he felt inside. Everything was fresh, exciting. The bikers, sitting on the wall nursing their beers, were rebels once. But they forgot. Hey faggot, they yelled. They always yelled, Hey faggot.

The family set a direct bearing for the cottage when Yakuza strutted up, mewing loudly to scold them for leaving for so long. DuBois picked up the cat by the scruff and ushered Dooby, Rufi, and Aspen inside. He shut the door, breathed easier and stroked Yakuza's black fur.

"Sorry, Yacky. We had to go on a mission."

"Meoowwwww!"

"Do you like cats, Dooby?"

"I-I I'm afraid of cats. Cats don't like rodents. They sometimes eat them."

"Dooby, you say the cutest, funniest things."

Rufi showed that she wasn't scared of the cat by stroking him behind the ear. Yakuza must have appreciated the attention and didn't make trouble. Rufi still wasn't sure what to make of Dooby. He reminded her of Brenda's kid brother. He bugged her without doing much more than exist. If anyone suggested that Dooby stole her momma's precious attention, she would deny that she felt threatened. For now, she fought the desire to ask if Dooby was a "retard."

"You know what? We should've got them a housewarming gift."

DuBois looked around the cottage for anything they could re-gift. He thought about the sandwich griller in the closet but remembered that EC had given it to them because she already had one. He picked up a box of wooden matches that had been sitting on the end table. Saw a book of Faulkner's short stories.

"What would Abner Snopes do for a housewarming?"

"Daddy, is there anything we can regift?"

"Rufi, you are just like your daddy."

"Give me a break, Aspen, babe. We learned the fine art of regifting from you. Do you think they'd like Faulkner? No, I guess not. Let's make a gift of the rent check. Have you got a pretty envelope?"

She handed him an envelope and a party bag with primary red, blue, and yellow balloons on it, which Rufi had gotten a Barbie Doll in for her last birthday.

"It's not much, but we help them pay the mortgage."

"It might cover the interest on their Megatool Outlet bill."

Dooby looked around the small house. He didn't know whether to sit down on the couch or remain standing, so he rocked back and forth. Yakuza sniffed one of Dooby's Pro-Keds.

They all took turns going to the bathroom. Even Yakuza got in his cat box and scratched around. Aspen studied her ear, since it looked sore, she popped a couple of pain pills. She piled her hair on top of her head and pinned it with chopsticks.

Outside, the music blasting out of the stereo changed to Top 40. Boy groups were in vogue—spin offs of Menudo, Synchronized Backstreet Pet Shop Boyz to Men at Work, ad nauseam. When relatives came over people who didn't care about music chose the tunes. Like bland food for the terminally ill. Why not let a chap who's studied musicology call the tunes? Why not listen to something good? He considered wrapping up a Blue Note album from his collection, Lee Morgan or Horace Silver, but remembered they didn't have a record player. He looked over at Toby who tapped his foot along with the melody.

DuBois saw that his eclectic, eccentric, maybe even erudite, taste in music limited the popularity of the bands he'd played in.

"What's the matter, honey?"

"You know how I can't stand this crap music. Or this banal culture that's always being thrown at us. Everywhere we go, it's like a shitstorm with pigeons dropping bad music, bad tv, bad politics, bad values on us. They're out there talking about property values. They're out there having fun, I guess. This party is a farce. Everything sucks."

"Babe, that's because you're ten years ahead of your time musically."

He liked when she said sweet things.

"Everything does not suck, I don't care if we go to the party, we can stay in here and watch The Simpsons."

DuBois let out a long stream of piss, which helped to assuage his anxiety. He washed his face and hands. Studying his own reflection in the mirror, he felt like maybe a party would do him good. He lifted the gun from his belt, took the bullets out, fingered and inspected each one, and stowed it in the back of the closet under Aspen's sweaters. He put the five bullets in a coffee can of collected nickels, dimes, and quarters behind some books on a tall shelf.

"Rufi, Dooby, I don't want either one of you to touch this gun. Guns are dangerous, even if you think they're not loaded. Too many kids end up shooting themselves in the stomach or blowing their friend's face off. Don't touch it. Ever seen a man shot in the stomach? Guts pour out like spaghetti. Rufi, I don't want you to mention that we have a gun to your friends at school. Don't show it to your bestie. Don't tell anyone. It's none of their business."

He had never made a speech like this, and though it screamed of responsibility, he felt good about it.

"What should we do?"

"Go to the party, turn off the lights. I don't care."

"Are you hungry, Dooby?"

"I-I I'm hungry, I like to eat stuff sometimes."

"So, let's get some grub."

"I-I ate a grub once."

Aspen went straight to the kitchen to say hello to EC. DuBois and Dooby each grabbed a plate piling food like they were half-starved and sat near the cottage away from people. DuBois didn't know anyone. The guests were friends of Toby's from work and members of EC's extended family. He grabbed a Mexican beer from the Igloo cooler—Negro Modelo. Rufi went to play pinball with the boys while DuBois sipped his beer. She would grow up to be a beauty, a gazelle on the veldt. Sooner than he could imagine a tuxedo-wearing hyena would be smiling at the door with a corsage in hand. Before that, maybe, she would be kissing him at the movies. He wanted strong parenting skills, wanted to spare her a painful initiation into the world of experience.

While her parents were chasing Chank at the stucco shack, Rufi had her first period. Things were changing quickly and he didn't want to be locked out of her adolescent world. He wished that she hadn't felt the need to hide her blood-soaked underwear from his parents. DuBois had tried to prepare himself by reading books on the subject. He felt ready to discuss menarche with his daughter. He'd tried to learn everything he could about the rag—from non-toxic sea sponges to pads with wings. Rufi had learned about menstrual periods in fourth grade, so she didn't fret about dying like the girl whose parents pulled her out of sex ed for religious reasons. Rufi told her momma about the blood, showed her the stain, but said, Don't tell anyone, even Daddy.

DuBois remembered holding up a box of tampons at the store, Hey, Aspen, do you need any extra-absorbent deodorant tampons! He wasn't embarrassed and didn't think anyone should be. It was nature. It was natural. But he could also see how stigmas were put on the body. DuBois's father noticed the menarche book—called *Cunt*—on his bookshelf in Little Italy and said DuBois shouldn't leave "pornography" lying around where his daughter could find it.

"You know that book on your shelf. Ahem. A certain four-letter word...starts with C."

"You mean *Cunt*?"

Funny that he didn't say anything about Melville's *Moby Dick* next to it on the shelf. He pulled it out of the bookcase and tried to hand it to his father, who retracted his hand, afraid of the book's cooties. It fell through space but didn't hit the floor as DuBois snagged it with his left hand.

"As porn, it's disappointing. No pictures. It's an owner's manual. Stories about abortions and yeast infections…"

His father stopped listening. Candor, a C word more people might learn. DuBois wondered about "bad" words, about shame around the body. Maybe Rufi's generation would relax. Church people would find some other natural phenomena to lay their taboos on. They needed sin to keep control over their flock.

Dooby sat on the porch like a trained circus bear.

Aspen stepped into her friend's house. The woman up front had actually vacated the premises. She was gone. Maybe things would start looking up. The interior had been painted a bright white and EC had furnished the living room. They had the hardwood floors refinished and most of the furniture looked new. The couch looked too pristine to sit on. Aspen pitied the first person who spilled on it. Bright curtains hung in the windows. Aspen wasn't ready to talk about her adventure and settled in to listen to EC rant about her gifts.

"Lucky, lucky EC. My aunt Linda got EC a new food processor and…"

EC referred to herself by name when she got super excited, which didn't bother Aspen but highlighted the need for two coffees and a beer. Berneece, the unseen note lady, had sent champagne. Would they become friends? Aspen realized, with a tinge of melancholy, that she didn't know the answer.

"Can I help?"

"Sure, sure. Dice up these strawberries and put them in this white bowl. I'm going to mingle."

Aspen poured coffee and listened to EC's mother telling one of her aunts about her son's credit card debt.

"Why did they want to buy a boat when they owed $10,000 already? Those children spend, spend, spend. They don't know the meaning of a rainy day..."

Toby held court at the barbecue, sporting a Kiss the Cook apron and floppy chef's hat.

"This is the Monster-Q 9000, the top-of-the-line propane multi-deck grill with precision flame dual side-burners."

The guests formed a line at the grill and held paper plates, which he plied with meat.

"I bought forty pounds of chicken, so eat up."

EC's Uncle Tomas filled his plate four times.

"Frank, you know EC's Papi, that son of a bitch loved barbecue. He could work a grill like a fry cook pulling a double, Camel hanging from his lip and highball in hand. Did I tell you when

I worked with that son of a bitch in a slaughterhouse? That was real work."

Every time he called EC's father a son of a bitch, one of the aunts would say, Rest his soul. Who said vaudeville routines passed out of fashion? Toby smiled and listened. He wanted to explain how being at the grill reminded him of his assistant manager days at Round Table Pizza but couldn't break through Uncle Tomas's monologue.

They made jokes and laughed. DuBois drank his beer.

"Toby, be a good kid and put the fire pit on."

Tomas heartily clapped him on the back. Toby had the wood set up well before the party, but Uncle Tomas explained how to place the kindling anyway. When the flames jumped up, everyone applauded until a column of smoke scattered a clique by the dessert table.

EC came back into the kitchen.

"Boy, oh boy. It has been so stressful getting everything ready for this party. We had a big fight about the blended drinks. He knows that I don't really like beer and go crazy for tequila. But he kept saying, Blender accidents make homeowner's insurance payments go up. Someone will break it or hurt themselves. I think he didn't want to be responsible for his coworkers. Dee Dee with the fake tits and her husband Jackie got wasted at the company Xmas party and made a scene just shy of an X-rated movie."

EC giggled like she'd let a dirty secret loose.

"I see you won that round."

"Hear, hear. Dee Dee's over by the blender wearing a tiny tank top. The one with the huge bazongas. The implants cost her husband five grand…"

Jackie, in an open-necked golf shirt, fell in next to Uncle Tomas. A drink in one hand, he talked with as many gesticulations as words.

"Yo, I'm from Brooklyn, *also known as Crooklyn*. Oh, ha ha. Fuck yeah. And in Brooklyn we know tits. In Detroit, you've got your ass men, in Chicago you've got your leg men, but in Brooklyn we love tits. Have you ever seen a rack of lamb like this?"

He gestured toward his wife, laying his left hand, the one with the gold wedding band, gingerly on Toby's back.

"I mean, on some broad who wasn't a hooker? Ha ha. Technically, my little plush toys belong to Mastercard, but two more payments and they're all mine."

Dee Dee must have relished being talked about because she twirled around as if to model them.

"What about San Diego?"

"I don't know… Out here in Cali, it's kind of a whole-package deal. They don't specialize. I heard they don't like fat chicks. In Philly, you got your gash men… you know, big pussy eaters. I heard that in Jersey they like to eat out the butthole, you know, rim jobs… That's what I heard."

DuBois looked over at Dooby and took a sip of his beer.

A guy with ugly, hairy, pale toes hanging out of a pair of Birkenstock sandals walked up and stood next to Dooby holding a plate of food.

"So, you live in the back house?"

"I-I I don't know."

"Well, a young lady in the kitchen said I could find her husband outside, so I…"

"I-I I'm not married."

"Oh, I'm sorry."

"I-I I'm not a dirty bird."

"You know you're a dead ringer for Toby. I like the goatee. Are you related?"

"I'm not Toby, I'm Dooby."

"They're twins."

"Ah, you must be the young lady's husband. DuBois? A Trolley called Despair—"

"Mmm."

"Hey, Doob, why don't you get yourself a soda? You want another drink, man? I'm getting one."

"Oh no thanks, we're going to be leaving soon. Don't drink and drive. Orr orr. I had a punker friend in high school… The

Warriors look like champs this year. The Bulls dynasty has fallen, sad. That Rodman, right?"

"I don't follow baseball."

"Oh, uh. So, what do you do?"

"I read a lot, play music. Raise my kid, cheat the system."

"Oh, there's my wife. Excuse me."

Across the yard, EC's Aunt Rita moved to rein in Uncle Tomas.

"Tomas, you shouldn't drink any more."

"That's what my doctor said."

Dee Dee danced alone. Jackie looked proud, he tapped Toby on the shoulder and said, Bro, check this out, like his baby boy took its first step or his dog had learned a new trick. He got in behind her and they fell into a kind of synchronized grind. People clapped and cheered them on.

Rufi played pinball by herself.

"Can I play?"

"Sure, Daddy."

He set his beer on the ground and managed to keep the ball in play for a long time by bumping and shaking the machine. On Rufi's turn, DuBois said, Don't hit both flippers at the same time. He sang in a low voice, *Ever since she was a young girl, she's played the silver ball, from Lemon Grove out to OB, she must have played them all.* Rufi banged the ball up into the upper bumpers and shook the machine to milk her score.

"Cool haircut, Maniac. I had a friend in college who had a mohawk."

"Hey, Toby."

"I gotta show you this sweet yard drill I picked up at Megatool Outlet."

"Cool."

"I saw you got another ticket."

"I need to stash that car somewhere before the man tows the mutha-fucker."

"You should sell it."

"You can't sell a car unless it passes the smog test."

"A guy at my last job bought broken-down cars…"

Dooby, standing alone by the garage, caught Toby's attention.

"Who's that?"

"That's our friend Dooby. He's visiting from up north. He's going to stay with us for a few days until he gets set up."

Aspen grabbed Dooby by the hand and brought him into a circle with EC, Toby, and DuBois. Rufi continued to play pinball.

"Dooby, this is… EC and Toby, they live in the big house up front. This is our friend Dooby."

Aspen finished her beer and picked up a margarita from the blender table.

"I-I I'm not Toby, I'm Dooby."

Their resemblance astounded everyone. Even EC and Toby seemed bewildered by it. They were the same height, the same size, the same shape, although Toby's work in the gym had forged muscle where Dooby was soft. Dooby must have felt the heat from the fire pit and took a step back. DuBois figured he better get inside the cottage before one of Toby's friends said, I had a retarded friend in college.

Rufi left off pinball and held her hands up to warm them by the fire.

"Ish something wrong?"

"I-I I don't like fire."

"Ish okay, Dooby. Ish okay."

Aspen gave him a kiss on the cheek and EC laughed at the big red lipstick print. Jackie held one of the tiki torches aloft for his wife to limbo under. Her tits almost caught fire.

"Are you supposed to drink with the pills you've been taking? You're slurring your words."

She glared at DuBois with devil hate, turned without saying anything and disappeared into the cottage. The front window vibrated like it was hit by a small earthquake when the door slammed.

"We should all go in. Thanks for the party. Congrats."

Aspen passed out on the futon. Tucking Rufi in, DuBois said, in a voice as harried and thick as the top string of his bass, I'm tired, baby girl. Can I read you two stories tomorrow night? She said she didn't care. He laid his sleep roll out on the carpet and handed Dooby a pillow. You can sleep here. DuBois slipped in next to Aspen. Her alcohol breath smelled sweet. Before he could get to sleep, he heard his own voice singing, *Daylight come, and me wan' go home.*

Suburb + Utopia

Dooby poured the last of the cereal into his bowl and a tiny stuffed Bert-from-Sesame-Street doll crash-landed among the flakes. Dooby let the surprise show on his face. He picked it up and examined it, thinking, What is Bert doing in my cereal?

DuBois and Aspen drank coffee from identical mugs and pressed Rufi to finish her breakfast flakes and get to school on time. Put your saddle shoes on in the car, let's go. EC's neighborhood had a school she could walk to, but Rufi continued at the school in Little Italy—a seven-minute drive on the freeway.

"Rufi, do you want this Bert?"

Dooby extended the Bert doll. She took it, looked it over, tweaked the black tuft of hair on its head and handed it back.

"No thanks, I wanted Rubber Ducky."

"A cloth rubber ducky? Is that like plastic silverware?"

"So nice of you to offer the toy to Rufi. You can keep Bert."

"It's like a wooden nickel."

"Quit distracting Rufi from eating."

"Or maybe like false advertising."

"Come on, it's time for school."

"That's not an oxymoron, Daddy, it's redundant."

"Let's go."

Yakuza sniffed at the base of the table with radar locked on the leftover milk. Dooby thought maybe he would try to overcome his fear and pet the cat. When he bent down, his pants sagged a little in the back. Rufi had an idea. She whispered into Dooby's ear and he stood up straight with his hands folded behind him.

"Momma, Dooby's got plumber's butt."

"I-I I'm not a dirty bird."

She jammed the Bert doll into the crack with his head peeping above the waistline and spun Dooby around.

"Look! It's Butt Bert!"

Dooby reached back and flung Bert into the air—Yakuza pounced and batted Bert around the floor.

"Yakuza's got Butt Bert!"

Aspen couldn't help but laugh, even though her head felt heavy from the pills and booze.

"How come I'm the only one who has to go to school?"

"Somebody's got to learn some skills and get a job to support us."

"Hey. Look at Dooby's head."

They gathered around Dooby and watched the pulse underneath his scalp where he had been trepanned.

"Dag.

"We can all look at Dooby's head later. Let's go."

Aspen pushed her daughter out the door. After they left, Du-Bois made himself another cup of coffee and carried Yakuza into the yard to see if the squawking bird might attack. Another beautiful day. The bird wasn't around, so he walked out to the street. Toby and EC had already gone to work, so he decided to pull the beat Toyota wagon into the driveway to prevent the man from towing it away. First, he broke down one of the cardboard boxes from their move and slid the cardboard under the oil pan so it wouldn't stain Toby's white cement.

"Hey, Dooby, can you help me pick up the cups and bottles from last night's party? It would be a big help."

"I-I I like to help."

"Thanks, Dooby."

When Aspen returned from taking Rufi to school, Dooby searched for beer bottles around the yard like a kid on an Easter egg hunt.

"DuBois babe, let's do an exercise walk."

"A'ight."

They walked down the driveway holding hands. His lanky gait couldn't match Aspen's quick steps in exercise mode.

"Pick it up. Pick it up. They say we've got to speed walk for at least forty minutes to raise our heart rates. Oh, look, there's a house for sale."

"What about our heart rates?"

"This one's so close to EC's. Wouldn't it be great to be neighbors?"

"The market's in the seller's favor right now."

"Let's look in the window. Oh, a sun room. Sweet. Take this flyer. How much is it?"

"Too much."

"I wouldn't mind if Rufi went to a better school. Rufi's teacher told her about an achievement gap. White kids score highest, then Asian, then African American, then Other, then Latino."

"Why do teachers say shit like that?"

"That's what I thought. And if the teachers know it, why don't they fix it?"

They passed another house for sale but didn't look in the window. It had two stories, five bedrooms and an immaculately landscaped yard.

"What are we going to do with Dooby?"

"He can't stay with us forever."

"We can barely feed ourselves."

"Maybe the state can take care of him?"

"He's too big for an orphanage."

"Maybe there's some kind of group home? I dunno."

Up the street, a homeless person picked through the refuse for aluminum cans and empty bottles. It might have been a black woman or a white man. His or her hair clumped like the Berber welcome mat EC bought at Pier 999 to put in front of the door. His or her rhinoceros gray hide was tanned by grit, sun, and wind.

"There's an achievement gap among the homeless. The Asian bums wake up early and snag all the cans. Their moms give them quotas and yell at their asses."

"Be serious. What if they turned him out in the street?"

"We won't let that happen."

"You like him, don't you?"

"Mmm."

"Even though he was a hippie?"

"Well, kind of my point."

"I don't understand. You're basically a hippie yourself. You like rock and roll. You don't bathe all that much. Hippies came up with Earth Day, protested the war."

"It started as a generation clash. Punks got tattoos to remind themselves not to sell out. The hippies just got stale. They found jobs they hate. Or burned out. They got into boring drugs and their songs, fuck, got longer and longer. Woodstock, Altamont. These big arena shows. It became a commodity. It was easy for them to become mindless consumers. Every classic rock station plays the same bands—Hendrix, Van Halen,

Stones… Every punk has a different experience. We have the touchstone bands—The Clash, Black Flag, but most of the bands come out of local scenes. No two punk rocks are alike. Hippy experiments with drugs and spirituality faded into new age magical thinking. It's true that a lot of punks died from drugs just like the hippies. Their parents' generation is worse though. They get a lot of credit for fighting Nazis in WWII. But it took a world to make a world war. Americans wanted to control shit too. I'm glad they fought the Nazis, but they also saddled us with the bomb. It's bullshit. And I'm against it."

"Your grandmother is not a generation. She voted for FDR. Her remedies don't hurt anyone."

"She voted for Reagan too. There's no scientific evidence that her cures really work either. She dabbles with things she doesn't understand. It's disrespectful to indigenous cultures."

"Dub, you have a mohawk."

"I know. It's stupid. I'm the simulacra. The copy of a forgotten original. Kids used to play Cowboys and Indians on our street. Yours too, right? Walk into any office and the ones who always wanted to be cowboys will be sitting in the boss's chair. The kids who played Indians became punks. Normal people don't like my haircut because it's a relic of a genocide they benefited from. They don't want to think about it."

"I can see you think about this a lot, don't you?"

"Yeah, well."

When they came back to the cottage, they found Dooby sitting quietly in the patio chair with Yakuza purring on his lap. Aspen logged onto the internet—browsed the NY Times headlines online and checked her email while DuBois finished an essay by Howard Zinn on the toilet. He'd been finishing the books he kept in the bathroom quickly and wondered if he'd found a bright side to hemorrhoids. Or maybe reading on the toilet encouraged constipation? He didn't know. He'd try more fiber and exercise before he quit reading.

"We should celebrate Rufi's last day of fifth grade. Get ice cream at Thrifty's."

"Sounds good."

"Do you want to go to a poetry reading tonight? My ex-boss the Jaguar is featured."

"As long as we don't have to listen to open mic."

"The flier lists him and one other person at that café on Fourth."

"The Devil's Whorehouse? I like that coffee house. What'll we do with Rufi and Dooby?"

"Bring 'em along, it'll be fun. There might be other kids. Dooby can stand in the corner or drink a soda."

Aspen gave him a kiss and he thought she might be up for sex, but Dooby sitting on the couch made it impossible.

"Maybe we could find a nice young girl with Downs syndrome for Doob."

"You can be such a pig."

"What? What'd I say?"

"Okay, guys, let's clean the house. I'll clean the kitchen. Here, take this brush and do the bathroom. Dooby, you can vacuum."

"I-I I never used one of these machines, Aspen."

"It picks up dirt from the carpet. Just don't push the vacuum over socks or things like the phone bill that DuBois left on the floor."

After he finished the bathroom, DuBois went outside and climbed up on the flat roof of the cottage. He was raking leaves that had settled up there when Toby opened the back gate. DuBois climbed down the ladder, the shorter of the two that Toby bought at Megatool Outlet, holding a barrel full of mulch in one hand. Toby had already noticed the limbs hanging over the cottage from Berneece's yard and was eager to try out his new chainsaw.

"Hey, Toby, what's up, man? I almost left Berneece a note that said, Please don't park your leaves on our roof, but cleaning up seemed less of a hassle."

Toby didn't say anything. He looked angry.

DuBois wondered how long the tree had stood there and who planted it. Did the original owners put it in the ground? Or could it possibly predate the housing tract? The strange whirring sound, which he'd heard intermittently since they moved into the cottage, started up again.

"What do you think that strange sound is? I didn't see anything from the roof."

"You can't park your car in the driveway, man."

"Hello, to you too, Toby. I wanted to keep it out of reach of the man. Got an appointment later in the week with a guy who might buy it."

"It's not your driveway. You cannot keep the car there. This is my house, my driveway. My roof. My castle. We have to keep that clear."

"All right, I'll move it. It's cool, at least you didn't write me a note. Had the guts to confront a man face to face."

DuBois went into the house to get the keys. At this point he didn't care what happened to the car—of course, repairs would have been nice—but they couldn't afford it. Toby disappeared inside the main house, looked inside the refrigerator. Grabbed a diet soda.

"What's his problem?"

"I don't know. Maybe he hates his job, maybe EC's not giving him any."

DuBois got into the Toyota, which started right up. He parked it on the opposite side of the street. On his way back into the house, he picked up the oil-splotched cardboard.

"Looks like turtles fucking."

An automated sprinkler clicked along in the middle of the block. The whirring noise had stopped. DuBois brought a coffee and lawn chair into the front yard so that he could watch for the parking insurrection guard. The pirate flag no longer flew from the flagpole a few houses down. The mail carrier stuffed a wad of junk mail in the slot and walked on, listening to a baseball game on his transistor radio. Eventually, DuBois decided to sit in the car and read a short story by Jervey Tervalon. He'd read Tervalon's first book *Understand This* and liked it. The parking guard, suddenly there, had snuck up on him.

DuBois got out and said, Hi, how's it going? He explained his plan to sell the car and to his surprise the grim agent of the state said, Since you are so nice, I'll let it go. But you have to move this car soon.

The Devil's Whorehouse Café

Poetry fans packed into the café like Jello into a mold, like mold in the grout, like trout in an artificial lake. The Jaguar had been featured in a Dap Jeans commercial, so there were as many star-seekers as poetry aficionados in the audience. Americans would line up for anything they saw on television. A group of his original fans sat off to the side near the coffee bar plotting to order vanilla lattes as soon as he started speaking. That always made a lot of noise. They hoped the hiss of steaming milk would spoil the experience for the neophytes, and maybe they'd be able to get close to him after gigs again. Each wore a black hooded sweatshirt with "The Official Jaguar Black-on-Black Insignia" embroidered on the sleeve. Dashing his fame on the rocks might keep him in the local scene. Besides, everyone knows that anonymity makes better poetry.

"Remember when he used to shout, This is not a poetry reading, this is a guerrilla war?"

"Remember when he used to recite from his first chapbook at Betty's Books?"

"He's too good for that now."

"Who does he think he is? Allen Ginsberg?"

"More like Neil Cassady."

"Oooo. That's low, girl. Might as well compare him to Byron."

"Seriously, I'm shocked that he's even doing this café. I heard The Smashing Pumpkins asked him to open a university amphitheater tour."

"Sell out."

DuBois and Aspen wished they had found a sitter for Rufi and Dooby since they couldn't find a seat in the crowded café. The rich smell of ground coffee beans had been rubbed into every wood surface. The empyrean odor competed with the human funk of too many bodies cooped up in a small space. Young people comprised most of the audience, though former hippies, beatniks all in black, and even a few Ezra Pound modernist types with elbow patches on their tweed jackets milled around the scene.

DuBois felt uncomfortable standing, since there wasn't a spot that didn't block a fan's view of the stage. Aspen felt good being out in public. They ordered two house coffees, a soda, and a hot chocolate with whipped cream. They'd shown up late and caught the last poem from the first speaker. She looked to be about forty, "a celebrated woman," rocking a denim jacket with leather and cowry shells stitched onto the back. She read a piece called "Dipsy was a Darky," which seemed at first listen to be about that popular children's program *Teletubbies*. After she thanked the audience, three people in the middle of the room got up to leave.

DuBois pushed Dooby into a red velvet chair with black leopard spots and slid onto a faux eel skin settee before anyone else could claim it. Rufi and Aspen squeezed in beside him. Dooby admired the iron sconce light fixtures hanging from the ceiling, but the brass devils, glaring down from each of four corners, were a little scary.

"I'm glad we got a seat."

DuBois spilled his coffee.

"All these people crammed in here make me nervous."

His leather jacket squeaked against the couch.

"I like those paintings."

"I haven't seen this many leopard spots since the zoo."

He looked over at Dooby and hoped that he wouldn't spill his soda. There were several colorful paintings hanging on the walls. Abstract. One might have been a nude or a landscape of a freeway. Another one could have been a family of wolves sitting down to eat or a group of sweaty young men listening to jazz piano in a smoky juke joint.

"Whoever painted this has an aggressive stroke."

"A rational sense of the spatial too. Rufi, Dooby, be careful not to spill those drinks."

"Don't worry, Momma. I like the scarlet Baphomet on black velvet, it's cool."

"Mmmm. Tijuana modern."

The walls themselves were painted deep purple and firehouse red, adorned with crushed velvet gold draperies. Several people who had gone outside to smoke cigarettes left place-holders on their chairs: a sport coat, a journal, a digital camera, a back-pack. Aspen pointed out Julie from work sitting next to Boring, who unscrewed the cap to a bottle of peppermint schnapps he'd had tucked in his belt and tipped a shot into his macchiato. Julie wore a low-cut blouse made from a thin material so that her nipples showed and Aspen wondered if she had a crush on the Jaguar. Something was going on between their glances. Aspen watched Julie unwrap an Atomic Fireball and roll the candy around her tongue as she eyed her boss. Julie had a way of flirting with her whole body.

At stage left, the Jaguar talked to a woman holding a clipboard. He wore a big suit and a 40s vintage tie—he combed his dark wavy hair back slick. He smiled and laughed probably at his own joke. Julie looked frightened and it occurred to Aspen that she'd never been to a poetry reading. She sat with a stiff up-rightness like a meerkat sentry on guard against jackals—likely compiling an inventory of what people were wearing and taking mental notes. But her furtive glances always checked back in with the Jaguar. Aspen waved, but Julie continued to scan the room. Susanna had come down for the reading and bought herself a piece of blueberry cheesecake. She'd probably come with Flores, who had found her people sitting cross-legged on the floor. Conversation, along with anticipatory energy, filled the room. Four girls between the ages of twelve and fourteen lined the edge of the stage. The youngest, wearing a short skirt, turned on her knees and peered over the audience from behind dark sunglasses.

"Rufi, do you know those girls?"

No, she said disinterestedly. Maybe they're in high school. Her attention dropped back to Crane's *Red Badge of Courage*. She took a sip from a steaming mug of cocoa.

There weren't many poetry videos on MTV, but the Jaguar's video had played in heavy rotation for a few weeks. People magazine proclaimed him the first poet without a backing band to be thought of as a sex symbol since Frank O'Hara. Aspen wondered if the girls would fling panties at him, like rabid fans (mostly women) at Tom Jones. When Toby took EC to one of his concerts, she felt compelled to follow tradition and flung a brand-new pair, still in its plastic packaging, onto the stage. Aspen heard that the Jaguar used to perform in the nude at art galleries and everyone supposed that those days were long gone. As he said in an interview with Rolling Stone, You only have to perform naked once.

Dooby sat in the leopard-spot chair drinking his soda and thinking about the Bert doll that had appeared in his cereal. Rufi could go home or stay here and read, she didn't care.

Photographer Bartholmé Chaos waited in the mezzanine, ready with his square format land camera. The alternative weekly published a smartly composed picture, one of the best he'd taken, which depicted a local soul stirrer who'd played guitar and sung his own songs at The Devil's Whorehouse a month before. A few more lucky shots like those and he might be able to move out from his parents' house.

The Jaguar stepped behind the coffee bar into the kitchen and the woman he had been talking to stepped up on the stage to the microphone. As soon as she touched it, the feedback caused hands all around the café to cover offended ears. Aspen felt like she needed a pain pill.

"Hello, everyone. I would like to thank Bonnie for letting us use the space in her café, she has always been a big support. Teri and Sonny are working hard behind the counter tonight, so please tip them. And of course, I graciously thank all of you for coming out to support Poetry."

The capital "P" in poetry popped in the mic because her lips were too close.

"Quit stalling! Bring out the Jaguar!"

Gauging the crowd, the hostess scrapped a plan to read a poem of her own composition before Velasquez came out. No one would hear it, a pointless exercise of the ego.

"If you aren't familiar with Benny Velasquez's work, be prepared, he will rock the house. If you're faint of heart, don't say you weren't warned beforehand. Benny has been featured on MTV's…"

"Jag-u-ar! Jag-u-ar!"

A mob of teenage punk rockers chanted with raised fists. The Jaguar groupies with the black Jaguar hoodies had lined up to order their lattés. DuBois hadn't seen any of these kids at shows. Wearing his old hand-painted leather jacket, he felt pleasantly unremarkable. He fit in. A cloud-like sheep, copied from Minor Threat's album, that had been painted on the back of his leather had faded—the words Fuck and Ewe underneath were barely legible. The three buttons pinned to his lapel—Toy Dolls, SubHumans, and Black Flag—showed rust.

"Jag-u-ar!"

"Okay. Okay. Ladies and gentlemen… Benny, the Jaguar, Velasquez!"

She pushed a button on a boombox next to the podium, sending the Jaguar's theme music in a shockwave across the room— a push of another button cut the house lights. Aspen worried that Dooby might get scared, but he remained indifferent in the red velvet leopard-spot chair, turning the stuffed Bert doll over in his hands. A punk rock pirate shanty rollicked out of the PA, and on cue, the Jaguar swaggered through the front door of the café dressed like the pirate Blackbeard in a tricorn hat. Lit fuses, weaved into a false beard, wriggled like snakes. He wore a billowy white shirt open at the chest and a patch over one eye. A plastic sword, in his left hand, cut the air.

"Arrrrrgh, me Arties."

"Arrrrrgh!"

From the back of the café, he leapt onto a table like Vatslav Nijinsky stunt-doubling for Errol Flynn across the silver screen, hopping in great balletic leaps from table to table, like parkour, a regular mountain goat, glancing the leopard-spotted chairs and thick oak tables through the audience toward the stage. With but a drop of coffee spilled, he hit the stage and kicked out the plug on the boombox—crashing the music—and broke into his first poem. The kids in front pressed forward. The teen girls shrieked. People in the back shot to their feet, afraid to miss a gesture between craning necks.

"How long you gonna wait for inspiration to send your inhibitions on vacation?"

The girls in the front let out another shrill scream. Everyone in the crowd pressed a step closer to the stage. Rufi and Dooby stayed seated—neither could care any less.

"Go down on your knees often to meditate or copulate."

This wasn't the MTV hit. An oldie from the spoken word graveyard. This number pleased his hooded cronies—slayed and buried the corpse of their cynicism in a fell swoop. Quitting their planned disruption, in a group they shoved closer to the stage. The piece ended with furious applause.

"All right, ya scurvy dogs!"

Tug-o-war had broken out over the tri-cornered hat. One of his hoodrats had a death grip on one point—a raccoon-eyed punk held another—and one of Flores's hippie sisters held on dearly, so not to be thrown to the floor. They spun each other around until they tore the hat asunder—a shred held by each party like they'd won the lottery. A lesser poet danced with the false beard as a merkin. The Jaguar uttered the first word of the poem from the MTV video and the madding fans in the mad café went completely mad. Transported to the high seas abreast of a strong wind, Her Majesty's treasure ship in their sights with a glint of murder in their pirate hearts. A college student, trying to stand on one of the café tables, fell in a dim crash when it broke beneath his weight. He bounded up without missing a stanza. Like dicing for laudanum shots with Coleridge or fucking Emily Dickinson. Everyone under twenty-five in the café chanted the refrain of the poem and mouthed each verse like an inane prayer in church.

He went straight into the next poem without slowing his fervid pace.

"1, 2, 1, 2, 3, 4! He wants to be black, because now it's cool to be black, next week he'll be toting a dashiki to school and back, just to be black…"

One of the punks, a lad with a thick pink scar under his left eye, reared back and threw a coffee mug that broke against the back wall like a gunshot. A shrill screech like a crow alerting the murder issued forth and a military-looking dude leapt through the crowd in a flying tackle. Fists flew in a melee and DuBois thought it might be prudent to lead Rufi and Dooby out the back door. Exhilaration pulsed through the catheter of the air into the veins. In step, if not a step ahead, with her boyfriend, Aspen picked up Rufi while DuBois, in his stiff black leather jacket, locked hands with Dooby, unphased by the chaos, with a firm grip on Bert, and pulled him along. A stray elbow wrenched the book from Rufi's hand, trampled in the tumult by frowzled feet, pages bedraggled and tattered, it was left for dead in a no man's land. A panicked stampede crushed toward the front exit and several cane chairs were overturned in a heap. Aspen, moving against the grain, saw Julie felled in the rush. Boring, right behind her, scooped her to her feet, copping a feel. He tap checked the bottle in his belt. The crowd pushed and they were spit onto the sidewalk.

The punks were now fighting the hoodrats—the military guy was laid out flat under an overturned table. The cacophony rose like a toilet flush and fell silent. A placid calm fell over the café. The cane chairs smoldered, like a burnt forest, with silence. Jaguar struck a defiant pose on the stage, determined to finish his poem, fists poised for any mug that moved to stop him.

Out Like the Garbage

A short strip of dental floss sawed between his teeth, disrupting bacterial growth that had occurred across the night. After that, DuBois brushed each tooth exuberantly until the foam dripped out of his mouth into the sink among Aspen's loose hairs. He rinsed and tried to spit the sleep taste that lingered on his tongue. Considering his early morning face in the mirror, back to bed felt like the most viable option, but the mockingbird was squawking loudly in the yard, so he figured he'd take in a show. The old orange cat, stretched out on the neighbor's side of the low fence, turned the other cheek so that the squawking bird could harvest more soft bedding for its nest. After that he went out front to check on the Toyota wagon, still parked across the street—he wasn't surprised to see another note on the windshield. It had been written by a man who concurred with Berneece that DuBois should park his beat car elsewhere.

DuBois tossed up his hands. He stuffed the note in his pocket for evidence. He looked around, thinking that there must be a hidden camera, that it was a test to see how much he could take. He held up matching sets of stiff little fingers for the benefit of whoever was watching from behind the veil. His unseen neighbors were asking for a brick through their curtained windows. He headed up the driveway carrying that brick in his pocket.

At the top of the drive, a large canvas was leaning up against the trash can—one Juan Carlos painted for EC before they split. The heat of the direct sunlight was already abrading the paint—he picked it up and carried it into the cottage. It was a large work and he moved slowly to avoid banging it against anything. It already suffered a small tear near the top, which marked it as one that previously contained a Sunday painter's impressionist landscape and had been left in the alley by a lady in one of those apartments in Banker's Hill that looked down on the park. Juan Carlos painted a black hole shooting dark rays into the void over most of the canvas. Toward the bottom he had written, "Racism is a Six-letter Word, so is Stupid & Fucked" in yellow paint. There was a sidebar with violent slashes of color: periwinkle blue, blood orange, ochre, iridescent green, lily white. DuBois had seen the painting hundreds of times over the years hanging in EC's condo above the couch. It had survived her entire relationship with Robert but was finally left for trash.

"Where are you going with that?"

"I found it by the trash cans."

"You know we don't have room."

There wasn't a blank space of wall big enough for a painting even half its dimension in the cottage.

"We'll keep it at mi madre's casa."

He leaned the painting against the boxes of encyclopedias he still didn't know what to do with.

"I don't mean to be disrespectful to Juan Carlos, but we already have several of his paintings. Why do your books, your records and your art dominate the common spaces wherever we live? Rufi and I live here too."

DuBois looked around. It was true.

"Because my aesthetic is the bomb?"

She thought she might assert her taste by covering the furniture with leopard print material and faux fur. They needed a pink flamingo. The world could be so bleak that only camp and kitsch could brighten it. DuBois focused on Dooby, who quietly turned Bert over in his hands.

"Hey, Doob, what did you think of the poetry reading?"

"I-I I didn't like it. I don't want to go down on my knees often to meditate or copulate. I'm not a dirty bird."

"Wow, Doob, that's amazing recall considering…"

Dooby was pretending Bert could fly.

DuBois went back outside to see what other treasures might have gone to waste. Aspen followed to keep anything else from coming into the house. She knew that DuBois hated to throw things away, but didn't know his fetish included other people's discards.

"Smells like trash day out here. Look, EC threw some books away. A bible, *The Prince*."

"Just leave it."

"It's funny that if people own one book, it will be the bible and if they own three one will be Machiavelli."

Dooby's dirty old stuffed animal caught Aspen's eye.

"Hey, Dooby dropped his old stuffty for Bert."

"It's lost filler over the years. It's dirty too… It's—"

"Greasy?"

"Looks like he splooged on it."

"That's disgusting. Go wash your hands."

DuBois and Aspen shared a laugh, kissed on the lips. He breathed in the scent of her raspberry lotion.

"Dag Babe, you smell good even next to the stinking garbage."

EC had thrown away the pillow that used to sit on the couch, which had been chosen to match the painting. DuBois plucked some stuffing from it. He found a needle and black thread and sewed the hole in Dooby's stuffed creature. After that Aspen put it in the washing machine by itself with extra detergent, and it came out looking comforting like a good stuffed animal should. Aspen wanted to give it to Dooby right away, but Du-Bois suggested that they save it for a special occasion. DuBois tucked it under Aspen's sweaters in the closet next to the gun.

When Rufi got home from swim practice, they decided to take a walk down to the playground. They walked past the thirty-six houses, still no signs of life, and crossed into Morley Field park.

The shade thrown by the eucalyptus trees felt refreshing. The mulched bark underfoot made them feel like they were walking on uncertain ground. Aspen and DuBois held hands, Rufi ran ahead while Bert and Dooby lagged behind. They passed the dog park where people brought their dogs to commune with other dogs.

"Watch out for land mines. Don't smoke those cigars."

Every tennis court was in use.

"White people wearing white clothes hitting yellow balls."

"We should get racquets."

DuBois pointed to a sign that read "Members Only." A water polo team practiced in the Olympic-sized pool. Rufi looked through the fence for a friend from swim team. There weren't any other children at the playground either. Over on the ball field, a group of boys and girls played a scrimmage soccer game. Their coaches shouted instructions. Morley Field had a new play structure that replaced the merry-go-round and tee-ter-totter. The traffic sign near the park depicting two figures balancing on a line stretched between a fulcrum would have to be replaced, too. Rufi's generation of drivers wouldn't know what it meant.

Whenever the city was flush with tourism taxes, workers could be seen razing outdated or broken equipment. The new play structures boasted bridges a foot off the ground and plastic tic-tac-toe. The short slides might thrill a baby falling into its mother's arms. There might be a tire swing or duck that rocked back and forth. The structures were always built low to the ground and didn't inspire daring. Not as many bones would break. But the children who played here would never build the Empire State Building with a zeppelin port in the steeple. The sturdy structures were excellent for playing tag, though, and as soon as she reached the sand, Rufi hollered, "One, two, three, not it."

Dooby sat down in the sand with Bert.

Aspen shouted, Not it, and took off running. DuBois smacked her on the rump as she climbed the ladder into the play structure.

"You're it."

She tagged Rufi before she could disappear through the tunnel slide and the girl tore off after her daddy up over and around the play structure. They did three laps. She couldn't catch him until he collapsed, winded.

"I'm it."

"The graffiti is base."

She leaned on a scrawl of indecipherable gang code. He waited for her to take off running, an excuse to regain composure.

"No puppy guarding."

"Puppy guarding?"

The game of tag had expanded its vocabulary. Even the word tag had acquired new meanings. Taggers tag their tags. He didn't know that he could call, Base on fire! and send her running. After catching his errant breath, he chased Aspen up the stairs and over the bridge and down the slide.

Rufi taunted him from her safe spot, Daddy don't wear no socks, a ding dong. I was there when they chiseled them off, a ding dong. Tossed them in the cafeteria and brewed a new bacteria, a ding dong dong dong dong, a ding dong. When she strayed off base, he changed tactics and let Aspen go. He cornered Rufi on the top of the structure, and instead of tagging her, picked her up and heaved her down the tunnel slide headfirst.

"I throw you out like the garbage!"

She enjoyed the experience so much that she ran up the ladder shouting, Do it again, Daddy, do it again!

"I throw you out like the garbage!"

"Momma, Dooby, come on and get thrown out like the garbage."

Aspen held Dooby's hand and they walked up the stairs.

"Okay, Dooby. I throw you out like the garbage."

Heavier than DuBois could lift, the two-hundred-pound boy had to send himself belly-side down the slide.

"Oh no, I'm not going down headfirst."

Wrestled into submission, Rufi's mother didn't have a choice as he summarily tossed her out like the garbage as well. At the bottom of the slide, they plotted their revenge. With determination on their side, they pushed DuBois into the mouth of the tunnel and kicked and kicked until he went down.

"I throw you out like the garbage, Daddy!"

But he hadn't gone down all the way and pushed himself, hand over hand, backward up the slide.

"I came back like a turd from the toilet!"

Rufi laughed like she had never heard anything funnier.

"Get the plunger."

The two girls kicked and pushed with all their strength, but DuBois would not go down. The walk home from the park felt labored as DuBois thought he might have thrown his back out or pulled a muscle in the game of Out like the Garbage, which Rufi promised to introduce to the playground when school started back in September. The sun had nearly set and they would have to prepare a late dinner. Toby had parked his car in the driveway. He and EC ate by the light of a red candle in the main house. DuBois, Aspen, Rufi, Dooby and Bert all waved. Toby clearly enjoyed the meal, smiling broadly after each bite, though the angle or the light made his hair look prematurely gray.

DuBois felt something odd down at his right Chuck Taylor, a pink Post-it note was stuck to the bottom of the shoe. He peeled it off, thinking it might be important. It looked like a laundry list of names: Robert, Samantha, Pia, Juan Carlos, Aspen & DuBois.

The Hit List

Rufi had twenty-five problems left to figure out before she could start her book report on science in the middle ages. The pencil had already made a sore indentation in her index finger. She scratched on the paper and carried the numbers around like a burden. This was the math, at her age, DuBois did in his head. She took her time, counting on her fingers. He wished that he could cut the gift out of his own mind and give it to her. She'd do great things with it. He didn't know how to teach it since no one had taught him.

"Rufi, after swim practice, I want you to do math and reading every day this summer."

Aspen turned to DuBois, who had his nose in a book.

"DuBois, you need to help, I can't do it alone. You need to take responsibility… Maybe teach Rufi algebra."

"It's all BS."

"What?"

"Institutionalized education is an oxymoron. They wanna train people to show up to work on time. Schools make automatons and squash innocent confidence. Rufi, what does a kid hear more than anything else at school?"

She thinks for a second and says, Quiet down.

"Sad but true. Be quiet, sit down. The school districts are under pressure from the feds to improve test scores. Expenditures need to be justified, but standardized tests don't quantify wisdom. A quiet world justifies real education. Peace, justice, liberty, respect. Not easy to quantify. I'm not worried about Rufi. She's a reader, she'll do fine."

"Fine isn't good enough."

"College, a scam, another corporate scheme. A filter—smart over here, dumb over there. A squared plus B squared equals C squared."

"Sounds like your crackpot bongo circle. Imagine how dumb people would be if they didn't go to school. They'd start thinking evolution was just a theory and stupid shit—like vaccines cause autism. Rufi's got to practice so she doesn't get overwhelmed by all the homework the teachers give out. We can't let her self-esteem get overrun. She's under the gun six hours a day. What's wrong with being good at it? Stress causes anxiety, which causes depression, which leads to drugs…"

"Give me a break with your domino logic. Self-esteem is another American myth… I know what you're talking about, though. I heard this story on NPR. Massive Homework. A new method out of Stanford. MH for short. They abandoned Phonics and picked up Whole Language so Massive Homework might just be another trend. The psychologist who developed the theory's a fucking quack."

"DuBois."

She'd won the discussion with a word and an unabashed stare.

"Okay, I'll return the coffee table book on Rocknroll Heroes Pops got me for Xmas to Borders and use the credit to get Rufi a math workbook."

"Dad, can you help me with my book report?"

"The encyclopedia's over there."

"Do you know how to turn lead into gold?"

"Oh, brother."

DuBois turned to Aspen and asked, Who's Samantha?

"You remember EC's roommate after Robert moved out. The girl with the monkey."

"Oh yeah, the blind albino chick with the monkey. What happened to her?"

EC knocked at the cottage door and DuBois crammed the Post-it into his shirt pocket.

"Toby went to fill in at Chinese Furniture Showroom. Do you want to go for an exercise walk?"

"I'd love to."

"Chop-chop. Let's go."

Her designer tracksuit—Hecho en Pakistan—and sweatshop cross-trainers looked new. When she saw the painting leaning against the boxes, she said, Oh... I was going to ask if you wanted that.

"Of course, we want it. I can't figure out why you'd throw it away. It's art."

"It doesn't match our new couch. Besides, Toby bought me a framed rhino print from Z Gallerie. You know I go crazy for wild animals."

DuBois carried the Zinn Reader into the bathroom.

Aspen put on her walking shoes and they set out past the thirty-six houses.

"Toby doesn't like me to go walking after dark. He says it's dangerous."

Aspen looked around, didn't see anyone. The streets were well lit by street lights and a blue light glowed from every window like the pulse of the city. She hadn't looked at the crime beat in the paper but remembered hearing about a stabbing on the other side of the Dirty Boulevard a few years before.

"I think it's safe around here. Besides, we're together."

"Toby worries about me. I think it's sweet."

"I suppose. DuBois doesn't care what I do."

"Robert was like that. He'd come home and sit in front of the tv. I would go for a walk and he would say, See ya later."

"He was nice, though."

"Yeah, we never got in fights, but he never did anything. I used to call him Slug-man. Toby has a lot more going for him. He's ambitious. He has strong leadership qualities and makes more money, plus he likes to spend time with me."

Aspen thought Toby wanted to usurp all of EC's time. She hadn't seen much of her friend lately. DuBois always said that the resolution to spend every minute together faded over time. Aspen looked dismayed.

"You know, I'll always go walking with you."

"I know. But when Toby's home, he says we should go to the gym and hit the treadmills. He asked me to organize the garage tonight, but it's way too nice of a summer evening to be cooped up."

The twilight gleamed through a clear and cloudless sky. Birds were busy singing in their nests.

"Why did you break up with Robert?"

"I met Toby, and he kept asking me out…"

They turned up another block where the houses were all set high off the street above retaining walls and had to be accessed with stairs. Some of them were Victorian mansions, which in Little Italy and the Downtown area served as law offices. Families couldn't afford the rent unless the big houses were carved into apartments.

"Wow, people actually live in these big houses?"

"Yeah, probably a spinster with her pretty wittle kitty cats."

A weather vane atop the widow's peak of one of the houses showed the wind blowing in from the north.

"I don't know. I guess I got bored with Robert. Our relationship wasn't going anywhere."

"Are you and Toby going to have kids?"

"He wants kids, I wanna travel."

"It's tough to travel when you have a kid."

"Thank god for birth control. I want to go everywhere. The beaches of Bora Bora, the baths of Baden-Baden. I wanna go to Africa and see the rhinos. I wanna go to Asia and walk on the Great Wall. I wanna climb a pyramid in the Yucatan… You know, see all of the biggest things all around the world."

"A story on the radio this morning said the Fresh Kills landfill on Long Island is now the biggest manmade… thing… Never mind. Won't it be hard to save money for traveling with the mortgage?"

"I'll say Toby, you're my hero. And will inform him that he's not getting any sex until he gets another job."

The girls both laughed.

"Maybe he could work nights at a travel agency."

They paused to look at a house for sale.

"Look at the asking price! Property values are going up in the neighborhood. We're already earning equity."

Aspen felt her dream slipping away but didn't allow a frown.

"What's up with this Dooby character?"

Aspen proceeded to share the whole tale of Chank's stucco house in the desert and how they found Dooby at Dan Petro's Bar and confessed that they didn't know what to do with him.

"Why didn't you call the sheriff when you found Chank?"

"At the motel, we called the Inyo sheriff and he said that area around Armagosa was in Mono County and the sheriff's office in Mono said it was Nevada…"

"And he brought the gun into the cottage? Is it loaded? With bullets? Tell DuBois to take it back to his grandma's house this instant. You know if Toby knew you had that gun, he would want to get one too. He would love to shoot the poor little gophers. And I hate guns. I won't have one in my house."

When she got home, Rufi had finished her work, gotten ready for bed and was playing chess with DuBois.

"Hey, Momma. My teacher says chess helps with reading."

"After this game, you need to get under the covers and go to sleep."

Dooby watched tv. DuBois and Aspen met in the kitchen over a steaming pot of green tea.

"I figured out the list. It's Toby's list. He wrote down the names of EC's friends and has been getting rid of them one by one."

"That's preposterous."

"Look. Robert was the first to go. Didn't Toby and EC meet while she was still living with Robert? Samantha left the picture. Didn't you think it was strange that Pia wasn't at the housewarming party? He had to get rid of Juan Carlos's painting, which was like purging the memory of EC's former lover."

"EC could have made the list. It could be a coincidence. It could be a list of people she wanted to invite for dinner."

"Juan Carlos is dead, Aspen."

"I know."

"This painting and his old punk records remind her of him, and Toby wants to expunge that. You watch. Toby will talk her into selling those albums. The Germs, Thunders at Max's, Flex Your Head, Hüsker Dü… Dag, Juan Carlos had every 45 rpm The Jam ever put out. Paul Weller was a god to him. You watch. Toby would liquidate god to have EC to himself."

"Well, they are her records. Juan Carlos left owing her money. She can do whatever she wants with them."

"But I loved those records. I grew up with them. We never bought the same record, our collections complement each other, like toast and jam. I bought The Clash and he bought The Jam. We were foolish, thought we'd be friends forever."

"Still, your hypothesis feels weak. Pia sucked as a real estate agent…"

"Sure, she messed up some paperwork, but, come on, Pia and EC had been friends forever. They had known each other since kindergarten. Toby called her a stupid bitch and they haven't seen her since."

"And we're next?"

"Yup."

The kettle whistled and DuBois poured a cup of green tea for Aspen.

"You want honey, honey?"

"No thanks."

They sat at the kitchenette, which DuBois contrived from two chairs EC cast off, a slab of plywood found in an alley and some encyclopedia boxes. Aspen blew on the surface of the hot tea, displacing steam.

"I'm still not convinced. What's the motive?"

"I haven't figured that out yet. What happened to Samantha anyway?"

"You know they were roommates. The reason we didn't see much of EC in those days was because she was out on the town with Samantha. They went out to bars, dancing every Thursday and Friday night, you know how EC is when she doesn't have a steady boyfriend—"

"Looking for one."

"Ha. Ha. Not exactly. She goes to clubs since she doesn't know what to do with herself when she's alone."

"Add vodka will travel."

"Samantha got a pet monkey around the time EC started dating Toby. The wittle monkey is so cute, EC would say. She called it Curious George even though its name was Bonzo. The cuteness wore off when it started shitting all over the condo. EC said, Sam, Sam. Toby sat in monkey doo-doo and I want you to keep Curious George in your room."

"See."

"Other issues popped up. Samantha wasn't cleaning the bathroom and she would come in late when Toby and EC were trying to sleep. Eventually, EC asked her to find a new apartment and she moved out thirty days later."

"Okay, so there's nothing conclusive. It could be a coincidence. Or it could mean that he's good at what he does."

DuBois enjoyed fomenting conspiracies he could never believe in himself. He ruminated on it in his mind and discussed it with Aspen for an hour after Rufi went to bed, until the plot grew so thick and complex that it wasn't recognizable. Eventually, both he and Aspen laughed it away. In one scenario, he proposed confronting EC with the note. But what if it were true? Would she wake up to Toby's manipulation and ask them to stay in the little house forever? For all DuBois knew, they could be plotting together? It could be a mutual pact to purge their lives of the renting class? What if... What if...

The Joy of Name Calling

"Stupid… Bitch!

"Go screw yourself, Asshole."

DuBois and Aspen sat on the futon with their ears cocked, trying to listen to the domestic row. Aspen turned down the volume on the radio. They'd been listening to *This American Life.* But Ira Glass signed off and Garrison Keillor announced The *Prairie Home Companion.*

"Hey, babe, turn that off. I'd rather listen to EC and Toby squabble."

When they lived in Little Italy, they used to sit in the dark and listen to the neighbors in the front apartment argue late at night. Before that, DuBois would listen through the walls as a drunken neighbor screamed at the bottle. Before that, he would sit on his first girlfriend's bed and listen to her father, a floor below, yell at the empty house. His rage seemed inexplicable to the teenagers. They didn't know what work was or how bosses could be, even relationships were new to them. A good fight was like winning a free pass to a movie premiere or getting a neighbor's magazine subscription in the mail by mistake.

"One of the networks should encourage people to send recordings—America's Worst Neighbors."

"*When Couples Clash* on Comedy Central. Reality tv sucks. It's all fake. Maybe it seems staged and phony because we live in a phony fucking world. *Jerry Springer, Cops, Judge Judy*, real people doing stupid shit. *Litigation Nation, Legal libation. You...done...me...wrong!* Didn't Shakespeare say, All the world is staged?"

"When did you see cable tv?"

"I guess I haven't actually watched a whole episode. You can't escape shit like that."

"Remember that guy we met in Wisconsin who said he made the *Shut Up Little Man* tape?"

"Yeah. He taped his belligerent psychotic neighbors."

 "I said don't touch that piece and you kick it!"

 "That's right. One of those dudes insulted the other by calling him women's names—Phyllis! Eunice! Barb!"

"And one would say, Shut up, little man."

"Yeah, hee hee hee."

Toby had been trying to repair the drainage pipe for a concrete laundry sink in the garage. EC wanted to help but misunderstood his instructions or had a better way of her own.

"EC needs a more creative riposte. She needs her own, Shut up, little man..."

"We used to fight like that?"

"No, no, no, not like that. We're not name-callers. My dad used to call my mom all kinds of names. You're a poor sad cow, he would say. I hated listening to that shit, in bed with the pillow covering my ears. Later I thought, maybe they enjoyed fighting. It let off steam… I dunno. Maybe, every joy turns to hurt. Maybe Toby and EC stage fights for our amusement?"

"They need better writers. It makes this room feel small."

"Come on, face it DuBois, this cottage feels more like a cupboard than a room, smaller than that one bedroom at the beach."

"I liked our neighbors at the beach."

DuBois thought they might save two hundred a month living in a one-bedroom close to downtown. The futon could serve as couch by day and bed by night. They would never find a palace like they had in Little Italy for rent they could afford—not with the city on housing shortage red alert. Dooby didn't take up much space considering his size, but having him around didn't help. His omnipresence wore on them like shoes that were too small.

DuBois thought of himself as a monk—he could get by with a straw mat to sleep on and space for his books and records. Of course, these simple pleasures needed the support of a record player, several bookshelves, a chair in which to read, a lamp, which led to the electric bill… He realized that Aspen both wanted and needed more and mulled over the fact in his mind until he ground it up into bits small enough to forget.

"How can you be so fucking stupid!"

"Remember how Gwen and Pretty Boy argued in the old neighborhood? Bombastic quarrels. They didn't quibble over breakfast because they didn't get up till noon."

"Remember when she called the police on him and had to hide in the stairwell to avoid getting picked up on traffic warrants?"

"She wanted to scare him, but the cops took him downtown?"

"A boy as pretty as him in jail."

"Ouch. When he got out, he was pounding on the door at 3am yelling, Let me in whore! I need my wallet. You're nothing but a whining stripper. You want money, you'll get money. I thought you made four hundred a night. I bet the IRS would like to hear that… But Gwen wouldn't let him in."

"She said, If you do bad things to me, I will do the most heinous things you can imagine. Fuck. Has anyone ever used the word heinous on you? That's heavy. The word heinous is like a sharpened toothbrush shiv in the joint. One week later she was the one outside pounding on the door, and he said, I paid the rent. Get the fuck out… People are messed up."

"Jacked up. And stressed out."

"Buying a house is stressful."

"They bought the house already. Even if they have to make payments, this should be a time of jubilation."

"Hey, that's my line. That's what I've been saying all summer."

"We should be hanging out, having fun."

"You stupid cunt!"

"Fuck yourself, you fat fuck!"

"Maybe they enjoy the bickering? My parents perfected it, ran it like a routine. They had four arguments, each with a hundred variations."

Aspen didn't shy from an argument but couldn't stomach any kind of debased language. She felt a knot tie up her guts. Du-Bois held words themselves sacred, including so-called bad words, since they usually expressed a precise sentiment. His philosophy teacher in high school said "War" and "Rape" were the real bad words, but when you drop a hammer on your foot, it would sound stupid to shout "War" and even stupider to hol-ler "Rape." Aspen skipped articles about war and rape in the newspaper, so usually finished the news quickly.

When the domestic altercation broke out around the same time the next night, Toby started with, You fucking idiot. How many times do I have to tell you to shut the door so Jay Edgar doesn't get out!

"Didn't we listen to this show yesterday?"

"Same bat channel."

Yakuza had aggravated the situation. He'd been lounging un-der the patio table and decided to tussle with Jay Edgar. The two cats came face to face. Reeeoww! Hisssss! Yakuza puffed up to three times his normal size and looked like a porcupine. Toby's cat cowered for a second, hunched low to the ground. He let out a low whine and shambled toward a chink in the fence.

Yakuza chased him and batted Jay Edgar's ass, tearing loose a claw full of fur, which, picked up by a light breeze, floated across the yard.

"I feel bad for EC."

She didn't like to hear her best friend get berated.

"Even the cops don't like to get in the middle of domestic squabbles."

DuBois picked up the baseball bat. The closet still smelled of cat urine. He'd done the same thing one night when Pretty Boy and Gwen's fight sounded like it was turning physical. He didn't even like Gwen, who couldn't speak without lying. EC had been his friend for a long time—they had laughed and grieved together. He pictured the bat hitting one of Toby's muscular legs, taking him out at the knee. It made a pleasant thump.

"DuBois, wait."

"I can wait. But if he hits her, I'll show him the bat."

Aspen looked at him. He flexed his fingers on the handle and adjusted his grip. She didn't know what to do.

"You're a useless fucking bitch!"

EC stopped fighting back. DuBois and Aspen waited, hunkered down, like a tornado was passing overhead, pressed by contentious swirling energy.

Dooby stood at the kitchen sink. He asked if he could wash the dinner plates and Aspen said she would appreciate it, calling him Sweetie pie. She made him promise to take his time and not break anything. He washed each dish with concentration and finished without material damage, but flooded the fake tile floor. Water pooled an eighth of an inch deep and he must have tracked in dirt on the bottom of his Pro-Keds because the kitchen looked like a muddy swamp.

"Hee hee hee. We're going to need a boat to get to the refrigerator."

"Here, Kitty Kitty! Here, Jay Edgar!"

A trace of nervous lamentation marked EC's voice like she'd been crying. Here, Kitty Kitty! Here, Jay Edgar! EC and Toby had been in the yard looking for his cat. The search proceeded like a road to nowhere, like a civil war or an execution. She called the cat's name like a child missing in the war. Jay Edgar! Empty, hopeless. Jay Edgar! Her voice rang out, heavy with regret and real fear, as if her future was locked up in the lost creature.

"I'm going to help them find the cat."

He set the bat back in the closet.

"Hey, Toby, I'll help you find him."

"Don't worry about it. I'll find him myself."

"No worries."

Dubois climbed up on the cottage roof with a flashlight and searched the adjacent backyards. He scanned the yard looking for a pair of red eyes in the brush.

"Hey, Toby, I think he's in Note Lady's yard."

Toby peered over the fence where DuBois held the light and watched his ample cat amble for the front yard. DuBois climbed down and saw the red eyes flash again under the beat Toyota.

"He ran under the car."

Toby put his knees to the asphalt while DuBois held the light. His hand bravely caught hold of the fat feline's scruff.

"Jay Edgar, bad kitty. Papa doesn't want you playing outside. You're going to need a bath and a flea dip. Bad kitty."

Toby treated the cat with more respect than he'd treated EC. At least he didn't call it a fucking bitch. Even his tone of voice with the animal betrayed pity and understanding. Maybe Toby loved the cat more than his fiancée.

Another note was wedged under the windshield wiper of Du-Bois's Toyota.

"These people are relentless."

An offer to buy it. Could it be real? It felt like a joke. He brought the note into the cottage to study it. The handwriting didn't look familiar. Aspen wouldn't mess with him this way. Toby didn't have a sense of humor. EC was capable, but, no. His prime suspect looked suspicious on the carpet playing with her dolls. Rufi was a joker after his own heart. He thought about tossing it in the trash. He even crumpled the note in his fist before he picked up the phone and called the number.

"Hello."

"Hola. This is Guillermo. ¿Qué pasa?"

"Uh, hey. You, uh, left a note on my car."

"You selling it?"

"Maybe…"

DuBois felt sick. An invisible man twisted his arm. He heard himself say, Come by tomorrow morning, bring $200, runs great, no smog. He'd panicked and asked for the amount he needed to cover the parking tickets. Shit. I love that car. It hurt like hammering your finger: sharp, then nothing, later it would throb. He also felt like he had no choice.

"Asp, I don't want to sell my car."

"Get it repaired."

"You know we don't have the money."

"Maybe you should get a real job."

"I have a liberal arts degree. Despite the bull market and the booming economy there aren't many jobs for a guy who cares about where his money comes from."

"I don't buy it. In fact, I haven't bought anything in years. Everything we have has been handed down. I need new shoes, new underwear, and new digs."

"People search far and wide for antiques."

"Not holy ones with stains in the crotch."

"You're exaggerating. We have everything we need."

"Except a bedroom and now we're short a car. Do you own a pair of pants without holes in the knees?"

"There are kids out there ripping holes in their designer jeans to look like us…"

Her thoughts were on Rufi's welfare and staying off welfare. He hadn't even noticed that she expanded the subject on him. He'd resorted to Danger Logic and wished he could retract it. DuBois thought that Aspen tended to focus on what her daughter deserved, overlooking non-material things that made their life richer. Rufi went to ballet class and swim team because her parents sacrificed time and hooked up free scholarships. She had a wider range of experience than other kids at school—music, books, art. But Aspen didn't like that she couldn't play outside in the old neighborhood. And they hadn't seen any kids running wild in the streets on Circle Circle. To be fair, Aspen wasn't the kind of person who craved unserviceable luxury. Rufi missed out on the free-range childhood Aspen had loved. She dreamed of a house on a street where Rufi could ride a bicycle or play hopscotch. Aspen got upset and considered a series of epithets that might cut DuBois down to size, but, conscious of acoustics and the proximity of innocent listeners, she gathered calm and nailed the case shut with its last words.

"So, you want to compare us to children who live with their parents?"

DuBois stayed up late on the patio wondering why Toby and EC weren't out here in front of the fire pit enjoying the night air. Summer dwindled through their fingertips. Use of the fire pit hadn't been written into the contract, so he didn't try to light it up himself. He would keep a low profile and avoid stoking the ire of his friends in the main house. He also started to think of his friends as landlords. A disturbing thought. Aspen was already asleep—attempting a lucid dream about the house she would buy with her lottery winnings.

He refused to feel guilty about not working more. You poor old Toyota, good riddance. Fuck nostalgia. Sleeping in the back of the car in Berkeley—a bed too short to stretch his legs. Getting drunk and falling asleep—cops banging on the window. Leaning out the door to puke, hee hee hee—some dumb dog lapped it up. There were road trips, drive-in movies, Sunset Cliffs after sunset, various escapades—but Aspen would rather have sex in her own bed. They'd had rip-roaring quarrels in the Toyota too. One time Aspen got so mad she slapped him while he was driving. He had traveled almost 200,000 miles in that car, but felt like he had never gone anywhere.

The punk band stickers alone were priceless, since many of the bands had broken up. The stickers proved he was into these groups before anyone. He still had his tattoos—it would take a lot of sunshine or an undertaker to efface those. A new owner would scrape the stickers off or plaster their own over top. He imagined seeing his car, parked at the mall, with a filthy baby car seat inside and one of those Xtian fish slapped on the back. He wouldn't let it stand, would have to carry a marker to draw on little feet. The little evolved feet of the first fish that crawled out of the sea. Speculation was useless—most likely the enfeebled automobile would be sold for scrap.

EC had allowed Toby to throw away Juan Carlos's painting, just like DuBois had to leave the mural Juan Carlos had painted on the wall in the house in Little Italy. What was the difference? Both a waste. He should have taken a skill saw to the wall, cut around the mural and carted his friend's sublime masterpiece away. He should have done something, saved it. Hmmm. At that time, the security deposit seemed more important than art. Maybe Aspen was right.

The next morning, after EC and Toby left for work, DuBois walked over to the main house and wiped his feet on the Berber welcome mat. Carefully lifting the screen off one of the windows, he climbed inside. The new decor reminded him of a visit to Chinese Furniture Showroom, even though the way out didn't involve navigating a labyrinth. Moving past the puffy couch and the glass-topped iron end table, he paused to admire an abstract painting that wouldn't look out of place in a hotel room and flipped it upside down. Satisfied with his prank, he hopped back out the window and replaced the screen. He bet they wouldn't notice for at least a month. EC, if and when she noticed, would flee the house screaming, Ghost! Ghost! My

home is haunted. EC wouldn't last ten minutes in an episode of
Scooby Doo.

Guillermo showed up with a buddy, the tallest Mexican DuBois
had ever seen. He started the car, looked under the hood. The
two men discussed it in Spanish.

"I'll give you one-fifty cash."

"Naw. It's gotta be two."

"One seventy-five."

"Hhhh. Three hundred."

"I've seen big shits ride down a toilet smoother."

Guillermo's husky voice felt like walking barefoot on gravel.
He pulled on the hairs of his goatee.

"Dude, I don't even want to sell this car."

"Okay, carnal. Two hundred."

He produced a roll from the front pocket of his blue jeans and
peeled off ten bills. DuBois folded the ten crisp Jeffersons and
tucked them in his wallet. Guillermo sat in the driver's seat of
the old Toyota. He slammed the door. The tall Mexican got
into the pickup truck. The beat Toyota started right up, sound-
ing rough as Guillermo picked up speed and disappeared
around the corner. DuBois used part of the money for a bus pass
and gave the rest to Aspen to buy new underwear. The parking
tickets could wait.

Assassin Bus Stop

DuBois could feel his hot feet inside his scuffed Doc Marten boots as he had been standing next to the bench at the bus stop outside of Undersea Planet for around thirty minutes. His Fender bass stood upright in its gig bag. He was humming a few bars from Jimmy Cliff, which he had managed to weasel into a set for the tourists, when a zit-faced white kid came out of the amusement park holding a crumpled greasy apron in his fist after an eight-hour shift at the batter-fried fish stand.

"Don't sit—hey. What the fuck's wrong with you? Didn't you hear?"

"I don't know, what?"

"You know that bus stop on Market and Seventh? A guy got killed by the bus stop. Not next to it. The bus stop killed the muthafucker. Five thousand volts of electricity—zap—into the bench. The guy burned for seven minutes. His fucking hair caught fire and smoke came out of his ears."

The kid had trouble comprehending.

"It wasn't smoke, you know, so much as steam, steam evaporating off of his brain as it dehydrated. Fuck man. There was nothing around there to knock him loose. People witnessed the whole thing. Groped around. Afraid to touch him."

"Wow. You saw that?"

"Naw, man. I read about it."

A one-in-two-million freak accident, according to the newspaper, but they also reported that the dead man had been drinking malt liquor from a bottle wrapped in a paper sack and said he was homeless, none of which turned out to be true. Just another bus-riding stiff trying to get home. An underpaid janitor in a big law office. There were, the paper said, four hundred and two benches like the one on Market & Seventh. Four hundred benches lurking around the city like hooded executioners. A heavy black mass of cloud roiling with lightning. The city set up orange cones and yellow tape around the bus stop, which the family decorated with red, yellow, and green crepe flowers.

"Go down to Market & Seventh and look at it. You can see the guy's outline in burnt flesh on the seat like a ghostly impression on a burial shroud."

The young kid stared at DuBois quizzically, tired from his shift. A splotch of tartar sauce speckled his hat. The grease hung on his face like a sausage casing. For a few days, commuters stood at benches all around the city. After a week, their flat feet and tired bones begged them to forget. The invitation to rest welcomed them: Come here, sit down. Risk could be damned. What were the odds that this temptation to lay back and close the eyes would be eternal?

DuBois flashed his bus pass and moved toward the back of the bus to find a seat. His guitar case bumped into a shirtless man with thick black braids hanging on each shoulder.

"Sorry, buddy."

"Stupid fucking white man!"

The shirtless man wore dark glasses and Dubois thought maybe he was blind. He kept one eye on him, but the guy didn't flinch or move at all.

Passengers on the bus went off for lesser affronts all the time. One time a gaunt little junkie nodded off on two seats with her knees pulled up into her chest when a tough-looking woman with a slipped weave and spanking-white Air Jordan kicks asked her politely to move her feet. The junkie didn't respond, so the woman, who had the name Foul Bitch tattooed on her left tit, said, I think you best move yo' feet, before I drag you off this bus and bang your dopey head on the curb. The junkie didn't move, so Foul Bitch sat directly on top of her feet. The junkie slit her eyes and whined, Why are you fucking with me? I'm sick. Foul Bitch chortled and bore down with all of her weight until the bus came to her stop.

Adverts covered the bus. Taggers hit it up with black markers and Madison Avenue ad men with colorful placards. Lomas 26 had been here and Megatool Outlet would hold a grand opening for a new store behind the graveyard.

A high-school-aged kid sat across from him with a gold medallion in the shape of a Glock 9mm. His khaki Dickies and white t-shirt were both neatly pressed and he sat with unchallenged confidence, holding his arms outstretched across three seats. His teeth were perfectly white. People filled up the bus. A man carrying a hard hat gave up his seat to an old woman, who took a full hard minute to get from the street, up three steps, each a steep hill, to alight on her perch behind the driver. Another woman sat pinned by three half-awake kids sprawled on her lap. A hastily packed bag, with clothes spilling out of the top, rested against her leg.

DuBois settled in to read Emma Goldman's autobiography, *Living My Life*, which he had checked out of the library.

A man got on the bus who was having a loud argument with himself. He must have forgotten to take his meds. The kid with the Glock medallion gave his partner a conspiratorial nod across the aisle. DuBois thought they might tell the guy to shut up, but they didn't.

Finally, the bus rolled on Broadway downtown. Glass and steel, hotels, law offices. The tallest building boasted forty floors. A few of the plaster façade shops looked abandoned, the windows were boarded up. A siren echoed over the rumble of the bus's engine. An ambulance raced past. Car exhaust and the close funk of the homeless nearly blunted a gust of stale sea salt blowing in off the bay. Ads for pagers and bail bonds blurred together across the sooty storefronts. The Hall of Justice had gone dark. Quiet at this hour—jurors sent home, lawyers headed out for a drink at their local and the penitents were secured inside the shabby gray jail. As far as DuBois knew, this was a real city. The bus passed the liquor store where he'd fished a bottle of champagne on prom night. The marquee at the Spreckels Theater announced "Pet Shop Boys: One Night Only." A new piece of public art at the trolley station looked like a giant hand grenade. And a midnight vandal had wheat-pasted twenty Andre the Giant posters on a wall around a construction site—perhaps ironically looking like communist propaganda. They passed the old brick Greyhound station and the C Street Inn: no visitors after 8pm. Tiger Jimmy could be seen through the window of his shop tattooing a sailor. Two more sailors with baby faces in white dungarees staggered down the sidewalk toward the Saigon Palace. As soon as the stores closed, you could see bodies in sleeping bags or covered by rough surplus blankets in every doorway. DuBois heard that one of the old sailor bars closed after a wide-eyed college kid looked askance at a bar hostess who'd said, Buy me a drink, sailor. One anonymous email to the Alcoholic Beverage Control board was all it took. Of course, that couldn't be true. Club Naha on Seventh still served rice or noodles and Coors or Coors Light on tap to drunks at 8am. The Chee-Chee raised a rainbow flag above the door. You could still ask for Seagram's 7 & 7 at the Hong Kong and expect to pay less than three dollars.

DuBois got off on Fourth to wait for the next bus and saw Eddie sitting on the bench.

"Hello, Doo-Boyz."

Queer Eddie thrust a balled fist out, which DuBois ignored, instead looking up Broadway for his bus. Eddie wore red vinyl pants and a half-t-shirt that gave his hairy belly a chance to breathe. The mall was well-lit behind him—with a long line of tourists waiting to enter Planet Hollywood.

"I've been working on a self-portrait, a collage of found objects. Hahahaha. Straightjacket nailed to plywood. Hahahaha. They're trying to cut me off SSI, so now I have to get a job. Can you believe it? I stopped drinking and place a blue pill and a prayer on my tongue each morning. Work got me drinking too much in the first place. Hahahaha. I'm taking the 7 uptown to catch a meeting. You know me—Queer Eddie. Crazy and sober. You want crazy, hahahaha. Crazy people show up to County Mental Health in their own straightjacket…"

Eddie didn't seem drunk or high, just manic. The #2 bus pulled up, and DuBois said, See you around Eddie.

"Not if you see me first, Doo-Boyz. Hahahaha."

DuBois pulled out Goldman's bio and read a few pages. She'd been right here, in a free speech fight, in 1912. A passenger pulled the stop cord and the bus driver let them off. The bus surged up the main drag, ten seconds, shifting right to let folk on and off. DuBois hadn't looked to see who got on and heard some fools shouting poetry up near the driver.

"Chiapas 45 Chiapas 45… I am the oppressor and the oppressed, but don't ever call me repressor or repressed, because I believe in speaking freely and do so…"

DuBois recognized the Jaguar.

Two younger poets wearing black hoodies stood behind him and planned to have their say as well. One mouthed his own rap over to himself so he wouldn't forget it when the time came. A Japanese student kept right on listening to his Walkman and paid them no attention. A woman sitting with an older man in a private security guard outfit looked at them curiously. She probably didn't speak a word of English. Kids in the back scribbled on the seats with thick black markers.

DuBois listened to the rap while the bus driver kept on driving. The lad with the thick pink scar under his left eye waited for his turn. DuBois recognized him from the café. The Jaguar finished and they all acted like they had done something impressive—hand-delivering culture to the downtrodden. They stopped short of exchanging high fives.

The Jaguar recognized DuBois and came back to sit with him. Dub moved his bass over next to the window.

"Oi, aren't you Aspen's man?"

"Yeah. Aren't you the chief telemarketer?"

"Shhh. I'm on a mission to infiltrate corporate America, but poetic terrorism gets my blood pumping."

Cocky like a gunfighter blowing on a smoking six-gun, he indicated to the young kids up front.

"I turned these kids onto poetry and they can't get enough of it. Sow feeling and cultivate belles-lettres, that's what I always say. I've got my own crew. We make it fun, do the late-night buses. We read Sundays in the park. Perform in crowded elevators or declaim at the airport. Do you write?"

"Naw, naw. Hee hee hee. You all are like Hari Krishnas. Seriously though, I wanted to ask you about the poetry reading—"

"That wasn't a poetry reading—it was a guerrilla war. Planned chaos. Man, we fucked shit up that night. The first step to enlighten—"

"Huh."

"What did you want to ask?"

"I guess you answered. You don't really care about people. You started a riot in a room with kids and handicapped people and old people. You didn't ask about Aspen's ear. You're another phony on the bus in search of street cred. Get your buster ass outta my face."

He looked down at the book in DuBois's hand.

"Emma Goldman, cool, but. There are those who read and the propaganda of the deed. I don't claim to know you."

In the Way

DuBois's bare toes sunk into the soft flesh like a fist into pizza dough. He hadn't meant to kick Dooby in the stomach, only wanted to slip into bed. Dooby appeared to be asleep on the floor. Aspen liked to tease DuBois about stubbing his toes and knocking things over. He would whip open bathroom cabinets and send sticks of deodorant tumbling out. His fast hands had a knack for catching loose objects before they hit the ground. He called it a talent. She said it was a skill.

"Did you see that? Caught it on the fly. It's my secret talent. Everybody has one."

"Sure thing, ya clumsy oaf. When I open cabinets, things don't fall out. Is that a talent? You're always in a rush. Maybe open the door slowly and practice mindfulness."

Yakuza curled up on his side of the bed. Aspen snored on her side. He would have liked to make midnight love with her, but not with Dooby on the floor like a living prophylactic. Maybe Doob could sleep out in the car? No, the neighbors would get upset and call the police. DuBois lifted the cat up by the scruff as he climbed into bed. Shadowy bulks rose in the gray light of their small room—a tv in one corner, an Apple computer, a large stack of books, a small stack of plates. Dooby was stretched out underneath a thin blanket. He set Yakuza on his chest and stroked the sleek black fur.

Aspen didn't like doing it in the middle of the night anyway. After coffee, but before lunch, under the direct power of the sun, but not on Sunday, as Sunday offered a chance to sleep late. Dooby lay awake and worried. He couldn't understand why DuBois had kicked him. It was the mystery of all mysteries. Maybe he should apologize? His face flipped between lugubrious expressions. He liked the sound of Aspen's breath rising and falling, a comfort not to be alone. He stayed awake, thinking about things in his own way.

When the sun filtered in the next morning, Aspen climbed out of the creaky futon to wake Rufi for swim practice. Dooby got up from the floor. He went into the bathroom while Aspen shook her daughter by the shoulder and coaxed her back into the conscious world.

"Time to wake up, kiddo."

Rufi didn't want to open her eyes and pulled the covers over her explosive head of hair.

"Come on, baby, time to get up. Come on, Rufi, you've got swim practice. Boo-daw, time to wake up."

Dooby and Aspen met in the narrow hall in front of the bathroom. Aspen had to step back to let Dooby pass. He didn't know what to do, so he stood in the doorway to the kitchen.

"Come on, Rufi, we're running late."

Aspen came face to face with Dooby again on her way to the kitchen, not ready for Harpo Marx, as he moved with her like a strange reflection in a mirror.

"I have to get Rufi breakfast. We're late for swim team."

"I-I I'm sorry."

"It's okay."

She got the nonfat milk out of the refrigerator, poured a small glass, and stirred in a spoonful of strawberry instant breakfast. She considered herself a morning person, but after coffee. After coffee, she could take on the world.

"Come on, Rufi, let's go!"

"I'm trying, but Dooby stunk up the bathroom."

"I-I-I'm sorry, I don't know how to un-stink the bathroom."

He turned and knocked into a lamp, which made a clanging noise.

"Dooby! Dude, be quiet. I'm trying to sleep. Cheese-n-rice."

The futon creaked like the bowels of a tall ship. Dooby set the lamp upright and looked around for a corner to stand out of the way. Furniture or boxes occupied each corner in the small cottage. He didn't know where to stand. The tiny room shrank around him and constricted his breath. He turned. Saw the front door and went outside—Yakuza followed. The sun rose for another perfect summer day—a calm brilliant blue sky was streaked by a wisp of white cloud. Birds sang in a chorus so that the trees seemed like living theaters. *Ba ba-ba ba*. Dooby didn't know what to do, but the air smelled fresh, so he concentrated on breathing. Yakuza scampered around the side of EC's house and Dooby decided to tail him. He watched the black cat squat to pee in the grass. When he unzipped his pants to pee out a golden arch into the yellow grass, he hadn't seen EC toweling herself off in the window.

"I am a funny fireman. Putting out the fire, putting out the fire…"

EC twisted the towel into her hair. Mistaking the bulky figure outside the fogged window for Toby in a kinky mood, she eased open the curtain and pulled back her shoulders to perk up her breasts. She wet an index finger between her lips and circled the dark nipple on her left tit, twisting it stiff. As a burlesque shimmy washed across her naked torso, the refrigerator slammed shut in the kitchen.

"EC, are we out of milk?"

The scream caused him to look up and catch her fumbling with the towel. Dooby stuffed his penis back into his short pants, but a trickle of urine dripped down his leg.

"Toby! Toby!"

"I'm not Toby, I'm Dooby."

He ran behind the cottage and tried to hide. Found an opening covered with a board and a brick. Pushing it aside, he crawled under the house where he heard Toby tromp through the yard and bang on the cottage door.

"Cheese-n-rice."

"I know you're hiding him."

"DuBois worked late, let's talk about it when I get back."

Aspen pushed Rufi out the door. Dooby stayed under the cottage with his knees pulled into his chest. I am a rock, he thought. I am a rock under a house.

"Dooby sure is dumb."

"Now, now, Aspen. There's nothing to talk about, this is not a boarding house or a flop house. He needs to go today."

Aspen pushed Rufi through the gate and down the driveway toward the Fury. EC went back into the main house. The yard got quiet after that, even the birds stopped chirping.

It wasn't long before Yakuza came snooping around the back of the cottage and found Dooby under the house. Dooby reached to pet the cat and hit the spot near the base of his tail where he didn't like to be touched—Yakuza hissed and scratched, drawing a thin line of blood on Dooby's hand—Dooby jerked and bumped his head on the bottom of the floor. A two-hundred-pound boy never wanted to cry so bad.

"What are you doing back here Dooby? I thought I heard possums burrowing under the house. Come out from there."

Dooby crawled out, covered with grey dust and cobwebs, staring down at the ground with the most sorrowful and shameful expression DuBois had ever seen.

"Did Yakuza get ya?"

Dooby nodded for yes and wiped his nose with his other hand.

Squawk.

DuBois picked up Yakuza and set him in the middle of the yard, he pulled Dooby behind the lattice. The bird squawked from its perch on the wire and Yakuza rolled over on the grass, absorbing warmth from the sun. The bird went for him in a headlong plunge, violently struck the mark and excised a chunk of black fur.

Hee hee hee. He slapped Dooby on the back.

"That'll teach that ornery cat to be nice."

"I don't understand why things are funny. Mr. Chank said not to be mean to animals. I like capybaras."

"Ahhh, well, he deserved it."

Dooby still felt sad and the sorrowful gaze poured back into his face.

"EC said I have to leave today."

"I heard her. What are we going to do with you? Do you have anywhere to go? Any other friends? Family? Do you have any skills? Can you get a jo—"

The vowel and consonant sounds erupted out of a subconscious magma chamber deep within, sounds became syllables and formed words he deciphered only as they hit the air. How many times had people said those same phrases to him? Do you have any other skills? Can you get a job? He felt nauseous, like a hypocrite.

Dooby's lips formed imperfect shapes as he tried to say, I-I I want to stand in the corner, so I won't be in the way. His yellowed, twisted teeth showed that he had never been to a dentist. Aspen had bought him a toothbrush, but he didn't like the way it made his gums bleed. DuBois tried moving the boxes of encyclopedias and Juan Carlos's painting into the hall- way, but Aspen said the feng shui felt wrong, so DuBois set up an island of boxes in the kitchen. Another wrong move, he real- ized as they would soak up a lot of water the next time Dooby washed the dishes. He opened the kitchen cabinet and a tin of green tea fell—instinctively, he insisted—his right hand shot out to make a basket catch.

"Dooby, we need to go someplace we can think and eat."

No Free Lunch

Dooby scratched his head.

"I-I I like to eat."

They got off the #11 bus in front of the Market Street Price Club. DuBois didn't have a membership card but flashed his driver license behind a shopping cart and strolled through the entrance. The door monitor waved them through. Dooby felt intimidated by the shelves of merchandise. He'd never seen twenty tvs and wondered why they were all tuned to the same channel. If I had twenty tvs, I could watch twenty shows at once. DuBois loaded the cart as they strolled through the aisles. EC has that coffee maker. EC has that frying pan set. EC has that iced tea maker...

"There's the crowbar Toby bought to take apart those old shelves in the garage."

Near the bread aisle, the boys hit the first free sample table where a lady hawked bread, buttering slices of rye toast. Dooby tried one and said, This toast sure is delicious. A man stacked two dozen six-packs of diet soda on a cart. Another man loaded up two cases of bourbon. A mother, trailed by three younger than school age brats, pushed a cart containing ten boxes of Lucky Charms and a cow load of milk. Seven people crowded around the next sample table as the sample lady lifted a tray of chocolate chip cookies from a small convection oven. DuBois didn't like to see people litter and swept three sample cups into a trash receptacle. Show some respect, he thought. Don't ruin a good thing.

"Alright, Dooby. We'll eat lunch one sample at a time. Try not to make an impression on the first round. The ladies are busy and won't notice who picks up what."

"Is this stealing? Mr. Chank said not to steal."

"Excuse me, ma'am. Are these samples free?"

"Help yourself, love."

"See."

DuBois pushed the cart past the next sample table without stopping and lifted two crackers with hummus in one hand. Dooby picked up a cracker and shoved it in his mouth. They ate Norwegian salmon, blueberry cheesecake, stuffed potatoes, tried a new veggie burger, drank green juice, and pocketed an energy bar for later.

An old lady doled out a sample labeled Dried Plums.

"Dried plums? Those look like prunes to me."

"Well, son, the California Farm Council changed the name of prunes to dried plums. Their purgative powers are legendary, but you might argue that prunes have a PR problem."

"No shit. Huh. I didn't know prunes and plums were related."

"I-I I never ate prunes before."

"They help you go to the bathroom."

"I-I I don't need to go."

DuBois steered the cart into the book section. He didn't see anything he wanted to read. Their book selection was like Top 40 radio. They had a set of Roald Dahl books in the children's section though and DuBois made a note to bring Rufi. They could tackle *Charlie and the Chocolate Factory* one chapter at a time. Dooby looked at pictures in a Dr. Seuss book.

"I like the elephant who hears Whos."

DuBois gave his baseball cap to Dooby and put on sunglasses. His mohawk, now dyed blue, popped into view.

"Crazy haircuts impede free sampling. It's better to be invisible."

DuBois retraced the steps they had made and put items back on the shelf, one by one. The toast lady slathered butter on the rye without looking up. DuBois and Dooby both grabbed two pieces.

"This bread has four grams of sugar, three fibers and two proteins… It's organic and each slice has only four calories…"

The old granny had been on the floor serving all morning. A terrible ache pulsed up from her bunions into her varicose vessels. Another crowd rushed in like pigs at the trough. This wasn't the kind of job that nurtured affection for humanity. A guy at the front of the line examined each sample for the biggest one. DuBois parked the empty cart next to the cigarette cage.

"Let's get out of here, Doob."

A security guard checked receipts at the door to prevent theft. DuBois recognized Toby too late. A line formed as he checked each receipt and waved the people past.

"What are you doing here, Maniac?"

"We wanted to try the new veggie burger. I didn't know you worked here."

"Just go."

They walked out the door and stood near the bus stop.

"What are we going to do with you, man? What happened to all those other hippies in the video? Maybe one of them could help you out?"

"I-I I think the kids are gone."

When they got home, Dooby wedged into a corner and DuBois logged on to the internet. It took about an hour, but DuBois found an article about the commune.

"A Dr. Cornelius Chank, a.k.a. Henry Chank, a.k.a. Will Chancre, a.k.a. Bhagwan Moksha, traded a warehouse full of psychotelekinetic mushrooms to government agents for a million dollars in federal gold reserves. The mushrooms were helping the government read our minds. The FBI later raided the farm and busted a handful of runaway youths for drug and firearm possession. They impounded a dune buggy but found no gold."

Welded-Steel Chain Fastener

A calloused finger walked along the top string of a bass guitar, thumping at a mournful, steady gait. A snatch of song almost forgotten. He hadn't wanted to plug into his bass cabinet and play the old songs in a long time. The neighbors would for sure call the cops. Even the finest music sounded like noise at this hour and his old songs were not the finest music. By the un-marred birdseye maple and gleaming Toaster pickups, it was obvious DuBois hadn't played this 1977 Rickenbacker 4000 at a live gig. He set the guitar down and climbed in bed. He'd switched off the light and securely locked the door. DuBois wanted to tell Aspen about this scruffy heavy metal guy who approached him at the corner store and asked when Welded-Steel Chain Fastener was going to play.

"Ha, never. Never going to happen."

"Bummer, dude, you guys were great."

Juan Carlos was dead. They could find another guitar player, but it wouldn't be the same. He hadn't talked to Hayduke in three years and their drummer, Duggie Pinctada, had his own thing going. When the moonlight fell onto her face, he saw that she looked sullen and forgot all about it.

"What's the matter, babe?

"I'm pissed that you took that gig at Undersea Planet on my birthday."

"I thought we were going to celebrate next Saturday."

"Yesterday in the morning, EC said she couldn't walk because she'd signed up for pilates at the yoga studio on the boulevard. I can't afford classes there. She said, I know, I know it's your birthday, but I'm going to be too busy tonight working on my house."

"Sorry, babe."

"Brenda's mom came over and took me out for frozen yogurt, which was nice—you know I like Rufi to have friends. We were gone about thirty minutes. Brenda's mom had to pick up the little brother at baseball practice, you know how she's always running around. So busy. When I got home, Felice and Moe were watching Toby grill pollo asado."

"I haven't seen Felice Harmon since Juan Carlos's funeral. Where are they living these days?"

"I don't know. I think her mom died and she inherited that apartment building in Point Loma."

"So, they're landlords now, too."

"It wasn't two months ago when the three of us were hanging out together. Felice wanted to teach us about candle magick and how to set our intentions. I overheard them talking about money and Moe said Toby should start his own business. And Felice said, with rental prices being what they are, the back house was a gold mine. She said they could charge a lot more for rent. After that, EC told about the time she bought clothes at Sears, returned them to Bullock's and pocketed the markup."

"Felice worked at Bullock's with Juan Carlos."

"Hmm."

"He used to mop the floors before the store opened and play Hüsker Dü on a boombox."

"Hmm."

"And she sold shoes."

"Hmm.

"Yeah."

DuBois stroked her hair and she nuzzled into his chest and he held onto her until they both fell asleep.

The Closet

Dooby's eyes shifted crazily between Aspen and DuBois. The whites looked blown out with bloodshot and the pale blue irises were occluded by gaping black pupils—like the openings to abandoned subway tunnels.

"Dooby, did you ever see any gold at the farm?"

"I-I I'm not a dirty bird."

DuBois doubted that there had ever been any gold. Aspen felt sure about it. She'd staked a claim and was ready to load up a mule with rations and prospect the hills. When the bank erred in your favor, you didn't question it. It would be like forsaking an unexpected inheritance or a fortuitous dividend. Would you walk away from a treasure because a crackpot seer pointed to it with a peep stone? Or would you bring a shovel and dig a hole? Finding the gold would be a long shot, like the lottery ticket her father held up coming across the line in a photo finish by a nose. A million dollars could buy any of the thirty-six houses on EC's block and put Rufi through college. That gold would be worth way more than a million by now. They could live off the interest. Their worries would be over. DuBois thought that much gold might create more problems than it solved. They would have to worry about the IRS and the FBI.

"Um, uh… Mr. Chank said, Don't even think about the gold until the day I die."

"Well, he's dead."

"I-I-I forgot."

"About Chank?"

"No, about the gold."

DuBois's mother would say, he's in a better place. Grammar would say, Dead men tell tales, if you ask them real nice. Pops would say, I never met a dead man I didn't like. His elders' wisdom couldn't help him now. He didn't believe any of it. He had friends who died, he had friends he hadn't seen in years. He missed Juan Carlos and thought Dooby might feel the same way about Mr. Chank.

"I'm sure he would want you to use the gold to set yourself up. Get your teeth fixed. Use it to take care of yourself."

DuBois decided he didn't want any of it. If it existed, Dooby earned it living with that stumpy old madman in the desert. He earned it the day Chank drilled too deep into his skull.

"I-I…"

"What is it, Dooby?"

"I-I I want to start a capybara farm."

Aspen looked perplexed. The fever flickered in her eyes like a flame out in the wind.

"That's a great idea, Dooby."

"I like capybaras too, Momma. They have them at the zoo, they're like one-hundred-pound rats."

"Capybaras are native to South America, but the rainforest is being depleted at a high rate. Capybaras are excellent swimmers. An adult capybara can weigh up to one hundred fifty pounds."

"Huh."

"You know, Dooby, you could do whatever you want with that gold."

"We could—"

"If Chank sold mushrooms to the feds, Dooby must be the rightful heir."

"But where's the gold?"

"The gold is in the closet, but I-I I don't want to go in the closet."

"Wow. I didn't believe this crazy story, but…wow."

"There could be a secret panel or a basement in the shack."

Dooby rocked in his corner.

"Um, uh… I-I I don't want to go swimming. Capybaras are excellent swimmers, but I-I I don't want to go swimming."

"That's it. That's how that fox in the video stayed underwater so long. The closet is a fucking cave in the muck pond."

"Fox?"

"Foxes are a natural predator of the capybara."

"She had a set of lungs on her, but held her breath way too long. The closet must be a hidden cavern in the pool."

"Anacondas also eat capybaras. Anacondas are big snakes."

"And they hid the gold in the closet!"

Aspen pogoed up and down like she'd won a dishwasher on *The Price is Right*.

"But I-I I don't know what an anaconda looks like."

Aspen wrapped both arms around Dooby and gave him a strong hug.

"I'll check the oil and water on the Fury."

Aspen packed the wicker basket and called Dubois's grand-mother.

"Hello, Grammar, this is Aspen."

"How's your bum ear doing, darling?"

"It's healing, thank you."

"Good to hear… How's Rufi?"

"Great, we're all great. My dad's having health problems, but they are way up in Canada, you know. We're driving back up your way and thought we might stop in for a visit."

"Tonight?"

"Well, yeah, summer vacation's almost over, you know, unless you have a hot date."

"I haven't had a hot date since 1939, when that fireman pulled me out of bed. The house was in flames all around us, but I made him shut his eyes until I was properly dressed…"

"We're bringing another friend of ours named Dooby."

"Dooby, what kinda fool name?"

Grammar's laughter broke into a cough and Aspen held the phone away from her ear as Grammar hocked up a gob of spit.

"Rufi's anxious to see you."

Rufi, hearing her name, looked up from her Barbie dolls.

"Grammar, we'll be in late tonight, so don't get scared when you see the headlights."

"Scared? Darling, I'm not scared of anything in this world."

"Well, I don't want you pointing that shotgun at Rufi."

"Okay, darling. Don't worry. Love you."

"You too."

Aspen found DuBois reaching into the top of the closet for the gun. He jammed Dooby's stuffed creature into his green bag. The weight of the pistol still surprised him. She watched him push bullets into the chamber. He picked up a book by John Fante that he had been reading from the floor and stuffed it in the bag.

"I talked to Grammar."

"Yeah."

"She didn't mention you."

"Figures. Told you she could hold a grudge. I'll get the silent treatment until the day she dies, then she'll haunt me with silence. What if the FBI wants the gold?"

"Your grandmother is scarier than the FBI."

They drove headlong into a traffic jam. The Fury inched forward in fender-to-bumper traffic. What adventure ever started with a traffic jam? Rufi and Dooby were buckled in and Aspen sat in the front passenger seat. Drivers traveled alone in most of the cars.

"This commute adds two hours onto the workday. That's like working sixty days for free!"

Aspen had been thinking about the gold, wondering if they should give it all to Dooby. He needed it more than they did. She hadn't begun to think how heavy it might be or how to fence it.

Rufi wished they would play the radio. Her parents had grown silent, mired in their own thoughts. She looked over at Dooby. He looked as dejected and downtrodden as ever. Rufi had always wanted a sister. Her grandma said she should pray for one, but it seemed like this big weirdo was as close as she'd get to a sibling.

"Hey, Dooby, I'll trade you this shiny dime for a dingy old quarter."

"I-I I really like shiny dimes, Rufi."

"This one's extra shiny."

"Rufi, give Dooby his money back."

"I'm just doing business, Momma."

"It's okay, Aspen, because shiny dimes make me happy and money can't usually make people happy."

"You should get at least two shiny dimes—"

"Cheese and rice! Cars are stupid."

"Momma, Dooby won't stay on his side."

"I-I I didn't go on your side, Rufi. That was Bert."

"Rufi, leave Dooby alone."

Rufi crushed an impulse to toss Bert out the window. If Dooby used his gold to buy her momma a house, he could become the favorite. DuBois turned on the radio.

"Dooby is so fat, Chinese people rub his belly for luck. Dooby is so dumb, he could get elected president."

The radio traffic reporter announced that the northbound freeway was at a standstill.

"Finally, truth."

"Don't start talking to the radio."

They inched toward a '55 Ford truck, overloaded with wooden pallets, stalled in the middle lane. The driver had jogged over to the freeway's shoulder to call for assistance. As they inched past, DuBois felt like putting the poor sap out of his misery. There would be witnesses but none would care. The gun in his belt pressed cold against his bladder. In his mind, at least, pulling the trigger felt easier than shooting a snake.

They stopped for gas in Hesperia and the sun hung at the edge of the sky like it was burned into the retina. Continuing up the 395, the coming darkness switched places with the fading daylight. The heat stayed right where it was, standing in the middle of the road, with no sign of backing down. When they hit the stretch patrolled by aircraft, DuBois wondered if the pilots worked nights. He stepped on the gas and Aspen's car thundered along the highway. They passed a multitude of cast-off dreck on the side of the road—black chunks of exploded tire, spent beer cans and sealed-up jars of golden piss. They passed Ballarat and Skidoo, Panamint and Leadfield, Greenwater, Badwater, no water, and Chloride City. They passed the place of dead roads and the cities of the red night. Around midnight, the Fury turned up the dirt road that led to Grammar's ranch. Rufi slept as soundly as if she were in her bed in the cottage. Dooby looked up at the sky, he had forgotten how many stars were pinned to the firmament.

Grammar sat on the porch with her shotgun across her lap, smoking a cigarette and drinking the neighbor's bootleg liquor from a tin cup. The Fury eased to a stop about thirty yards from the house. Grammar pulled the hammer back on the shotgun but didn't get up.

"Grammar, it's us!"

DuBois wanted to holler, Don't shoot, but tempting the old lady would be a mistake. Aspen popped the cap off of the orange prescription bottle, which she had refilled before they left and swallowed one of the pills. Her ear felt a lot better, but the meds worked wonders to calm her nerves. She eased open the car door and stepped out on the gravel.

"Hi, Grammar!"

"You girls sure know how to worry an old lady."

"Sorry, Grammar, but we got a late start and hit traffic back in the city."

"I won't live in a city. Cities have dark vibes. My husband Marcus used to cuss and change lanes like channels on the tv."

DuBois stepped out of the car. Grammar held the shotgun with her finger on the trigger, so he moved slowly.

"That your friend Dopey there in the front seat?"

"His name is Dooby."

"Sleepy, Grumpy, Dopey and Doc. Does he have to be told to get out of the car?"

She acted like DuBois was invisible.

"Dooby, come on out and meet Grammar. Oh, I bet he's afraid of the shotgun. Dooby doesn't like guns. He's had bad experiences."

"Poor boy looks shell-shocked."

Grammar set the shotgun on the porch and Dooby stepped out of the car. When DuBois picked up Rufi, his back twinged. He brought her inside the house and laid her on the cot. One of Grammar's chickens pecked around underfoot.

"Is that a chicken? I-I I've never seen a chicken before, only ate one."

Grammar offered Aspen and Dooby a cup of moonshine, said how much Rufi had grown and compared her beauty to Aspen's. She continued as if DuBois didn't exist, except once when she muttered the word snitch. The best course of action, he thought, would be to carry his book and his sleep roll out to the barn.

Decorative Reminiscence

EC pressed a photo of Aspen into an album. She felt settled into her new home. The house had been furnished by Chinese Furniture Showroom, where Toby had been moonlighting, and her mother's maid had been cleaning twice a week to keep the place looking like a model home. EC had focused on finding, buying, and fixing up the house for so long, that she needed a new project.

Toby divided the foreseeable future into four home improvement theaters: front yard, back yard, garage, and infrastructure. He'd spent the better part of Saturday trying to organize the garage. He'd put up drywall over the termite-chewed wood and sprayed the interior with white paint. As the paint hissed out of the mouth of the gun, he imagined his future domain: a card table for Friday night poker, an extra refrigerator stocked with meat and beer, a workbench loaded with every conceivable tool from awls to zinc nails and a big tv. The biggest tv he could find. Maybe I'll get an extra job at Mad Jack's Electronics, he thought.

His mouth felt like drying paint.

"EC, would you mind bringing me a Diet Pepsi from the refrigerator?"

She was organizing her photo albums on the dining room table in the main house. One of her coworkers planned to throw a Decorative Reminiscences party, and EC wanted to get her photographs in order so she could decorate them with puffy paint and pressed flowers. She heard they had cartoon bubbles with funny sayings you could stick on the photos like "Are we Having Fun Yet?" "Uh Oh SpaghettiOs" and "Where's the Beef?" The women took turns selling each other Tupperware, lingerie, and Xmas ornaments. Decorative Reminiscences would be popular until something else caught their fancy.

Her photo albums had been organized chronologically, but when she reflected on the new wave big hair days of the 80s, going to see Echo & the Bunnymen or Duran Duran every weekend, she wondered what happened to her youth. She didn't like the way she got older and heavier as the pictures moved forward in time. She'd only changed three dress sizes in nine years, but comparing the early photos to the current ones, left her feeling fat and old. The pictures would have to be organized in a new way.

EC carried the cold can of diet soda outside.

"Whoo hoo hoo hoo. You scared me. I thought you were a ghost."

"All I wanted was a Pepsi."

Toby hadn't realized that the paint sprayer he picked up at Megatool Outlet left his hairy body dusted with white paint. He looked like a ghost in a snow flurry. EC tried to picture him as an old man and decided that he wouldn't go bald like his father.

"Come over here and kiss me. I dare you."

"No, no. Not until you take a shower. I cooked a romantic dinner, so maybe tonight we can make whoopee."

His face swelled with anticipation. He had imagined that buying this house for her would lead to more action in the bedroom, but so far it hadn't. The three-hundred-thousand-dollar aphrodisiac had been less effective than a placebo.

"I need to clean out the paint sprayer and I'll hop in the shower."

"I just need to press the photos of Aspen and DuBois into the last album."

"You organized albums for all of your old friends?"

"I finished one for Robert, Juan Carlos, Samantha and Pia."

He wanted to complain about the inclusion of her ex-boyfriends, her shitty roommate and their lame realtor but didn't want to throw her out of the mood. He couldn't control his expression though, which looked to her like he'd bitten into a rancid Brazil nut.

"Don't worry, Toby. I want our babies to see what an improvement I made in their Papi."

She leaned in, careful not to make contact with the white paint, balked and kissed air. The pink Post-it note, which she'd been holding in her fist, floated to the cement, and was picked up by the wind. It stopped near the trash cans on the pathway between the gate and the back cottage.

Toby stepped back inside the garage, which smelled strongly of fresh paint. He disconnected the paint sprayer and rinsed it meticulously in the concrete sink. The white paint spiraled into the drain. After that, he washed the residue from the sink. A quick survey of the painted area made him think of a pristine alpine wilderness. He fantasized about being an abominable snowman in his natural habitat. I'm going to ravage the snow queen tonight, he thought. He beat his chest with balled fists and finished the job whistling.

EC pressed the last pictures of Aspen and DuBois in place. The album contained so many memories: EC and Aspen crushed in front of the stage at a punk show // DuBois and EC drinking tequila from a bottle after the show // Aspen and EC with matching go-go boots // EC holding newborn Rufi at the hospital // Aspen looking bloated after giving birth // DuBois with his mohawk holding his daughter that first day // New Year's Eve with DuBois and Aspen kissing in EC's old apartment // a portrait of Aspen taken by Juan Carlos. // EC dancing a cha-cha on girl's night out // DuBois passed out drunk in his Toyota // Toby serving DuBois a tofu dog at the housewarming party // Aspen, drunk, sitting on EC's lap at the same party // EC and Aspen at the beach // EC, Juan Carlos, DuBois, and Aspen in Mexico eating lobster.

She wasn't sure whether to put that one in the Juan Carlos album or the DuBois & Aspen album. Aspen had that same picture in a cardboard box stored in DuBois's parents' garage… Durn it. Juan Carlos made me so happy. Why did he have to be such a no-good alcoholic loser bum? She wondered if she had stayed with him, if he would have lived, or if they would have died together. How romantic, she thought.

She put the photo albums on the bookshelf across from the entertainment center, wiped a tear from the corner of her eye and set a candle on the dining table. Her mother had brought over a pot of the family recipe spaghetti sauce, which Toby couldn't get enough of. She would have the pasta boiled and the Chianti opened before Toby got out of the shower. She struck a match and held it to the wick. A red candle to inspire passion. She poured herself a glass of wine and reflected on where she had been and where she was going.

The Sex Part

DuBois watched the steam lines rise from a tin cup of the blackest, richest java he'd ever smelled. Aspen leaned over him. The morning air seemed unseasonably crisp and Aspen could see her breath. Not a single cloud superimposed itself on the solid blue mat of the morning. DuBois picked up a faint hint of her raspberry body lotion underneath the smell of the coffee. His mouth tasted dry with sleep and his joints rusted in the damp night. Stretching his arms made his shoulders crackle where he carried stress.

"Where'd you sleep last night?"

"On the couch."

"Where's Dooby?"

He thought maybe Grammar would have Dooby sleep in the Fury. Aspen didn't reply at first. She didn't know what to say. She thought maybe DuBois would be jealous that Dooby slept in the house while he slept on the stiff mat in the tool shed.

Aspen decided to kiss him.

"That's the first night we haven't slept together all summer."

"Since my last exile to the tool shed."

Aspen unhitched the first button on her blouse.

"I thought the black coffee you brought woke me up, but that black bra, man, wow, that's somethin' else."

It wasn't out of character for her to initiate sex, but he'd never seen her do it with relatives close at hand. When they stayed at her parents' house, they slept in separate rooms. When they stayed with his parents, they were allowed to sleep together, with emphasis on the word sleep.

"What about Grammar?"

She laid on another wet lip kiss.

"I think she'll be sleeping late after the moonshine. We drank the dregs of it last night. She's acting like you're invisible anyway, remember."

"What about Rufi?"

"You know the girl won't wake unless woken."

"Dooby?"

"Asleep."

"How can you tell?"

They shared another kiss. His hand moved over her shoulder, along her arm. His erection had risen before sunrise and he realized why both roosters and dicks were called cocks. Stroking it to relief felt like a viable option, but rooting around the stable for an oil rag to wipe off on diminished any charm the idea had. Her mouth tasted like coffee, her neck like the faintest breath of a raspberry. Soon his erection hoisted up like the center pole in a circus tent.

"I'm not wearing panties."

A snap of the latch and the black bra slipped off her perfect breasts. He bit into her raspberry-smelling neck like a pie. Holding breath inside his lungs—twelve years now—until he gasped. His exhale carried the decaying corpses of bacteria, which turned her head but not her mood. He touched one soft nipple with his tongue, lips plucking a hidden fruit. The trigger behind the ear chased the hardening nipple into the cold. Hoping she didn't see the widow hanging in the corner—he kissed Sailor Jerry's mermaid on her breast. He couldn't have managed a toddler sentence as he crucified the nipple with playful, animal-like biting. Pirate desire swelled in his heart as one finger slid under the joy-fold where the left tit rested on her rib cage. He tasted raspberry-flavored sweat and pushed his finger into her mouth. He wouldn't ask her to go down, since he wasn't fresh out of the shower. Maybe she'll want to, he hoped, as he pulled back on the finger and pushed it in up to the knuckle. If there was an international gesture besides pushing her head down, he didn't know it. A man could get castrated pulling a trick like that. He pressed his ear to her bosom and listened for a rapid heartbeat, finding her surprisingly calm. Like meditation, like medicine. Codeine hangover, opium sucked through a water pipe. Strange Sanskrit dreams. Finally, a god to believe in. I'll pay tithe. Enough for gold candlesticks and a Cadillac for the minister. Cheese and rice. He felt like he could lose it, so he mounted her, thankful that her liquid was on. Jesus with sweaty long hair in his eyes. He didn't thrust twice before his muscles surrendered. Arms shivering, he collapsed. Staying small inside her. They continued kissing until he felt himself harden. Black Jesus hair like wool. That first thrust made him feel like a man, the tenth thrust like a pimp in a book he'd read, the eleventh, twelfth and thirteenth like a great orator at the proscenium, chorus clapping out an artless rhythm, Hey Now! Fourteen, fifteen, sixteenth thrust—pornographic. Skin graphic real, beyond real. Cinema lit, with the morning sun rising over the hill filtering through cracks in the wall—choreographed—a musical where characters burst into song without warning. Hey now! Her moan, a soprano in the art of song. Aaaaah, ah ah ah aaaaah. The crystal palace shattered in shards of sweat. He had to cum (explode into space) and couldn't see her to the end. Summoning his will, he pulled out and slid his tongue down the length of her raspberry torso, between the vanilla milkshake breasts along the centerline of her being, looped once around the navel, squeezed her soft stomach with both hands, strategically locking palms on each protruding hip bone—hip bones that ached to buck—dragged his forehead across her rough pubic hairs—Hey now! A darkening fell over the old horse barn as if by a passing cloud, he sensed that they weren't alone but couldn't have broken his desire for anything—he plunged the spear—like a warrior tongue deep into her sex organ—Wurlitzer sounds—a train whistle, a thousand drums, a crescendo of clitoral violins and a tuba to keep the beat—Oom-pah-pah. Oom-pah-pah.

"Mmmm."

"I don't understand how anyone ever gets out of bed. Why don't we do this more often?"

"I ask you the same question every day."

"I want us to be closer, more passionate."

Aspen heard a noise outside, like wood creaking, which might have been Grammar stepping onto the porch. She pulled her blouse over too quickly and buttoned it wrong. Had to redo it. He felt her liquid and his own seed drying on his face like a papier-mâché mask.

"Maybe we should leave Rufi and Dooby here…"

"Anything you say, doll. But I'm not jumping in that pool."

The Gold Bricks

Dooby had slept on a rug at the foot of Grammar's bed. A habit practiced long enough to feel natural. Grammar hadn't thought much of it. She woke up with an ache in her head to meet the one in her bones. She mixed her remedies in the dark, unready or unwilling to meet the sun.

"What a strange world."

After that, she rinsed her face in the sink and chased the chicken outside. The coffee made on the stove was a pleasant sight. DuBois should marry that girl. The coffee looked strong and black, the way she liked it, and the first sip didn't disappoint. Seeing Rufi asleep on the cot, she regretted living so far away for so long.

"Oh, my goodness, what a precious beauty."

Grammar brought her tin mug of coffee onto the porch and sat down on the bench, which creaked and moaned under her weight. The herbs threw open her sinuses like a window and the clean morning air rushed in. She sat like that until Dooby came out on the porch and sat next to her on the bench. He didn't speak and neither did she. They didn't have to. Looking across the expansive desert sand and her acre with the chickens and her old grey cat, she decided that it was too late to change her life, much, even if she had a million dollars.

Aspen and DuBois came out of the stable and their daughter stepped onto the porch with sleep in her eyes and asked, What's for breakfast? Aspen adjusted her shirt. DuBois seemed cheerfully awake.

"Come here, little darling, and give your Grammar a big hug."

Rufi would swear it the best hug in the world, even if Grammar smelled like old people. It lasted longer than most hugs too, because her great-grandmother liked it that way. DuBois remembered that crush, a smothering close to death that filled you with more life. Grammar looked over at her grandson, and he felt suddenly visible, even though she didn't say his name or anything at all, he felt her love as he'd always felt it, buried in the marrow. Aspen squeezed his hand.

"Good morning, Grammar."

"Good morning, DuBois."

"Morning, Dooby."

DuBois mussed Dooby's hair, saw his scalp pulse.

"I second Rufi's motion for breakfast."

"Before I scramble grits and eggs, I have an announcement."

Aspen smiled. Dooby blushed under his patchy morning stubble. For a second, DuBois thought maybe Grammar and Dooby hooked up. He thought of his Grandfather's bones moldering in the grave.

"Charles has decided to stay on here with me and work around the ranch. Lord knows I'll be dead and buried before anyone else in my family offers to do it."

"Charles? Who the fu—heck—is Charles?"

"I-I I'm Dooby, but also Charles."

"Grammar has a special way of talking to Dooby. They communicate. I think he said more to her last night than in his entire stay with us."

"Huh."

"He can sleep out in the old horse barn. My handy neighbor can fix it up nice. Insulate the walls. Put up sheetrock. We'll get him a space heater. How about grits and eggs?"

She boiled grits and scrambled eggs with wild herbs and fried up the last of the bacon she had in the freezer. She sliced up prickly pear and set that on the table. Rufi sat upright clutching a fork, ready to eat. After breakfast, Dooby went outside to pull weeds and make friends with the chicken.

"Daddy, can I stay here and help Grammar make dumplings and stomp lemons for lemonade?"

"I think Grammar would like that. Save us a dumpling."

The Fury pulled up under the tree, which may have been a poplar or a cedar. DuBois tapped the gun under his belt and they hiked past the wrecked car, making their way down the trail. He kept an eye out for the snake, mindful of treading on its territory. Aspen held his hand all of the way to the cabin. The muck pond smelled worse than she remembered, which might say more about memory than the awful smell. A stretch of freeway tarred with human shit. A stinking wound in the Earth left to fester.

"Dooby told Grammar that Chank sold his magic mushrooms to men in suits who paid with eleven solid gold bricks. Chank told them they were government agents, but he wasn't sure. One of the hippies in their commune was a narc. Dooby thinks that the mushrooms gave Chank the power to read minds. Chank couldn't trust anybody. He asked Dooby to stash the gold in the closet before the agents raided the farm. They took his friends to jail, the cops, he said, planted hard drugs on them—the kids who came from money were shipped off to de-programming camps. The others went to prison. Chank traded his freedom for a different mushroom, which Dooby said he bought at a health food co-op outside of Inyokern."

"Dooby said all that."

"Charles spewed it all out after Grammar fed him those herbs. It wasn't that clear, more like remembering a dream. She sang to him too and the song felt so… lulling… I might have fallen asleep forever."

"Wow, it's hard to believe."

DuBois crept along the base of the shack and peeked through the window. Everything seemed as they'd left it. The sign still hung by a corner and rapped against the stucco—Thou Shalt Not. He wanted to laugh, but it stuck in his throat. Around the far side, they found Chank's body in the wheelchair.

"Looks like an animal picked at it."

"A millionaire's death."

"I asked Dooby how Chank got this way, you know, in the wheelchair and all, but he stuttered and rocked back and forth. Grammar's potion must have worn off or he slipped out of the trance. It might have been a car accident."

A large black raven, which could have been a crow, flapped down onto the wheelchair and pecked at a piece of carrion. Its feathers were as shiny as crude oil. Its beak rent the flesh. One of its horned feet was missing a talon. A hoarse cry from the bird, sent a sudden chill rippling across Aspen's body. DuBois felt sick. He remembered the first riff Juan Carlos worked out on guitar.

At the edge of the pool, the surface was crusted and moldy. There were patches of dirty alkali froth like the head on a pint at the local scattered over swirls of deep brown, black and yellow sludge. Aspen thought she would vomit if she opened her mouth. DuBois tossed a pebble into the placid murk, which vacillated on the surface and sunk into the depths.

"I wouldn't jump in there for a hundred million dollars."

Aspen thought about the gold and the house she would buy.

"We could get scuba gear or drain the pond."

"You know how much it means to me."

They heard the rifle shot before it kicked up dust right at DuBois's feet and repeated in echo through the hills around the canyon. They both hit the ground.

"Jesus fucking Christ!"

The shooter had the high ground. Aspen scrambled to her feet, pulled DuBois up and ran toward the stucco shack. Another shot rang out and the bullet whizzed over their heads. The rush of air displaced by the bullet was the most terrifying sound she'd ever heard. DuBois pulled the gun from his belt and without aiming squeezed the trigger. The sharp report sounded louder than he expected. Aspen covered her bad ear. On a run, both slid into the base of the shack like stealing second. The crack of his shot, reincarnated in echo, came back to them as scornful laughter while the dust from their mad run floated back in place. The wind had died off and the world felt still, quiet, and calm—save their hearts, of course, which pounded like a bebop drummer who'd rubbed coke into his gums before the set.

"Who the fuck is shooting at us?"

DuBois peered around the side of the stucco shack and saw Chank's decomposing corpse. The raven was already in flight and about to vanish over the rise. He scanned a line of scrub oak up the canyon wall and down a naked crag. In contrast to the sandy hill face—spiny chollas, creosote, and scarlet loco-weed grew in sparse patches. A man wearing a fishing cap raised the rifle from behind a boulder and squeezed off another shot. A chunk of stucco exploded above DuBois's head. He wanted to shoot back but one of the remaining four bullets might represent their last chance. Aspen waited by the door. The dead phone and the black and white tv waited for her inside. She almost started crying when the phone rang.

"You okay?"

"Well, I'm not shot yet."

He closed his eyes and tried to imagine the man with the rifle. He heard glass break up on the roof of the shack. A few pieces of glass tumbled down in front of Aspen, who pressed tighter up against the stucco. She bent to pick up the wood ramp by the door to use for a shield, but dropped it when a rat scurried out.

"The roof's on fire."

The dry shingles on the roof would go fast. He peeked around the corner and another shot exploded near his head. The flames surged and the roof fell in a rumble of smoke and dust. DuBois wheeled around and squeezed off a wild shot. A small explosion rocked the house.

"Run, Asp, get away from the shack."

Smoke billowed up and the walls were on fire. There was no place to run. DuBois dashed out in the open toward Chank's wheelchair and threw himself on the ground behind the old man's skeleton. The rifleman had made his way down the canyon and posted behind a tree. Another wall of the shack disintegrated with a rumbling hiss of flame and rising ash. Smoke as dense as fog fell across his eyes and the air tasted of filth. Aspen appeared in the haze. The man came out from behind the tree and aimed the rifle at her. DuBois grabbed the wheelchair and made a screaming run. He let the wheelchair go like a shopping cart in the supermarket parking lot and sent his last three bullets one after another streaking toward the man. The first bullet struck the man above the eye and the third followed the second through his chest with a popping sound. The smoking rifle fell to the ground.

"Jesus fucking Christ."

"DuBois! DuBois!"

"Aspen, you okay?"

"I'm not shot or burnt."

The smoldering fire sent up a weak smoke signal.

DuBois and Aspen held each other. He'd killed a man and felt nothing but relief. They walked to the fallen body. Chank's limbs and bones and rags had fallen out of the chair in a pile and tangled with the freshly dead corpse.

"Hey, that's the rude guy from the bar."

"Dan Petro."

"Yup."

"I would stay away from Chank's place if I were you, buster."

His shirt was soaked with blood above his exposed belly and blood spilled into the sand. The fishing cap slumped onto the ground and the top of the guy's head was an ebullient swollen red where the thin layer of skin across his tonsure had peeled back. DuBois could see two gaping bloody holes in the chest, another darkly bored through his eye. His jaundiced face drained of fleeing blood. The open top of his head might be considered a fourth hole.

"It looks like you shot him four times."

"Four times with three bullets? Huh."

Aspen kissed him on the neck. He was still holding the gun. She started laughing and DuBois worried that she'd lost her mind.

"Petro must have gotten his head drilled like Dooby. He must have been in their cult."

"Let's get out of here."

"I have to do something."

She sprinted for the muck pond, pumped up with crazy adrenaline—at the edge of a cliff or peak of a high dive—if you want to go, you go. DuBois looked down and saw that a bullet had passed clean through his leg. He put pressure on both sides of the hole to stop the bleeding, but didn't really feel anything at all.

Aspen held her breath as she dove headfirst into the shitty crud water. DuBois hobbled to the edge. A drunken sleep on a white sand alkali beach while his girl swam out into the sallow sea. He looked back at the burning house. The plume of black smoke dissipated in the pineapple sky. Another wall collapsed and a burnt plastic smell joined the reek of the muck pond. He hobbled toward the water, thinking she had been under too long. Her left arm grabbed for the side of the pool. On his belly, he grabbed as she slipped away. She strained, he pulled, she knew that he would not let go, he knew that she would not let go of the gold brick dripping with black slime that she heaved up into the dirt.

"Charles!"

She didn't even feel her exhaustion. The shit sloshed over her skin, into her hair, under her nails and threatened her orifices. Dirt packed in her face. Worms burrowing through her pores. DuBois grabbed her arm but didn't have the strength. The pain, which had been slow to wake, began to shoot through his limb like a radio signal from a tower. Aspen looked like the Creature from the Black Lagoon. A fish come to walk. Chunks of offal fell off her in a lump. A seabird in an oil spill. She wiped her hands on DuBois's pant leg and wrapped his wounded leg with his shirt to staunch the bleeding.

"I'm okay."

DuBois struggled to lift himself. They leaned on each other, felt sick and exhausted, stumbling through the canyon back toward the car. Passing the rusted wreck at the bottom of the hill, DuBois thought maybe he could die and become another fixture in the landscape. Aspen puked in a bush. Pressed one nostril shut and blew a glob of stringy black slime into the sand.

"I wanna rest here."

The salty sand felt hot through his jeans.

"Don't close your eyes, honey. Rest in the car. I'll drive."

"You never offer to drive, I must be dying."

"Come on, baby, time to get up."

He struggled dizzily to his feet. Under the shade of the poplar, or maybe it was a cedar, leaning most of his weight against her, sharing her filth in specks and splotches, he paused for a good long moment to apprehend her beauty. Thinking to himself or possibly out loud, in a filthy fog of buzzing flies, how incredible it was, cloaked in such vile excrement, that her exuberance could shine through like a black sun behind a tempestuous thunderhead winged with red lightning. They had been living their life in the whirlwind and found as much adventure in each other as in the world. They could argue about who was whose sidekick, later. A Panza to her Quixote, a Batman to her Robin. A Daffy Duck and a Bugs Bunny. He saw in her a good lover, a worthy foil, and a truly rare and reliable friend. And then, as might be expected, everything went black.

A Friendship as Good as Gold

The whereabouts of the gold had been a well-guarded secret. One man died protecting it, another, smothered in blood and sand, died hoping to uncover it. The two of them stone dead from nostalgia and bitterness. Lives had been altered in pursuit of a wisdom made trivial, lost as easily as a teenager's wallet or a girl's virginity. Dooby lumbered down the hill past the shade tree and found DuBois on the ground next to the wrecked car, a dumb grin in place of his dolorous mien. Dub felt wobbly as Dooby helped him to his feet and they stumbled like bosom chums in a drunken after-hours ramble. Grammar and Rufi were waiting in a reddish, mud-caked 82 Dodge Ram, which they had borrowed from the neighbor up the road. Grammar took one look at her grandson's blood-soaked leg and rummaged her bag for one of her remedies.

"We brought dumplings, Momma. Grammar and I made lemonade."

Dooby didn't recognize the woman, caked with reeking mud, who Rufi had called Momma. He walked right past her down the trail toward the shack, by now a heap of ash, and looking around, he discovered the body of Dan Petro, nudged it with the tip of a Pro-Ked, saw that it didn't move and dragged Petro and Chank both to the sandy edge of the muck pond. He may or may not have connected the corpses with the people they used to be. He couldn't think of anything he detested more than the pool. He had left the farm the day Mr. Chank asked him to dive through the dross and check his treasure. No one understood why better than Aspen. Did he think it dissolved? Did he think someone stole in after midnight and carted it away? Dooby decided that he would be happy living with Grammar, who made him feel useful. He asked if they could get a capybara, and she said, Sure, why not, darling? He hadn't been away from the farm long enough to forget the awful smell that assaulted him. Capybaras are excellent swimmers, he thought.

He waded into the crusted muck, plunged in and swam out to the middle of the pool. The smell was awful and all over his skin. He dove, trying to get to the bottom and disappeared in the black inky mess. The surface of the pool settled and the bloody sun set again to baking a crust. An arduous minute passed before he popped up, face dripping with shit, spitting and grasping for a breath. Oh, my goodness, he said, kicking and heaving the first gold brick out of the pond into the sand. He swam to another spot and dove down, out of this world a few seconds longer each time, breaking through the crust and kicking in the thick muck to drag up another gold brick. Oh, my goodness, I-I-I hate the closet, he said. He collected his breath and dove again and again, rifling the bowels of the earth, hauling ten gold bricks in all back into the world. He wanted a breath and vomited the brackish water back into the filthy pool. He flung his arms wide against drowning and kicked and kicked against the pool, which wanted, as if it were alive and malicious, to drag him under. With a final huge inhale, he slipped below the surface again. The sun beat the water. The shack smoldered in a ruin. He thought about Mr. Chank and his friend Dan and one of the young girls who used to smile at him and the night they spent up in the hills, together, wholly with each other under the stars, of which there were so many. He stayed down at the bottom and groped around, found a last bit of courage, and pushed with everything that he had left back toward the surface. He turned toward the sun, breathed easier and tossed a black mushroom into the sand next to the gold bricks. Through the smoke of the ruin the farm looked like a bad dream. Houseflies buzzed around in confused loops. He rolled the bodies of his old friends into the pool—and buried the secrets that killed them both under the muck. He saw the pistol coated with blood and sand like a leg of fried chicken and tossed it into the muck with the bodies.

"Give me a hug, Boo-daw."

"No way, Momma. No way."

Dooby coughed as he carried the bricks to the truck. He wouldn't miss the stucco shack or the farm. He understood now that Mr. Chank had finally died, and in a way, he felt glad. He held one hand out to Grammar and handed her the black mushroom, which she accepted, wrapping it in cloth and placing it into her bag.

At Grammar's ranch house, DuBois fell back onto the couch and propped his leg up. Aspen disappeared to take a bath. He had his eyes closed and didn't see his grandmother approach with the wooden cup.

"What's the matter, darling?"

"It hurts."

"Mmm. Well, drink this. Nature's antibiotic."

DuBois drank from the wooden cup and winced at the bitter taste.

"That will fix you right up. You rest, darling."

He didn't know how much time had passed, couldn't say whether it dragged on or flew by. He opened his eyes to find Aspen next to him on the couch, daubing his forehead with a cool cloth. She'd scrubbed her face rosy and looked clean and bright in the spar of illuminated dust filtering in through the window. He thought she smelled fresh of a harsh soap.

"Dub, honey, how are you?"

"I dunno. I'm not gonna cry."

"You can if you want."

"I didn't want to kill him."

"He was trying to kill you."

"Is that a good enough reason?"

"He was trying to kill me."

"That must have been it. But still."

She moved the cloth and set down a kiss on the top of his forehead.

"That's what scares me. I never thought I could kill anyone. I didn't want to kill Petro, but there must be something inside me."

His voice betrayed steady contentment. He hadn't seen Dooby standing in the middle of the room and was startled when he spoke.

"Mr. Petro was a friend of mine. But he charged too much for soda."

They stayed at Grammar's for three days. Dooby took a broom out to sweep the stable. Stopping to poke a wasp's nest under the eaves, he ran when the buzzing wasps took flight. Along the way, he fumbled but didn't drop the Mason jar tucked under his arm in the canvas sack. He found a screwdriver and poked holes in the lid. Dooby plucked the widow from her web. He would feed it and they would be friends. DuBois thought his grandmother looked tired after muddling up an old wives' remedy and rubbing the salve into his leg. She didn't mention the maggots slipped under the bandage to scour his wound.

A few days later, bedeviled by husky horse flies that buzzed around his head, he brushed the air with a thoughtless hand. When Rufi brought him a glass of water, he thought she looked taller.

"Rufi, get my green bag."

He unzipped the green bag and pulled out the reanimated stuffed animal.

"Cappy!"

Dooby sat at the end of the couch and caressed his old friend. Rufi stood up back-to-back with her mother.

"Wow, she's taller than you, babe."

"Still my little lamb."

"The capybara, the capybara, my funny friend, my animal twin."

Aspen sat near DuBois and stroked the fuzz growing in around his mohawk.

"What's your animal twin?"

"I used to think of myself as a tiger, but maybe you're the tiger."

"We could both be tigers."

"You could be a goddam mudskipper. Hee hee hee."

"I want to be a tiger too, Momma."

"You will be, little cub. I'm sure of it."

DuBois walked with a limp and thought he might get himself a cane to lean on back in the city. Aspen couldn't fully wrap her head around recent events. One question nagged above the rest—why didn't Mr. Chank cash in the gold bricks?

Driving past the thirty-six houses on Circle Circle felt more alien than ever. The street felt ghostly quiet. Inside the cottage behind the main house, they kept the door shut and the blinds drawn.

"I need to listen to those old albums."

Big A, little a, bouncing B...

His stereo speakers sounded tinny and small. Nothing like he remembered. He turned the volume all of the way up, but it didn't sound right. Rufi packed her Barbie dolls into a box and left them out on the curb. In the old neighborhood, they would have been swept straight away, but the next morning the box with the dolls was still out there. Aspen had the gold bricks arranged around her on the futon, she swallowed three pain pills with a gulp of water, closed her eyes and tried to sleep. Fiendish dreams left her restless.

Toby and EC noticed the light on in the back house and knocked on the door.

"What. Who's there? Oh, sorry, I was asleep."

"Where oh where have you guys been?"

"We took a few days to visit my grandma."

He figured no one could relate the whole truth in any situation even if they tried. There were always going to be details left out, interpretations.

"We talked it over. And decided that you guys need to find a new place to live."

"We let you live here for almost nothing, and… you've been using us."

"You're evicting us?"

Aspen remembered the pink Post-it and slit her eyes at Toby. DuBois said it all along, that Toby would push them out of EC's life. EC didn't answer, didn't say anything at all, and

Aspen couldn't find enough energy to protest. She watched her friend walk back to the main house and shut the door.

"She said we used them."

"We haven't been paying much rent."

"EC asked us to move in, she set the price. We didn't haggle. Our agreement says six months and it's been... one, two, three, four and a half."

"We can find a new place."

It took about a week to find an apartment that would allow cats. Even then, the new landlord asked for an extra security deposit. It was a small apartment with one bedroom that had enough space for a narrow bed against the wall. The bathroom was a toilet, a shower and a basin. In the kitchen, you could stand over a pot at the stove, turn to the right and pull a can of beans down out of the cupboard, turn to the left and wash a dish at the sink. DuBois said the place felt big considering the square footage and Aspen said, Don't get too comfortable, it's temporary. This place is not our home. They had no idea how long they would stay. Aspen would use the time to think. They would be okay through a long dry drought or a hard rain. They lived as if it were temporary, biding their time, sitting on a fortune like sitting on their hands, in the moment, always on the lookout for something better, a bigger place that they could afford that wouldn't attract too much attention. You see people in their great big houses, living as if it were permanent, unaware of the precarity, the balance, with fat old age weighing heavily on one side of the scale.

DuBois packed what he could into the Fury on a Thursday, and his father, who moved into a single wide trailer closer to the city, said he could use the van on Saturday. EC's SUV was parked in the driveway, so DuBois parked the van in front of the note lady's house. They were surprised to see Rufi's bike and their armoire sitting in the yard.

"What's our stuff doing out here, Daddy?"

"I don't know, Boo-daw."

The key wouldn't turn in the lock. He pulled it out, inspected it, shoved it back in. The locks had been changed. He wanted to set the key down and be rid of it. The yard looked different. Very clean, very bright, expansive. But something was missing. He didn't know what it was but felt sad. The plants he and EC set into the ground had been dug up. The familiar squawk of the mockingbird up on the wire couldn't be heard. The old orange cat couldn't be seen basking in the sun. The gopher holes had been covered over with green sod. Toby must have rolled the Monster-Q 9000 into the garage too—summer was officially over. That strange whirring sound whistled through the air.

"What the fuck is that noise?"

"I don't know, Daddy."

"Something's missing here."

"It's the lemon tree. Toby cut down the lemon tree."

"Ah, yeah. That's it."

DuBois limped out to the curb and hoisted the bike into the van. Toby stepped out of the main house and walked out to the street with his arms folded across his broad chest.

"Yo, Studboy, EC wanted to know if you still had any of Juan Carlos's records."

"I don't know, maybe a few."

"Can you bring them back tomorrow?"

"I'll flip through my collection."

"Tomorrow, we're getting the carpet cleaned. You left it kind of dirty."

"Yeah, well."

"I'm sorry we're not very good landlords."

"Naw, man. You guys were great landlords, just not very good friends."

His wounded leg twinged as he bent to pick up one last box by the curb. Leave that one, Daddy. School starts tomorrow and my friends don't play with Barbie's any more. The box looked like an orgy of sexless naked limbs. He looked back at Toby as he drove away from the thirty-six similar houses on Circle Circle and flashed a wry smile that glittered like gold.

A Playlist

Social Spit - Riot on Palm Street

Black Sabbath - War Pigs

Sonic Youth - Shadow of a Doubt

Jon Spencer Blues Explosion - Full Grown

Fishbone - Another Generation

Dead Can Dance - Black Sun

The Damned - White Rabbit

Stiff Little Fingers - Law and Order

Jerry Lee Lewis - Great Balls of Fire

Roy Ayers - Everybody Loves the Sunshine

Chumbawamba - Sometimes Plunder

Garage Sale Score! - Divest Yourself

The Selecter - Three Minute Hero

Toots & the Maytals - Pressure Drop

Lightnin' Hopkins - Big Car Blues

Big Joe Williams - Highway 45

Mose Allison - Highway 49

John Lee Hooker - Goin' Down Highway 51

The Blasters - Highway 61

Bob Dylan - Highway 61 Revisited

The Cramps - (Get Your Kicks) on Route 66

Wayne Hancock - 87 Southbound

Cadillac Tramps - Drivin'

Jonathan Richman - Roadrunner

Buzzcocks - Fast Cars

Leon Payne - Lost Highway

Tom Waits - San Diego Serenade

Big Bill Broonzy - Key to the Highway

Memphis Minnie - Hoodoo Lady Blues

Victoria Spivey - Telephoning the Blues

Chuck Berry - No Particular Place to Go

Bad Brains - Pay to Cum

Banda Machos - Sangre de Indio

Toy Dolls - Dig that Groove Baby

SubHumans - Reality is Waiting for a Bus

Black Flag - Nervous Breakdown

The Bags - Babylonian Gorgon

The Plugz - Mindless Contentment

The Zeros - Rico Amour

Thee Midniters - I Found a Peanut

The Disposable Heroes of Hiphoprisy - California Uber Alles

Curtis Mayfield - Readings in Astrology

Parliament - Aqua Boogie

Adolescents - Kids of the Black Hole

Lee Morgan - The Sidewinder

Horace Silver - Song for My Father

Minor Threat - Bottled Violence

Thee Milkshakes - Jaguar

Jimmy Cliff - You Can Get It If You Really Want

Crass - Big A, Little A

A Box of Books

Stewart Home - No Pity

Howard Zinn - The Zinn Reader

Toni Morrison - Tar Baby

Jervey Tervalon - Living for the City

Peter Plate - Police & Thieves

William Shakespeare - Macbeth

Fyodor Dostoevsky - Crime and Punishment, Notes from Underground

Albert Camus - The Stranger

Franz Kafka - The Trial

Emma Goldman - Living My Life

Oscar Zeta Acosta - Revolt of the Cockroach People

Jim Thompson - The Killer Inside Me

John Fante - Dreams of Bunker Hill

Rigoberta Menchu - I, Rigoberta

Frank Baum - Glinda of Oz

Stephen Crane - Red Badge of Courage

Jaroslav Hašek - The Good Soldier Švejk

WELDED—STEEL CHAIN FASTENER

SIDE ONE

Motel 69 (Fuller • Carlos • Hayduke • Pinctada)
Summer of 65, Route 66
taking in the sights & snapping the pics
We spent the night
At Motel 69
That's where we stayed
At Motel 69
Laid us down and prayed
At Motel 69
Never been to church, never needed a crutch
Tried to skip out
Want to disappear
Tried to pull out
There's nothing to fear
Phone rings off the hook
Clerk knocks to look
We wanted to stay
Now we gotta pay

The Gold Bricks (Fuller • Carlos)
You're lazy, you're lazy
You never wanna work
You're a lazy shiftless goldbrick
And a real fucking jerk

Grammar (Fuller)
Watch how you talk
Watch how you speak
Don't say ain't
Brush your fucking teeth

SIDE TWO

Litigation Nation (Fuller)
Litigation Nation, Legal libation
You done me wrong
sue sue sue sue sue sue
Above average station, Attorneys chasing patients
Assume the position, brutal deposition
You done me wrong
You done me wrong
Prison vacation, Out on probation
Lost in translation, legal fixation
You done me wrong

Suburb + Utopia (Fuller • Carlos • Hayduke • Pinctada)
Sunlight fills the picture window
The magic hour is on
The neighbors are in their own light
The cocktail hour is gone
Get to bed and get to work
The grind can't touch me here

Back in the garage, the fridge is filled with beer
I've got 2.3 children, a wife and a dog
I do the crossword in the paper
But my brain is all a fog

Suburb and utopia
My home is but a dream
Suburb and Utopia
I wake up with a scream

I have written poetry, short fiction, long fiction & non-fiction. My history of DIY publishing extends to the early 90s, though my novel *The Sub* was published by Incommunicado Press in 1996. I was also honored to be the featured writer for City Works in 2002. I spent six years writing *The Book of Books* which Rich Ferguson called my "magnum opus."

I was born in 1966. I lived with my daughter's mom for 30 years before we got married on our 30th anniversary. I choose day jobs that leave me energy for writing, the best was The Museum of Death. I love books and have a home library with 3,423 volumes. I collect books from small presses like AK, Exact Change, Manic D, Black Sparrow, New Directions, City Lights & Re/Search.

I'm a veteran spoken word artist, fortunate to have shared a stage with many of my favorite writers:

Steve Abee, Linda Albertano, Dave Alvin, Don Bajema, Liz Belile, Iris Berry, Angela Boyce, Derrick Brown, Dennis Cooper, Creedle, Kimberly Dark, Sharon Elise, Maggie Estep, Raymond Federman, Rich Ferguson, Larry Fondation, reg e gaines, Weba Garretson, Pleasant Gehman, Gary Glazner, Daphne Gottlieb, Barry Graham, Cecil Hayduke, Stevie Harris, Michael Hemmingson, Stewart Home, Hank Hyena, Tamara Johnson, Shawna Kenney, Michael Klam, The Last Poets, Mary Leary, Beth Lisick, Lob, Jon Longhi, Richard Loranger, Lydia Lunch, Douglas A. Martin, Ellyn Maybe, Larry McCaffery, Jeffrey McDaniel, June Melby, Joe Milosch, minerva, Mindy Nettifee, Matthew Niblock, Alexis O'Hara, Nicole Panter, Peter Plate, Clebo Rainey, El Rivera, La Ruocco, Michelle Serros, Several Girls Galore, Shappy, Bucky Sinister, Hal Sirowitz, The Taco Shop Poets, Jervey Tervalon, Juliette Torrez, Tarin Towers, Quincy Troupe, Chris Vannoy, Lizzie Wann, Pam Ward, Ted Washington, Saul Williams, William Upski Wimsatt & The Watts Prophets. I have performed at The SDSU Avant-garde Festival, The Fringe Fest, SXSW, The National Poetry Slam & Lollapalooza 94.